JENNIFER DAWSON was born in 1929 and brought up in South London. She has published eight books. Her first, *The Ha-Ha*, described by Susan Hill as 'so startlingly unusual, so original, so accomplished ... quite simply, a perfect novel', was published in 1961, winning the James Tait Black Memorial Award. It was produced on television as well as on the Edinburgh and London stages by director Richard Eyre, and broadcast several times on BBC radio. She went on to publish six further novels, *Fowler's Snare* (1963), winner of the Cheltenham Festival Award; *The Cold Country* (1965); *Strawberry Boy* (1976); *A Field of Scarlet Poppies* (1979); *The Upstairs People* (1988); *Judasland* (1989); and a collection of short stories, *Hospital Wedding* (1978).

Jennifer Dawson has worked variously as a teacher, subeditor and on two encyclopaedias and a dictionary. Her spell as a social worker in a huge mental hospital in the late fifties gave her the background to much of her fiction. She now lives near Oxford with her husband. Her new novel, *Troy Wharf*, will be published in 1991.

D0196987

STATE OF VERMONT
DEPARTMENT OF LIBRARIES
MIDSTATE REGIONAL LIBRARY
RR #4   Box 1870
Montpelier VT 05602

WITHDRAWN

JENNIFER DAWSON

JUDASLAND

VIRAGO

Published by VIRAGO PRESS Limited 1990
20–23 Mandela Street, Camden Town, London NW1 0HQ

First published by Virago Press Limited 1989

Copyright © Jennifer Dawson 1989
All rights reserved

*A CIP catalogue record for this book
is available from the British Library*

Typeset by CentraCet, Cambridge
Printed in Great Britain by
Cox & Wyman Ltd, Reading, Berkshire

I

The youngest Fellow of Sanctus Spiritus College put his head round the office door and smiled at the college secretary, still typing away serenely at seven o'clock as though she were ambling along on a nice horse. Clare Bonnard was the college 'tower of strength' or, to the younger Fellows, 'our central nervous system'. The youngest Fellow had bright eyes that he seemed to switch on just above his beard as he leaned on the door of her office and called in cheerfully: 'Clare.' She was small, fair and plump. She stopped her horse and raised her head, maintaining her neat controlled smile as he went on, 'I've got tickets for *Aida*. Tomorrow night. Can you come?'

'Derek, I'd love to.' The words came out pat as though someone else had showered them there. Clare always longed for certain words and enthusiasms not to come so readily, and for her free time not always to be so available, because the bearded young don seemed already to know what her reply would be and kept his eyes twinkling as he added, 'But mind. Don't read anything into it, because your escort has got a wife back home in Upsala.'

Clare's horse ambled steadily on. She tried to feel insulted instead of amused at male assumptions. But she had always suffered from *l'esprit de l'escalier* . . . she always only thought of the right retort when it was too late. And, in any case, the heavy chestnut trees out in Great Quad overpowered everything, as though only they could make real claims to existence. So she went back to her typing and her smooth professional smiling. Dr Alec Smale, the second most junior Fellow, had asked her to finish his book, check its index and get it off to his publisher before next Tuesday as he was off to the States himself. And there was the pile of dirty laundry he had dumped with amused self-consciousness at her feet before he went, like a dog who had triumphantly brought its mistress a bone and waits to be patted.

Once he had delivered it when she was standing in the butcher's in Judasland, the district where she lived. He had lowered the dirty and unsorted clothes into a pile at her feet for sorting and despatch on the sawdusty floor with a modesty and sheepishness he must have thought rewarding for someone. It was only afterwards that she wished she had said: 'Haven't you laid on a press photographer to record the distinguished young Oxford academic's boyish eccentricities?'

Alec Smale at the age of twenty-six had already produced five books on the subject of north Icelandic poetry metres. Perhaps American tourists would see him trailing across Great Quad, weaving in and out of its Inigo Jones colonnades with his galley proofs under one arm and his pants and vests under the other, rather like Treplev with a bandaged head in Chekhov's *Seagull*, the innocent victim of life's momentous indifference as he cried, 'Clare, what shall I do? My publisher's signed me up for four damn more. The whole damn series, in fact.'

'Good dog. Good jobs,' whispered the voice Clare never used. She often wondered what Alec did when no one was watching him. She tried to picture him alone in the desert at a table spread with sheeps' legs where no one had heard of Oxford. Or suppose it were 1940 again, and the Germans had succeeded in invading the country and had settled themselves here in the university? . . . But perhaps Clare herself would have got up from her typewriter with her professional smile and asked the SS man standing in the door, 'Can I help you?'

The unpleasant thought was interrupted because Alec Smale's dog had put its dirty wet nose between her thighs and was licking her crotch with leisured enjoyment. It was her job to exercise it and feed it while Alec was away. She stared with hatred at the dog but she knew she must be giving her Girl Friday smile just the same, because the dog seemed to be smiling back at her in collusion. An unpleasant smell came from its sticky belly-fur. The tough black jelly round its mouth glistened as Alec's voice sighed, 'I've been stampeded into the editorship of the whole bloody series.'

The dog's pink inner ear shifted as Clare gazed into its stupid and smouldering eye. Why did she let them use her as a kennel-girl with a very sliding scale of payments, varying from a picture postcard from New York to some duty-free scent? Why did she collude? Why did she let herself go on being the college's 'tower of strength'? Perhaps one day she would be brave enough to introduce the Fellows to that other little 'staircase' and that voice would cry, 'The opera? Tomorrow? *Aida?* But can't you get the lady who cleans out the telephone to make up your foursome? She surely wouldn't read anything into Egyptologists from Upsala.'

But the dog was sniffing at Clare's neat tights and the calves of her legs where they joined her good leather sensibly heeled shoes, and she could hear her college-treasure voice, as real a fixture as ever, calling down to the dog, 'Walkics, Anson? Anson come walkies. Good dog.' Would she ever get her own voice back – the voice she had in London?

Once Alec Smale had rung her from his house in North Oxford just as she was leaving for work.

'Clare, be a pet and come and see me. Can you call in on your way to the academic factory?'

'Certainly Alec,' she had said in her efficient way. 'Are you ill? Can I bring you any balms?'

'It's a possibility.'

She had got on her bicycle and cycled out to Alec's house. The front door was ajar and she had gone in.

'Alec? Where are you? Are you alright?' she had called.

'I'm upstairs.'

She had climbed the three flights of stairs and found him lying in bed naked on a large fur. He had smiled at her, 'Be an angel and clear up here for me. I had a party last night and my flight to New York goes in just over an hour . . .'

He had caught her by her neat grey skirt and pulled her over on to him and she had laughed nervously as she toppled over a pile of his proofs: 'Oh dear!'

She had got up, flushed, and straightened her skirt. She had gone down to his kitchen. His girl friend had walked out on him, he said, and left ten greasy plates covered with chicken bones. Cigarettes had been stubbed into bread rolls, and there were greasy wine glasses and table napkins smeared with lipstick and snot. And Alec's unwholesome dog was tearing at the remains of a squirrel it had found in the garden.

'Oh dear,' Clare had heard her voice say, then heard another, a deep woman's voice, interrupting her: 'Darling. Alec-Al-o . . . there's a rat, a bald ratty, on the windowsill in herc. Could you come and give him a tap on the nose with my powder-puff and tell him "Not here and not now." What were you saying? Someone in to do the washing-up? She'll need more Fairy Liquid if she's to tackle the *Saucisses Savoyardes*. And tell this rat no. Tell ratty-kins one thousand times no. This is a no-go area, so go lovely rat, tell him who wastes my time . . .' How Clare envied that voice.

'Oh dear,' she heard her own voice exclaim as she pedalled back to Sanctus Spiritus College as fast as she could. 'Anson has been naughty and torn a squirrel apart, broken it into . . . four pieces.'

The words echoed over her office. That had been the first time she had really heard her college-self. She had been on the stage before she got this job, after a long period of 'resting', and she expected the producer to cry, 'No, no. Clare darling. You've got to put more anger into that squirrel bit.'

'Alec. Your dog has eaten a squirrel,' she tried again. Then the 'staircase' voice called, 'Shall I pick up the fur and the tail and put them in your stock-pot? And there's some ribs and paws. Oh dear.' It was no wonder she had never made a career on the stage.

Today, however, the typing and dog were the lesser of the several evils being an Oxford college secretary brought with it. At least today she had a real excuse for not attending one of the Master's guilt parties, so she would not be hauled across his drawing-room to help out with a senile don or Labour Councillors, women JPs or foreign students unhappy about their Ph.Ds, their contacts at Oxford and their supervisors' permanent absences.

Last time Clare had been led to a couch where one of them told her about his rare blood group for half-an-hour and another had told her about some glorious grapes he had eaten in Sicily before the Second War. 'That must have been a rewarding experience.' Then she had been as enthusiastic to a couple of college wives who were talking about last year's sabbatical trips, mock O-Levels, ferrying their daughters to ballet classes, and their husbands' dressing rooms recently refurbished by a brilliant young designer at the college's expense. Then the subject ran on to the cost of running the little heaters in the electric towel-rails that kept the towels in the dressing rooms warm and dry.

From that Clare's thoughts had run to dry-cleaners, then the retex smell of the room she had once lived in above a dry-cleaner's shop in London. And then she was flying over the roofs of Regent's Park and Kentish Town with Ambrose, a long way away from the neat clipped voice reporting in its unimpeachable way, 'Of course, all these items have to be taken into consideration. And electricity is so expensive these days.'

Clare sighed and stared down at her crisp cotton dress. She noticed, as if for the first time, that it had tiny red Father Christmases down the front, and yellow teddy bears, guitars and drums.

She didn't know whether medieval schoolmen had really argued about how many angels could stand on the point of a needle, but she wondered how many Clare Bonnards there were to each of the tiny drums and guitars spaced evenly over her dress. She went to Ellistons and bought a black velvet sheath for the Master's party, hoping the Clare Bonnards would be released from the tiny drums. But when she got to the Lodgings Alec Smale saw her and came over.

'New dress, Clare? Did you buy it to dance the Farandole at the Albert Hall last week? Five hundred women all in tartan and black velvet under Queen Victoria's pink lighting. Did you carry bow and arrows? Or tambourines?'

'And how is Ba-ba and Suki and Tim?' the party went on.

'My dear we've spent so much on having them house-trained.'

'And vets can be so expensive,' Clare could hear her own well schooled voice run on. What would Ambrose have said?

'Clare's telling us about doing the Schottische at the Albert Hall,' she could hear Alec Smale reporting at the other end of the room.

The huge sash windows of the Master's Lodgings had been open and the loaded May trees hung like great presences almost inside the big Georgian room. Clare had always felt uneasy in May, and was growing to dislike it actively. Its full lush headiness unnerved her, reminded her of her own unlived life. She left the window, but a voice called after her from the flowerbed on the other side, a deep woman's voice with a slightly American drawl.

'He's in a bad way, the Master. It must be his age. It makes them like that – does the male menopause. But I'll have to explain to him, just the same, why I've got to have that *Laborenda* out. Overplanting and it's sure to rain too, poor Master . . .'

The Master of Sanctus had leaned out of his window and called, 'Grace, dear, leave that border. Come in and have a drink.'

Grace Plasket had once worked on his huge Hausa Dictionary and still gardened for him after a long affair. Her voice was soft yet powerful and it flooded the party drawing-room. She would stand out there every day working on the Master's garden as though it were his body. He would come out with the deadly politeness that he meted out to everyone equally: 'Grace dear, I wonder if you could spare this particular patch for the time being. Anna and I were planning to use it as . . .'

But then Clare could hear Grace sigh on the other side of the window and call back in, 'You're still overplanting, Master.'

'Grace darling, that's marvellous work you're putting in,' the Master would repeat, 'but why won't you come in and have a drink?'

Mrs Plasket would come gracefully round and into the Lodgings, tucking her muttoncloth shirt into her jeans and drawing back the fine grey and black hair that flew out of her chignon and round her high cheek bones. She smiled at Clare as though they had both shared the same lovers beyond the Kalahari or the Sind.

'The Master's still a good friend to me, now though,' she would confide. 'All the same, it's difficult to have a non-sexual relationship with someone you've copulated with in Tashkhent.'

Her eyes were large and grey and gentle and she looked round the room for someone younger than the Master, murmuring dreamily as the party hobbled on, 'The Master was always crazy about me, but now I just don't feel that way about him any more. A black became his mistress after I gave up the struggle. But even this petered out. Or so I heard. It upsets us both a lot. However, my Indian lover from Bombay has written. His son, Hari, is coming to Oxford. He's a doctor like his father. Writing a book on Placebo Therapy in Indian village practice . . . You must meet him . . .' The party had jolted on like a three-wheeled waggon.

But this evening Clare only had to listen to the bouts of controlled laughter floating out of its drawing-room and in at her office as she typed out Alec Smale's last chapter. His dog sat under a chair with bleary eyes scratching its coat. Dandruff and fleas flew up into the air and on to Clare's ryvitas. She had promised Alec to shampoo it and delouse it too. She had even promised to feed it charcoal biscuits and take it back to her bed-sitter, which Alec always conveniently referred to as her flat, in Judasland.

As she stood there at the window of her office looking over Great Quad and down the leafy tunnel into Long Quad, she could hear music coming from its other side. From 'the maze'. The college band was rehearsing for Bishop's Benediction Night in July when the students had gone down. Fragments of Handel came.

The Fireworks Music. Then snatches from one of his oratorios. The band was being rehearsed by the college's only woman lecturer, though on Benediction Night itself she would hand the baton over to Dr Joseph Conroy, who was more of a celebrity but wasn't able to appear until the night itself. He had been an absentee Fellow for nearly two years now.

Clare could hear Grace Plasket's husky and half-American drawl trailing away over the quad: 'If the Master takes my garden away from me . . . You know he was involved in this CIA plot to get me out of Havana? And now he's trying to take my garden away from me. Next to a body, a garden is the only thing I see as at all important . . .'

From behind her came a snatch of the Fireworks Music. Its steady beat and its certainty seemed for a moment to make up for life's meagreness. For a moment Clare was separated from her cotton print dress and her college secretary's voice. Perhaps Mrs Plasket would find her lover again. Perhaps the trees' great spring brain lobes would stop presiding over the world to mock them, to strangle them with all they unleashed each year, round these bleeping humans.

Grace Plasket stood there fumbling in her carrier-bag, pulling out volumes of Sleep Diaries and Dream Diaries and making a few entries into them while she reminded Clare that her Indian lover Anil's son Hari, the doctor, was coming to work in Oxford.

'Hindus are truthful people. We met in a bus shelter in Byelo-Russia when Anil's son was still at school. But does that matter?' She fixed her huge grey eyes on Clare. 'Have you ever loved anyone for long enough to go to Yykkhuiti with them?'

Clare stood there in her crisp knife-pleated skirt, a crisp cotton blouse and cashmere cardigan. It was all in the best of English taste. The pleated skirt had such a well bred restrained look, as though Clare were destined only to grapple with brown scones and porcelain thimble painting and footpath-rambles. Mrs Plasket looked at her and laughed, then looked at Alec Smale's gaping and stupid dog. The dog seemed to be imitating Clare as it sat back from its wet explorations in Mrs Plasket's basket; seemed to sit there also saying, 'How true . . . How simply gorgeous . . . Oh you poor darling . . . Let me make you a cup of coffee . . .' Clare had never had more than bit parts when she was on the stage.

Mrs Plasket was still laughing. 'It's our fault really,' she was saying as she fumbled in a trug full of plants she had nicked from the Master's flowerbeds to take back to her cottage out at Hedgencote. 'Men like to be mothered, and we women need to mother them because we need to be needed. Of course, if you've never made love at a high altitude, Clare, such as Lima, then you've never experienced men's need for mothering at its fullest. When I was living with this Peruvian water diviner . . .'

'Oh Grace, we must leave these high altitudes to you.' Clare folded her arms and protested, but the trees outside seemed overpowering. The pregnant reminders of a spring elsewhere. Trinity Term had just started. In summer, the heavy trees would shrink back. Sunlight would fall unclouded across the quad. The air would be full of student noise. Light would run round corners and dive into spaces and summer places would jump up like children in a game. The menace would be gone once the lush green had retreated just a bit.

Clare tried to picture Ambrose here in the Tudor alleys and the Inigo Jones quad. But when she tried to think of him, she kept thinking instead of the kitchen at home when she was a child and how she had gone down there alone very early one winter morning and found Jack Frost on the windowpane, very loud and exclamatory and exploding into movement. It was his laughter on the window that had caused this fantastic shake-up on the pane. She always thought of it afterwards as in colour, in flames of green and purple and blue, and she expected him to come dancing across the grass with leaps and bounds, in striped trousers and a checked jacket; and that the frost would break into flames.

Perhaps life would be like that with Ambrose, dark and polished, laughing and elastic. She tried to think of him in his flat above the dry-cleaner in Slack Street. But each time she tried to picture him, she found herself back in her father's flat in Drawberry Road, with only her mother's big old-fashioned treadle sewing-machine. Clare's stepmother still sometimes used it, pumping with her feet as though they were all standing round the harmonium on Sunday evenings singing 'O Blessed Watch' or 'It is Good to be Out on the Road'.

Clare tried again to picture her parents' new son-in-law, but she could only see him dancing up and down behind their big heavy settee, wearing a mask, carrying a gun, smoking cannabis, then running down the empty street and away from Drawberry Road, Clare following. She wished it had been like that. But she had been thirty then and now she was thirty-five. She had never heard from Ambrose afterwards, but she once dreamed that he had spent fifty-five years studying an alternative reading to a Middle English poem called 'See you Later, Alligator'. Then Clare had woken up thinking of her father again, and his second wife, Mardi, at Drawberry Road, London NW6.

She would soon be forty and then fifty and still she couldn't stop being their big girl; and when at last she came to retire, there would be more speeches about college linchpin and college treasures. She could see two academic sisters on huge twin tricycles zigzagging erratically down the Woodstock Road like angry bats. She could see dons in their coloured robes stomping round the Sheldonian Theatre chanting Latin on degree-giving days, and herself carefully easing the Professor from his gown and hanging it up reverentially, reminding herself not to forget to give it to him when he came back for Hall and not to recite: 'Wherever I go there's always Pooh. There's always Pooh and me.'

But Clare said nothing like that – living on a wreck and first casting out this and then that to lighten it, and living finally with only very small rations, but never actually disappearing as ship-wrecks do. Her father would beam though, and shake her shoulder gently: 'Fortunately, our big girl won't be in danger of that particular shipwreck. She's slim, eh?' Dad would smile at Clare. 'She's beautiful. Intelligent as they send 'em, so everything's going for her, and for us oldsters too, for as long as she's around . . .' Then there would be an awkward silence, as though Clare had just eaten something terribly wrong. She would smile miserably trying to get it from her stomach, but this was her food, her parents and friends seemed to assure her. The tiny trumpets and drums that spattered her clothes were her destiny.

II

'Cheers,' Clare's father would repeat, lifting his glass at Drawberry Road, before Clare's departure for Oxford.

'Here's to us,' her stepmother, Mardi, would add.

'When shall we three meet again,' her father took up his glass even further, 'by wind, by lightning, or by *liebe Fräulein* Clare?' He had leaned over the table at his thirty-year-old daughter. 'Are you sure you won't come with us and partake of that lobster salad and *truite au bleu*? Sure the "ding" won't win instead of the "dong" in the ding-dong going on inside that cranium of yours?'

'I'm sure, thank you father. Though, thank you, all the same.'

'Go on. Be a devil.' Mardi cleared her throat. 'Tell them you need some sunshine after all that office air-freshener. Some fresh, newly grown air. It's so beautiful in Switzerland in the spring.'

'I'd love to.' Clare had shifted the supper-table that rested uncomfortably on her legs. It was really too small for three. Almost just a telephone-table. Knives and china sometimes fell off it as they were eating. And yet they always ate there. It seemed to symbolise how things had been and how they would go on. Clare had leaned over her stewed plums and sipped at her home-made ginger-beer, looking at the cold, decent fruit in her bowl as though it wouldn't go away ever either – two neat golden plums, like twins with two neat golden stones inside them. 'I'd love to come on holiday with you, but you see, I'm expecting my agent to ring.'

'Yes, of course you are.' Mardi would nod and understand, though the agent had not rung for months.

'Is it the money side you're thinking of?' her father asked gently after a generous pause, knocking out his pipe into the coal-scuttle. 'Mardi and I'll take care of the el-ess-dee, Clare-chum.'

Clare winced at the last word and said in her small cool voice, nasally as though she had a slight cold, 'It's not the money, Daddy.'

She pushed her spoon carefully into a plum, lifting out the stone and transferring it with her full attention to the side of her plate where it slipped back into juice and she caught it and grappled with life as she went on: 'It's just that summer work is beginning to turn up,' she finished sorting out her left-hand plum, 'and I'd like to stay near the phone.'

For five years now, Clare had been 'resting' from her acting career. It had puzzled the neighbours and Miss Pugh below.

'After all those years she's had off them, you'd think she'd start looking for a proper job now. *Diawl*. Wouldn't you now?'

'My husband says he could get her a nice little job at the Social Security DS/Elevens, he says.' They would mention it to Clare's father and wait.

'Warm enough for you, Mr Bonnard?' They would lean over the low brick walls of the Kilburn gardens that ran like sheep-pens down to the railway-cutting.

Clare's father would smile and look up from the bed he was weeding and wait till the train had shaken itself away at the bottom: 'Indeed.'

'I see that Boone's is advertising for someone again, Mr Bonnard. And Clare, she speaks the foreign languages they're asking for, doesn't she? After that acting school ... There's no harm in a side-line, is there, with the languages?'

'Of course not,' Mr Bonnard would call back cheerfully, plucking at crackly rose leaves. 'Three languages our Clare-girl has. And if she keeps on like this at night-school, she'll sooon have the whole bang-lot.'

'If you'll forgive me saying, but there's too much of the foreign languages as it is. *Diawl. Duw.* Some of them round here now. You'd think they were monkeys, the way they chatter on so. As though the whole world was theirs. And speaks *their* way, the cheek!'

'Live and let live,' Mr Bonnard would signal the end of the conversation. 'It takes all sorts to make a world, and if you don't give, we always say in our home, you'll never get. Our big girl's got her head screwed on the right way, you may be sure.' Clare's father would raise himself slowly from his knees, a little red round his ears and forehead, and return to the flat upstairs.

Sometimes Clare got bit parts in pantomimes or tea-matinees at

Richmond or Llandrindod Wells. Sometimes her agents would get her commercial TV work, smiling over tins of catfood and saying, 'If Fluff is happy then I'm happy too,' or spreading margarine over her golden-haired son's sun-licked bread, or clasping pastel toilet-tissues against her childish rosy cherub face and exclaiming at their softness.

Once when she was blowing bubbles advertising inner cleanliness, a camera-man had kissed her: 'Shame the Shakespeare or Ibsen of inner cleanliness hasn't turned up yet to give you a break.'

'No prizes for guessing who I saw on the box last night,' the supervisor in the typing-pool where Clare often did temp work would say.

'I was so proud when I went into the Post Office,' Mardi would add. 'They'd all seen you. Even Mrs Lovidge. They all said: "We saw your big girl last night."'

When Mardi said this, Clare's feet would suddenly feel heavy as though they were being dragged down by shoes made of clay soil locked into the whole obdurate earth. She felt impaled somehow, and her clothes suddenly felt leaden too, as though they had been hung there in cladding panels by system-builders and there was no real reason why they did not drop off.

'Still, Mr Right will come along, eh, Clare-pod?' Her father would look at her face that was growing less chubby, more bony, with a jaw that would obtrude and obstruct where it should have withdrawn. Every time they sat down to a meal at their small table in the corner or carried it, laid for three, into the centre of the living-room behind the settee, where they ate like visitors in a tea-room, Clare would resolve to get in touch with friends from her theatre days.

'Did you ring Nickie and Hanny and Deb and . . . ?'

'And the four terrible T's,' her father would add. 'Running four men at once. Did you ever? What a daughter. Running four boys at the same time!'

Her father suddenly seemed hot and too near, and Clare wished the four legs of the small table were not so uneven; wished the table didn't shift from leg to leg under her father's laughter, permanently keying out the same family meal.

Some of her friends had made names for themselves and she thought it would be a cheek to try and get in touch again; some had married or shacked up, and she grew tired of being an ear for stories of joyful infidelity or enriching sex-experiments she wasn't sure were advocated for her or not by her telephone-friends. Or the friends invited her round to the studios where they worked and let her recognise them at the consoles where they directed chat-shows or perceptive drama; or sometimes in return for baby-sitting they would shyly offer her a 'go' of Mat or Bruce or Roger – they never quite spelt out the details of these contracts, and Clare stopped apologising for being so dull and having no fruits to pull down off the trees and offer.

She took to hanging about in coffee-bars when she got in from her Temp-Types at night.

'Yes, I met friends. That's why I'm late back,' she would tell her parents when she got in. 'Married friends. . . . TV. . . . I expect you've seen James on his Wednesday night slot.'

They would nod. 'Good. Must be fun. Bring them home.'

'So do come with us to Switzerland, Clare-thing. Montreux is so beautiful in the spring,' Mardi would plead.

'*Chère amie*,' her father would add, '*aimez-vous une* dance?' He would hold out his arms. 'Have you ever thought of acting in Shakespeare? I can still remember quite a bit of it, and there's this company I read about, *The Royal Shakespeare Company* it's called. Somewhere in the West End. "To be or not to be".' He would blend plum-juice and custard in his mouth, custard and sips of tea, and plum fibre. '"Friends, Romans and Countrymen."'

'You see, Daddy, I'm expecting some festival work.' Clare had lifted both her plum-stones off her plate and put them over the Royal Scots regimental badge decorating the saucer of her teacup.

'Tinker, tailor, soldier, sailor . . .' her father watched and waited. 'Friends, Romans and Countrymen . . .'

'I've booked to hear Tito Gobbi and I wouldn't miss that for the world.'

'That's right. Get up and go. At 'em. That's the young spirit of today.'

This was the first time Clare had refused their invitation. She had been on holiday with her parents ever since she had left her repertory company five years ago. She would ramble round old castles and towns with her father as escort. They once, for about ten pounds, took a glass of sherry with *M. le Duc* in his chateau, and once squatted in the desert in Gaza outside a nobleman's tent eating sheeps' dugs and offering coca-cola to a too fastidious camel. Whether they had thrown pennies for small boys to dive for, or watched Americans teach Highlanders traditional bagpipe pibrochs, Mr Bonnard would always beam over at his daughter when they got back to their hotel, beam at the tall handsome waiter or *patron* and introduce his daughter. 'Our belle mamselle.'

'Our big daughter,' Mardi would add. The waiter would bow politely. 'I expect he's very busy at the moment,' she would say in the empty echoing restaurant. 'I expect he'll come back later and give us all the news since last time. You could see he remembered you.'

Or they would walk quickly along the boulevard till they came abreast another family from the pension or the hotel. 'Hullo, is it? Am I talking to some of our fellow-countrymen from *Les Marécottes*? Are you as snug as we are up there? Can I introduce our daughter?'

'Our very own daughter.'

'I have a thing and a very pretty thing, and who is the owner of this pretty thing?'

Clare wasn't sure whether it was she or someone else who murmured this question. At any rate, she vowed not to go on holiday again, and went back to her Temp-Types saying, 'Yes, we had a marvellous time. A crowd of us. Borrowed a house near Bellagio. Not all that near. Didn't want to get too mixed up in the *va et vient* of the more routine lifestyles.'

As she said this she would see her stepmother in her mind's eye, plump and short with a saddle-bag on her head to keep off the exceptional sun and baggy pyjama trousers, standing with her legs wide apart in front of the smartest dress-shop in Paris.

'Clare, there's just the dress for your concert-going . . .'

'We want a very glam dress for the world's greatest music-buff,' Mr Bonnard would smile.

'I wouldn't miss this London concert of Gobbi's for the world,' she told her parents finally, still shifting her plum-stones and transferring them back from the regimental badge to the bagpipes on her bread-and-butter plate. She sipped tiny drops of tea, then sips of the glass of sweet sherry the family allowed themselves after Sunday dinner for a treat. 'And I've got several parties and "do's", and I've told my agent I'll be at home.'

'Quite right,' her father said, 'always stick to your commitments. Then there's the – what's it called? – the National Theatre? Why not give them a try? Or stay awhile with us, pretty maid, dallying in the Alps a time, eh?'

And so, until now, Clare had gone with them, the good daughter, the continuous reminder to her father that not all women were sluttish and debauched. It had taken him a long time to believe that his first wife had become ill and not a tart; that a form of pre-senile dementia was behind the change in her character. When Mr Bonnard had at last accepted that diagnosis, sitting with his wife in the grounds of High Lodge Hospital in the early summer among the beds of hot-eyed Phastia, quilted Pluck and Christ Lilies, Clare had started to dress carefully, wash scrupulously each day, get up early to clean their house, and even after her mother's death and her father's remarriage, the scrupulous way of life remained written on her soul. And might she too not have the disease if she did not prove that her personality was intact each hour of the day?

But now at last at the age of thirty, she was refusing to be the true female. She let them kiss her goodbye: 'We shall miss you, you Clare-pod. Don't do anything we wouldn't, *liebe Fräulein-o-mine.*'

The taxi came. Her father grinned and bowed and they were off. The morning sunlight in their flat suddenly seemed tawdry, wrinkled and dirty.

The first thing Clare did when they had gone was to plan a party. She cleared the living room of Mardi's work-table and her father's reading-lectern and the plump armchairs with wide fat sides and backs, and the big cut-glass fruit bowl and folk-weave mats on the dining-table in the corner. She carried out the big chocolate-coloured radio set with a brown bakelite sun setting over the green satin of its front, and took down the curtains and pelmets and modesty nets from the windows. Then she went out to the off-licence for rum and cider to make a punch bowl.

It was eight o'clock, and as she passed a church hall a few doors away from the off-licence she heard the sound of music and saw a big yellow poster flapping on the hall's doors:

DANCE TONIGHT. MUSIC BY THE
BLACK PLANETS SHOW GROUP
And the wonderful Eastern Flame Dancers and Baritone (Recent successful performance, Albert Hall.) Friends and well-wishers of all nations cordially invited

She followed the arrows chalked along the side of the hall down a flight of stairs and into a small crowded basement. It was only the thought of her big parents and their big furniture looming so near that stopped her from running in fright.

She stood there cold and sweet and English as a sugar-pig. The room was so crowded and smoke-filled that she couldn't see beyond the door, and the pop-group played too loudly for her to hear what the black man pressed up against her was saying. He was olive-skinned, with a long thin pointed face and rasta dreadlocks. He pressed himself dead-pan against her and picked up her hands as though they were cutlery, then let them drop and took her by the hips and pressed her against the hard shape of the great circular buckle that covered his navel. As they danced she felt his emaciated loins and his glistening skin and his rasta dreadlocks on her neck and arms. He glanced at her only cursorily as they danced to the Dancer Juno Big Presence Band. He pressed her against the tortoiseshell clasp on his belly, then pushed her away from him, stooped as though he were crouching on a bicycle then drew her up against him. The big buckle made her breasts stir. When the musicians stopped for a breather he sat down against the wall and drew her on to his knee and she felt the warmth of his thighs and groin. He said his name was Ambrose.

'Where are your friends? Bring them along next time.'

When Clare said nothing, a black girl in bright green with a huge Afro wig called out, 'Maybe them too hoighty-up. Too many white kid gloves folks round here.'

'So what do you think's cause all this hoighty-up and bad attitudes round here?' Ambrose asked Clare. She saw he had green eyes. 'That poster said specif this was for all nation, no matter what colour the skin. No matter what pigmentation.'

The girl in the Afro shouted something at Ambrose. He shook his head: 'These small-island people. Don't take nothing of her,' he told Clare. 'Small island.'

The trumpet was playing tentatively. The drummers came in. Ambrose lifted Clare's wrists up and drew her towards him again, but suddenly the music stopped and sirens wailed outside and a heavily-built youth was lying on the floor being dragged along by two policemen. The dancers rushed forward to protect him.

Ambrose took Clare's wrist: 'Let's go.'

They took a back door through a kitchen laid with cups and sandwiches and streamers to welcome the neighbours who didn't come, then they crossed a yard.

'What happened?' Clare asked. '*What* was it all about?'

'Probably some small-island chap got found with drugs or pinched someone's woman. Where shall we go?' he asked softly, almost sadly.

Clare could see the lights burning out of her own sitting-room where she had pulled the curtains down from the big Victorian windows. She unlocked the front door. Miss Pugh, the ground-floor tenant, watched them go up from her kitchen door. Clare took Ambrose into her sitting-room and locked the door.

'A party, uh?' he stared doubtfully.

She had pushed the big settee to the side of the room and he flopped down on it. He drew her on to his knee and touched the tips of each of her fingers in turn, then stroked the mounts of her palms with the fleshy mounts of his, fingering the connections of her knuckles, her elbows, shoulders and spine, then feeling underneath her spread shoulder-blades, marking out the shape of her hips till she felt her uterus small and hard and hungry. He was cupping her breasts to his lips and they were rising up and following him as though the dead could walk. She called out to him to come and come again till she enclosed him and wept for joy at this simple ending to her own enclosure. Then he put the backs of his hands into her armpits and mended her again. She hung pinioned against her father's wall, suspended between her lover's hands and knees and crying, 'Come on. Come again,' till he had cancelled her frightened past.

Then they lay there side by side on the sofa. Perhaps that was why Clare had been 'resting' for so long. She had never given anyone anything, so no one had ever come back to her.

Ambrose drew her on to him again and then felt the wet patch under him and saw the bloodstain on the floral chintz and frowned. Then he lowered his head and laughed delightedly.

'Oh no,' he exclaimed, almost protestingly. Then he patted Clare's head and felt for the halo round it. 'Little girl, I didn't knew you was like that.' He laughed silently now.

She laughed too and thought of her vanquished father. Ambrose was only the second black man she had ever met. The first she had met through her parents. He had been a sidesman at the church the Bonnards went to, and her father would cry when neighbours grumbled about immigrants, 'Fair play. Give our new fellow countrymen a chance. Let's welcome the stranger in our midst. Our brothers from over the deep.'

The Nigerian sidesman would smile as Mr Bonnard grasped his hand after the evening Communion service was over.

'Will you take a bite of supper with us? Pot-luck?'

'Ah yes,' he would smile and reply vaguely.

'Will you come back next Sunday to our home and partake of soup and cheese?'

'Ah yes.'

But the Nigerian had always just smiled and had never turned up. Nothing more happened.

Mardi though he might have lacked confidence and made a point of saying to him again, 'Sometimes you must come round and tell us about your jazz. It sounds simply gorgeous to me. I often switch on when I'm washing up or ironing. You know?' She made ironing-motions with her arms as though he were deaf and dumb.

The Nigerian had been invited again but he still didn't turn up. Mr Bonnard had thought that perhaps West Africans had different mores but Clare had been relieved to think that he wouldn't have to sit at their rickety overcrowded table while her stepmother asked him how to cook chicken with ginger or about the little red beans you got in tins, or the winds of change blowing over our colonies.

Now both parents retreated as Ambrose and Clare lay side-by-side on their sofa, love-juice trickling down her leg.

'You don't live here alone then?' Ambrose asked, looking round at her parents' heavy upholstered chairs and carved wooden bookcase full of Book Club books and *Readers Digests*.

'I share it,' Clare said unconvincingly, as Miss Pugh's voice came up the stairs: 'Clare-bach, did your parents leave the milk-discs and the Tidy Tilly out when they went?'

Ambrose looked at Clare and then at his watch.

Clare asked him what he did and he told her he had been a student. His father had studied medicine as a young man, 'To be a doctor, only the Mission Training School wouldn't give him full medical training as this might take the British power away and destroy their supremacy. So my father sent me to England to get what he missed.'

But his father had died and left no money, and Ambrose was still trying to get a Commonwealth grant. He sighed and looked round the flat, wandered into her parents' room, stared at their mahogany wardrobe with the mirror on the door and the mauve-and-green-leaded lights above.

'This flat isn't empty then?' he asked, feeling the thick embossed counterpane.

'My parents won't be back till next week.'

Ambrose wandered round the flat, frowning slightly at Mr

Bonnard's reading-desk, the dried flowers beside the faded crepe paper spread in a fan over the empty grate, the leg-rest, the harmonium and the oleograph, *Jason's Leap*.

'How old are you?' he asked suddenly staring at the shoulder-cape hanging on a peg that Mardi wore on winter evenings to protect her from draughts.

'I'm getting on,' Clare laughed apologetically. 'I've hit thirty.'

'Oh? We could go round to my flat. Maybe it's easier. It's in the city.'

'You mean the West End?' she corrected him.

'Oh?' he stared.

'What do you do now that you're no longer a student?'

Ambrose said something about lift-operators in Harrods, short-take, and accountancy. If he could not get the punch-card then an uncle at Harrow Weald. Training to be a painter. Three one. Depending.

It was Clare's turn to stare. She understood all his words but she couldn't fit them to anything else.

'You're not a West Indian then?'

He raised his hands in disgust. 'Small-island trash.'

But when she asked him where he did come from he said he'd been a student in Los Angeles.

'I jess start my studies there. In LA. But that was before BB Ray, and they took his passport away, and so he had to come to London. Then I took it on.'

Ambrose's eyes went round the room and again rested on the huge Readers' Digest Map of the World and the *Book of Great Rivers*. He stared at them and picked up her father's reading-desk in one hand and held it above his head.

'They're both away,' Clare assured him. 'On holiday. This is the first time I've stayed behind . . .'

She laughed nervously as Ambrose said, 'His shit. You stayed behind? What brought about that revolutionary dang? So you want another rolly? Do you want some more?'

He wandered back into her parents' bedroom. There was a faint smell of the Morgan's Pomade her father put on his hair, and the Wintergreen her mother used on her swollen joints. The bed was huge and daunting.

'Come on,' Ambrose said. 'Some more jollies, eh?'

Clare stared at the bed and the shoe-trees under the bed. The room had its own kind of swallowing silence.

'I don't usually come in here,' she said.

There was a pierglass in the window with brushes and combs on it. Ambrose opened the cupboard and brought out her father's old Air Raid Warden's uniform. He tried the jacket on and saluted.

'Come on,' Clare urged him, 'don't go in there.'

She stood timidly in the doorway till he pulled her on to the bed and she felt the weight of her parents' demands lift again and laughed, repaired again.

'You see, I've always had to behave so well here, ever since my real mother died. I call her Mardi,' she pointed at the wedding photograph on the dressing table, 'but I'm so tired of being a good daughter,' she let him draw her on. When he came back next day he leaped at her like a ferret till she lay back exhausted and laughing on her parents' bed.

Ambrose laughed, fingering the cotton sheets. It seemed to Clare as she heard the tick of her parents' clock that the world had come to her for the first time freshly-washed by a salty tide. The sound of Ambrose's teeth going into an apple. The tearing sound of a lettuce as he gulped at the sink. The hiss of paper. The kiss of the gas being lit. The sound of Miss Pugh's fleshy legs rubbing together outside on the stairs. The rubber wheels of a big red bus squeezing out a puddle in the street. The glassy kiss of bath-water being run. His fingers going into her ears and down her as he took her again and then asked, 'Had enough, eh? The women always want more, eh?' The sound of blood before it weakens. The sound of its fading then rearing again like a fountain.

Ambrose woke her at last, pointing at the big wooden clock ticking on the dressing-table: 'Is that the right time, eh?' Mardi had been given the clock as a farewell present from the school where she taught. Ambrose suddenly laughed. He thought it was Clare's.

They could hear, above its ticking, the clicking of Miss Pugh's nose as she stood there on the staircase outside the bedroom again. When she had shuffled away, Clare told Ambrose about her mother. The Bonnards had kept a shop in a seaside town until the war drove out the holiday trade. They would have had to give up the shop in any case, because of her mother's habit of stealing from it and giving all the sweets away. Clare didn't tell Ambrose this, but she told him how she and her sister would lie on their backs discussing why their mother had 'let herself go', appearing in the morning in wellington boots and a dirty wet nightgown and wearing a child's ribbon in her long straggling hair. 'Ought I to know who you are?' her smile would say.

'You are my two good girls,' Mr Bonnard would reply as they ironed their mother's clothes. The Bonnards had been regular church-goers and one day when Father Peters had been passing, Mrs Bonnard had called out to him, 'Did you have any success?'

'Indeed,' he had replied, 'with all due thanks to such a willing band of helpers, we managed to raise nearly ten pounds for the organ fund.'

'And did you manage to get the blood turned into wine?' Mrs Bonnard went on in her slurred voice, 'And the bread into whatever it is that brings on the dancing girls? We must all jubilate, what?'

The clergyman put his biretta on again and walked on. The girls looked at their mother. She seemed unaware that she had said anything out of the ordinary. She would turn on her family: 'What exactly are you doing in my house?'

'You two are my good girls,' their father would kiss them at night. 'Two of the best,' he hugged Clare on her birthday. Her mother's present had been a filthy old petticoat with a torn lace hem and three sucked mints wrapped in newspaper. 'Sorry Clare-pod, but you two girls are the bestest,' their father would almost weep as they washed and ironed their mother's clothes to take up to the hospital where she had been admitted. Mrs Bonnard now wore a straight pink cotton skirt and a straight pink blouse because these garments had no pleats or gathers and could be ironed simply by one bang from the heated collander that came down rhythmic-ally with a clap from the laundry-beam. Clap-bang. The noise never seemed to stop. Clare and Hazel dreaded its rhythm as the background of their visits to the hospital.

Hazel had emigrated, married young and had an immaculate house; had twins and changed their costumes three times a day. Clare stayed at home and received Mardi and entertained her for her father and was confused when he told her very gently that the three of them would continue to be pals.

Ambrose cleared his throat, then yawned. He came again next day but Clare could hear Miss Pugh shifting the big clock in the hall below, and making it jangle as she dusted behind it. Then she could hear her heavy breathing as she came up the stairs again.

'Clare-bach.' She stood outside the stained-glass door of the common bathroom, then touched the bedroom door. 'Those

25

curtains you've taken down . . . I'll have them in the washing-machine for you. But it's your turn, look you, good-gel, to sweep the stairs. It's dusty they are, and no mistake.'

'Yes Miss Pugh,' Clare heard herself call out as though she were merely washing her hair. 'I haven't forgotten.'

But Miss Pugh still stood on the staircase breathing heavily. Ambrose had lit a cigarette and she sniffed and coughed very loudly, leaning against the bannisters and saying: 'This won't buy the baby a new bonnet . . . If you give me the curtains, good-gel, I'll have them washed and back up in two shakes of a lamb's tail.' Then she went slowly down to her basement.

Ambrose stared at a photograph of the Bonnards. Clare and her sister were standing one each side of Mr Bonnard and his new bride. Two Maids of Honour in little round hats like fancy cakes, and carrying posies of Sweet Williams. Ambrose smiled at these small-island people.

Clare told him about the honeymoon and how she had gone on it with her father and stepmother. 'You see, I was resting at the time. Somehow after that I always seemed to go on holiday with them. I never had the courage until this time . . .'

Ambrose suppressed a yawn and ran his fingers along her palm and rubbed and asked, 'Didn't you get enough of the jollies? Didn't I roll you enough?' Clare stared and was silent as he asked, 'So what's come over on you this now?'

'If you like, Ambrose, I'll have that sweater of yours into Miss Pugh's washing-machine downstairs and have it out again in a jiffy . . .'

Ambrose had stared. Then he rubbed the inside of his palms again and said, 'Uhu. I've got to get to Salvo's . . . some guys seen this banger. What's your number?' he added. 'I'll call you.'

'There's only one phone for the whole house and it's by her stairs down.' For some reason the small table the telephone stood on matched the one the Bonnards ate off. Clare could see them all sitting round it, Ambrose sitting beside Mardi and facing a dish of tinned plums and like her, trying to fit each stone to a regimental badge on the plate's decorated edge, four neat chairs round the table and four neat plum stones, and one of the neat plum stones bleeding a little as Clare's father raises his little egg-cup of sweet sherry and calls, 'Here's to the stranger in our midst. And we hope it won't be long before Ambrose feels at home in Drawberry Road.'

'Hear, hear,' Mardi is adding. 'Here's to all of us. Who's for upwash? Not Ambrose, as a newcomer on the scene . . .'

'. . . the scene of the crime . . .' her father goes on boldly, 'I suppose we won't ever get Ambrose to feel that the Brits weren't an entirely bad thing out there . . . ? You and daughter Clare, Ambrose – why don't you take off for some high-jink place and leave us oldsters to wade through the pots and pans?'

'Please,' Clare begged Ambrose as the Bonnard voices grew louder in her mind, 'please take me again.' She drew his hands on to her breasts and then down to her belly. It was a shock when he yawned. He looked suddenly irritated. But after he had gone for the third time, Clare smiled to herself. How could it have been allowed, she asked as she saw reminders of her parents all round her. No sudden father angrily reappearing. Or Mardi. No suddenly reappearing Miss Pugh, even. How could Clare have been allowed to get away with it? Perhaps she would get pregnant? She laughed recklessly as she thought of Mardi pushing her first grandchild round Drawberry Hills, the little patch of green before the shops, and explaining to the neighbours how Clare always had been a citizen of the world, and her father always had looked for the day when we'd all be coffee-coloured.

The next time Ambrose came he seemed slightly distracted. He kept wandering over to the window and would peer down into the dark street. Some black men outside were laughing. Ambrose called down as though he knew them. A car hooted several times. He said he had to be off, but he would call her. Call her? Was he an American? He wasn't on the phone himself but there was another big gig again tomorrow night. If she liked. He gave her his address. He lived above the dry-cleaner in Slack Street. He was looking for a job in the Motor-Licensing Department. 'I've just come back from Sweden,' he confused Clare even more, 'so I must take the bite and jump me clear.'

After Ambrose had gone Clare suddenly felt rich. She could still hear Miss Pugh banging about below as though she were working another heavy great hospital colander, and she could still hear her father calling, '*Liebe Fräulein*, is it me you favour? Gentle maid o'mine we've had some good times, so why not bide at home till Mr Right comes along?'

But Clare was free now and searching for a suitcase to pack a few clothes. Sometimes when she'd had luck and got a part in some provincial theatre in the fifties, she would leave her father a note: 'White wine, Daddy. I'm to be Gwendolen in *The Importance of Being Earnest*. Perhaps it will be a hit and transfer to London. Then it will be champagne . . .'

But now she wrote, 'It's a small bit part . . .' But that seemed even worse, and suppose she were pregnant? So she just wrote, 'Shall be away for a few days, job-hunting. Love C.'

She got out her London A-Z book of maps and found Slack Street in a maze of short streets between Islington and Clerkenwell. She needed her father's magnifying glass to find its course between City Road and Grays Inn Road. She took a bus and then walked, congratulating herself on her newly found freedom.

III

The dry-cleaner in Slack Street smelt of retex. Two children played among the returned clothes and another shuffled himself along the board floor on his potty. A white-faced woman appraised Clare and asked her if she too was 'on the turn', and sighed. She called up to the children who were now playing on the stairs up to the rooms above, 'Daren. Come down out there or you'll know . . . "Suck or fuck", that was what he asked me each time I come up the lane, cheeky bastard . . .' No, she'd never heard of Ambrose, but she pointed up the stairs behind the racks of rustling plastic-draped clothes.

At the top of the first flight a black girl was peering down.

'Ambrose?' she frowned. Clare waited on the landing. There was a tap dripping into a stone sink and beside it a small hob where something was cooking. The reek of fat filled the air.

Ambrose leaned down from the floor above and looked at Clare as though he hadn't recognised her. 'Hi,' he called down. She clambered up the stairs feeling foolish with a big white week-end case her father had bought her on her twenty-first birthday 'to go places'. His room was a narrow slot with a narrow bed that took the length of one side and a table that took its width. Ambrose kissed her and pulled half a can of beer from under the bed and drank.

'You can stay the night if you like,' he looked at her casually. He hadn't seen her in daylight before. She sat on a rough, stained army blanket that covered the bed. 'You can stay here while I'm away,' Ambrose repeated.

Clare sat there and grinned sheepishly at her white suitcase. It reminded her suddenly of her mother's white dancing slippers and loomed near all of a sudden, like an aircraft's sudden war drone.

That May when her mother's illness had started, Mrs Bonnard had wanted to go to Bognor Regis to buy new clothes. 'But you're not sixteen,' Clare and her sister had objected, so their mother had gone to Bognor alone and come back wearing a child's dress with loud stripes like a beach umbrella, and carrying a ham sandwich tied up with pink ribbon she had bought for her husband's birthday. She laughed lustily as she dangled it on its string at his nose.

'You can stay here if you like, till I get back,' Ambrose interrupted Clare's thoughts.

'Will you be away for long?'

'No,' he said, with a neutrality that might easily have meant yes.

'Will you be away long?' Clare repeated, as Ambrose flung open the window and called out into the narrow street.

Two black men were on the other side, standing beside a car. They were all talking together, then Ambrose was gone and Clare could hear her father's voice call, 'Have fun while you may.'

Clare was beside him at their little round table, sliding an apricot stone to the side of her fruit dish as her father asked, 'What's the harm in it?' tipping his head provocatively on one side. 'Some people would say we Britishers are a stuffy lot. But here's proof we can live up to the best of them sur le continong. Ambrose, let me fill your glass . . . Take more. More. We are generous people once you get to know us well . . .'

Clare felt less light-hearted now, and she might be pregnant. She was alone when she woke next morning in the narrow stuffy room. It was very hot, and the room seemed now to be full of shabby wigs and hair-pieces, burst nylon stockings, gaudy rosaries, skin-whiteners and hundreds of documents that smelt of cheap scent and letters that began: 'Dear Sir, I am writing to ask of you a great favour . . .' Letters asking for assistance, letters to the Presidents of African republics, letters to African leaders and generals, offering to interpret their dreams for them; booklets on how to write begging letters that would succeed if certain rituals were obeyed; what rituals to perform if the letters failed, how to cast spells and manage omens. These couldn't be Ambrose's, Clare assured herself as she stared out of the window. His room looked over rows and rows of terraced grey houses; rows and rows of streets with small shops that sold West Indian vegetables, junk or electrical seconds. Clare wandered out on to the narrow landing, then looked out of the back windows where the staircase led up and down.

The weather was suddenly hot, and the house airless. Behind the smell of cooking oil Clare could smell Air-Wick and Lysol. A transistor was playing loudly down below. She washed her hands at the cracked stone sink on the landing. The hot tap was stuffed with rag; the cold sent only a secretion down. She heard noises down below and went on to a fire-escape to look down into the yard. An emaciated black man was stooped on the ground crying as he dragged himself over the hard yard earth. A black girl came out calling back to him in an unfamiliar language, and two small children followed her crying as they eased their father to a bench that stood there. 'Yani,' he called the girl.

Clare climbed further up and found herself on a black flat roof. The pencil line of Slack Street on one side was straight and grey, but on this inner side it grew erratic like a village. At some windows people were cooking or playing cards or sunbathing or reading, feeding babies, making love or washing their hair. From others steam came out, the hiss of a dentist's drill or the sound of voices over the intercoms: 'Mr Baxter is wanted at Unit TS.'

'Come over to the Prayer Palace and see the difference.' Clare expected to see a little shrine beside the notice, but down below, the yards were all as grey as this one. In the one on the left, a woman was standing by a mountain of rubbish with a stick, thrusting out a thick red moist lip as she poked at a thick red strawberry toppling out of a pot. Beyond, in some tenements with iron verandas children were playing with a dismantled fair, stained plastic tub-seats, bits of a Magic Carpet and a Jazz-High's electrical tentacles.

How could she have got here? And would Ambrose come back? What would he say if she were pregnant? Clare felt terribly clumsy. The stairs were dark and narrow and uncarpeted. The bannisters wobbled or didn't exist, and the smell of dry-cleaning and cooking and Lysol followed her up to the top of the house. She could see girls working in a paper factory, dropping packets on a small lift or counting pages with their toes. They told her she had escaped, even if Ambrose didn't come back.

She gazed out fascinated at this world going on so independently of the blank grey faces of the city streets. She expected to see a railway terminus next at their backs, a great Gothic barracks or a naval dock, all held there by the same trust that held every city up. But the sight of the Holy Bread Church of the Latterday Outpourings brought her sense of reality back. Shouts and songs came from it, and there was this pile of half-written begging letters and half-cast horoscopes and spells. They couldn't be Ambrose's. But more shouts came from the church and there was a banging on the front door downstairs. It couldn't be Ambrose so Clare took no notice. But there were footsteps suddenly behind her and two smartly dressed white women stood there.

'Was he your landlord?' they asked her angrily.

'Who? Ambrose, you mean?'

'No, Mr Hood. Do you happen to know who cleaned for him?'

'I don't know who Mr Hood is.'

'He was our uncle and he's been run over and his room's been gone through. Ransacked. All his stuff's taken, his pieces, his spoons, his clips, his cuff-links.'

'I've never met Mr Hood, I'm afraid.'

'I don't care whether you have or not. The stuff's gone.'

Behind the angry women Mr Hood's rooms had been torn apart. 'And he still lying there. No respect even for the dead.' Clare could just see into the room beyond. Its curtains were drawn but she could just see the big black shiny shoes Mr Hood was still wearing. His room smelt worse than the rest of the house. The stuffing had been ripped out of his chair and a dog was digging at it and turning up old tins filled with greasy white chips.

Another white woman stood inside his flat. 'Mr Hood's dead,' she repeated. 'The car didn't stop. It was a black. Hanging's too good for them. And you know how heavy Mr Hood was . . .' They went on tonelessly. They wanted to know where his will was. They felt behind the drawers and up the chimney and inside the tears in the wallpaper, and they jumped on the floorboards to see if they could bring them up. They looked accusingly out of the window at the black girl in the yard.

After they had gone she came up and sighed, 'Oh dear, oh dear.' She said her name was Yani Toshidi and Clare helped her carry boxes of Mr Hood's festering food out to the bins. They lifted the heavy loads as if struggling to get his huge body out. Then a bin lid burst off and out spilled a dead rat and dozens of pulpy tomatoes that wetted them both with red juice. Clare pinched her mouth up with distaste. Lard and bright tomato were smeared down her white dress. She wiped it slowly while Yani said 'That may mean that his life-spirit gone.'

Then an ambulance arrived to take her husband to the day-centre. Eddie was ill, she explained sadly to Clare. 'Brain nodules.

Caused by this country's bad spirit. In Bomba the operation would take place in a private clinic. You would give your date-line and they would say, "We operate tomorrow. For Sure."' But here Yani stared wearily as the ambulance man tried to raise her husband on a lift. 'This country has brought him into such brain illness . . . revenge because Britain has lost Malawi and the rest of Africa too . . .' Yani's husband leaned out of the ambulance in terror. The whites of his eyes dazzled with anguish and his mouth was open and searching for a word.

The ambulance drove off and they went back to Mr Hood's rooms. Yani gave a faint enduring smile as she searched through the landlord's things, wearily taking a pile of his shirts and trousers, some big hotel plates and six sherry glasses.

They didn't go into the back room because of the undertaker. They stood there while Yani explained about Mr Hood, then Clare went back to Ambrose's room and started to pack her clothes, tights, bright blouses, sponge bag and tampons. But suppose she were pregnant? Yani assured her Ambrose would be back: 'Probably just went to the DOS offices to get his chit. Or the coin-op job.'

Clare unpacked her case again. But it grew hotter and it seemed useless to try and remember what it was she had been going to tell Ambrose about her parents and herself. Instead she would just give herself to him, and if she were pregnant, she would perhaps have cured her racial prejudice.

She walked down Sacred Lane. There was a market on. The racks over her head were hung with old clothes that stank in the warmth, stockings turning green with age and old braided jackets. A deaf-and-dumb coster stood outside an eel-and-mash saloon gesticulating with his little red tomatoes, throwing them up and down like yo-yoes. A woman called at the pigeons that rose and fell in undulating waves, 'Come, my beauties. Come my lovely ones.' The pigeons slumped over Sacred Lane.

Clare went into the church she had seen and read a notice about taking care of handbags and valuables while communicating. She sat down beside the Virgin Mary. Someone had draped a white satin cloak round her and put a Ponds Face Cream jar beside her votive candles. Suppose Clare were pregnant?

She went back to Slack Street. Yani had spread a thick brown velour tablecloth over the bed in Ambrose's room, but she hadn't seen Ambrose yet, she said. Her husband, Eddie, cried from the yard. He had woken suddenly with a bad dream. Yani went out again leaving a load of china and shirts from Mr Hood's room on the narrow bed. On the other side of the street, pigeons strutted between the cracked chimney-pots, weaving themselves in and out of the long red pot ranks and scraping their claws free of the cigarette-stubs that had got caught on them, and disentangling themselves from bits of dirty plastic. She was pregnant, Clare thought again, and things were falling apart.

It grew even hotter and the window wouldn't open. She went to the top of the house to get cool. Then she went out again, down into Sacred Lane, went into the church again because it was so cool and white. She prayed for Eddie Toshidi's health and for the soul of Mr Hood. The church was peaceful and smelt of incense, and the baldachino over the high alter was lined with cerulean blue. The altar cloths were red for Whitsun and the saints stood silently and elegantly round, boy saints in white-and-gold tunics like young Roman patricians. And the Queen of Heaven had been newly dressed in violet nylon and white chiffon and she seemed to be smiling at this latest guest of hers.

Clare felt better and went back to Slack Street and the small hot room that was beginning to smell of almonds.

Yani stood there smiling in the doorway. 'It is very hot,' she sighed, and fanned herself with a book. 'They have not been for the corpse yet. In Bomba this would not be so. London is a very poor city. In Bomba that lavatory would not be tolerated.' She nodded at its cracked pan and beckoned Clare up to her room where Mr Toshidi again sat frightened.

'Do you want me to get Ambrose back for you?'

'Oh please,' said Clare, hearing how jolly her voice sounded. She felt funny sitting on a greasy chair, her fresh white skirt draped decoratively round her legs and her hands clasped together round her knees as though she were on a garden party lawn, talking to colonials and District Officers, nodding her enthusiasm as Yani went on, 'The she in the Sacred Lane – the she from the Planet House – she no good. She jes tell you put a stone under your wig and inside your body bottom. And that's five quid she wants, and it don't work.'

Oh dear,' Clare could hear her own best party voice. 'A lot of money, true.'

Yani stared at her. 'Have you got a dead on you?' She scrutinised Clare. 'I could fix it.'

34

'Oh thank you.' How kind, Clare almost heard her voice add.

Yani was telling her how she got 'a dead' on a woman. And how she got it out of her too. There were jars full of dark oil and black ointment along the window sill, hair-straighteners and hair-tints to hide African malnutrition. Mr Toshidi cried out in his sleep again, and a huge wooden clock ticked in the corner. Yani's two children huddled under the table. Then Mr Toshidi woke and twisted round so that he could see the television set. Some morris men were prancing round on the screen doing leapfrogs and shouting as they knocked each others' sticks, 'How do you, and how do you do, and how do you do again?'

A police siren drowned them for a moment and Yani sighed. 'In Malawi the police don't meddle with you so, and they don't meddle with a man's spirit and say it's just brain diseases this doctor's come to cure.'

Clare could see the faces of the two children peering up. Then Mr Toshidi's face fell forward and tears were running down his cheeks. He tried to walk over to his children, then he fell back in his chair.

'They do not do this to you in Malawi. The whites. Not allowed. No more.'

'How do you do, and how do you do,' came from the dancers on the small screen, mincing round in a circle.

'Back home we have coolers and screens and air-conditioning for the heat. Maybe soon my thesis will be complete and we shall return to regain our professions. You were alright in Britain till you lost your empire. Before you translate your Holy Books into the low tongues of the black people and trash. It was then you lost your power, with your Bible-spells. So you lose your empire and the trash comes over here to buy the things to take back there . . .'

Yani stared out at the pigeons still strutting between the chimney-pots and pacing across a rusty tin tray full of pebbles that someone had started to paint black and then abandoned. A pigeon turned the pebbles now, shuffled among them, then it too stopped. Yani sighed again and looked at her sick husband whose eyes were imploring them. The pigeon coughed up feathers and a cigarette stub it hadn't been able to digest. A wind rose. The two children crawled under the table and drew close to their mother.

'Do you want me to bring him back?' Yani asked, indicating Ambrose's room. 'If you give me one of his hairs and some of his excrems . . .' The wind blew along the yards, first from one direction then from another. The children started to cry. Clare looked at the mysterious books on dreams along the shelf. The wind blew again, and she saw clay models there too. Stout black deities.

'How can you believe in the one God?' Yani was asking Clare, 'when there are all these spirits running in different directions everywhere? If there was only the one god there would be only one wind and one . . . water . . . and one . . .'

'I don't know that I believe in God myself,' Clare said, in a voice that she had once thought rather adventurous.

'No. No. No. Nor do we. No longer. Five is the number of the wind-spirits and five of the water. Five,' she held up her fingers. 'Do you want me to get your man back for you? Or the dead you're carrying, eh?'

Clare laughed nervously and felt the weight of her white frilly blouse. She got up saying she must go and make a phone call. She went out again and down Sacred Lane. She came to a butcher's stall where bruised brown meat was spread. Curling yellow fat ran off it like a dirty nose. Beside the stall a filthy white poodle crouched quietly quivering while its owner shouted down at it, 'What's the matter with you?' The butcher turned to her customers, 'She's a little girl dog, and she's been all over the place, so now she's old it all just drops out of her . . .'

Clare climbed a flight of stone steps up on to a viaduct lined with great palatial planes and chestnut trees. The chestnuts were still in full flower but their pinks and whites seemed suddenly heavy and unpleasantly throbbing, full of viscous green substance suspended precariously up there, waiting in a flood stopped by only one thin membrane from descending on to her; such a weight up there that Clare almost understood why Yani revered stout and ugly clay deities grinning and presiding over this pagan moment in spring.

Yani was washing out the bath when Clare got back. It seemed to have been full of blood. 'My grandmother was a wise woman,' she called out at Clare. 'All our people used to go to my granny before they come to Europe. Even our Malawi ambassador, he come to our granny for words. Good words to help him in Europe against white power spells. Good words she used to write for them before they come to white man's country. Want me to get your man back for you?' She leaned over the bloody bath and breathed heavily as though she were simply leaning over to do her children's washing. 'Give me a few of his hairs . . . My grandmother work so that no white man can ever do this kind of thing over a black man in black man's country. But not here.'

They went back to Yani's room. The morris men still seemed to be shaking their legs on the television, and making the bells on their calves ring as they beat each others' sticks and twittered to Clare, 'Good Prince Hal shall be our king.'

Yani made a stab at a cockroach that was running smoothly over the table. 'In our country,' she sighed, 'we have servants to keep these things out.'

Then the undertaker came and took Mr Hood's body away and that seemed to release a stream of cockroaches. They ran up and down the hot walls in straight and diagonal lines as soon as the lights were switched off. They cowered in corners as Yani waved a rolled newspaper at them or threw a shoe. Clare had never seen a cockroach before. Yani sighed and called them 'English gentlemen' as they ran, as though they were on wheels, from Mr Hood's cooker. Clare caught one by putting a jar over it, but when she lifted it off it stank of menstrual blood and the rest of them seemed to be hugging each other and laughing at her, then running away like beads of blood down the wall to the wainscot again, to hug each other down there in reunion, laughing as her parents at their supper table discussed whether to invite the Nigerian sidesman at their church to come home for a meal. 'We live in a time of great changes, Clare-girl,' Clare could hear her father saying. 'We must keep our standards high but we must also adapt or perish.'

Clare pounced on a cockroach on the wall behind her and stamped it into the ground, but it only shammed dead and was up again and rolling along laughing as soon as her back was turned. Things were falling apart. They whispered, 'You didn't know there were still slaves in the world, did you?'

Clare could hear Mr Toshidi crawling over his room to the door and the stairs and the yard. Yani was calling to Clare to come and help her get him back into his chair. They pushed him back into it and he sat there leaning back like a saint in agony. The wind grew louder and the two children cried and clung to their father who moaned and shook and clutched the wall. Yani stared at him and sighed.

Loud singing came from the Church of the Holy Bread.

'Healings and Praises Daily' was written up outside its corrugated-iron door. The singing was drowned by a police-siren. Then the singing came even louder, then cries for healing.

'They no good,' Yani sighed. 'We tried them when we first come here.'

Mr Toshidi cried again. On the television the morris dancers were still crying as they clapped sticks demurely at Clare, 'Good Prince Hal shall be our king.'

'Once I was ashamed because my grandmother was a witch.'

'We with them to the merry green will go . . .'

'The missionaries cursed my grandmother. Come down the line of women and cry, "You, and you and you." And when they come to my granny they stopped dead: "And you the very wickedest of all evil women." So they did not let her pass on all her writings to me. But I learned enough. Then you lost your empire,' Yani gazed out of the window again, 'so our country came back to us, and our writings . . .'

The pigeon outside came right in at the window and pecked at Mr Toshidi's plate of food, pecked at the mattress on their bed till he cried again. Yani tried to put a plastic bag over its head.

'We are not so poor. We take the Koran instead for our knowledge now.' The rough pottery busts stood on burnt clay plates now. The deities had horrible eyes and big breasts and they seemed fiercely naked. Mr Toshidi cried out again, fiercely naked too. 'And look at him now your hospitals have lost their power and white man's only Bible powers gone.' Yani propped her husband up again. Clare felt hypnotically stuck to her seat. Drawberry Road seemed decades away.

Next day it was even hotter and the cockroaches grew stronger and tougher in the heat. Clare heard a voice downstairs and felt fixed again. If it were Ambrose . . . she felt sure it was Ambrose, but Yani shook her head and said it was just the ambulance men again to take her husband to occupational therapy. They watched a cockroach race away from a plate of food beside Mr Toshidi's bed. Heat pressed down from the slate roof. The two clay deities seemed to be singing and clapping. Clare went to bed and dreamed that the railway-lines had been taken up and that they had to hop instead, and keep on hopping. Only the cockroaches were allowed to run smoothly on runners.

It grew like an iron basin under the slate roof. Yani was writing on lined white paper sprinkled with heavily-scented talcum powder.

She said she was studying for a doctorate: 'The Role of the Grandmother in Nineteenth-Century Malawian Society'. When they got home to Bomba, she said, Eddie was to work in the Ministry of War and she was to teach sociology. 'Most Nyasa customary law is unwritten. I will have to return for the interviews before I submit my thesis.' She gave Clare a bracelet that would bring her a husband. She gestured towards the two ugly clay images with bawling mouths and huge breasts: 'I could clear your "dead" for you,' she indicated Clare's stomach. 'Three pounds.'

Clare dreamed that night that the moon was hairy and sticky. Yani bought sliced meats next day, damp and colourless and wrinkled and squamous. She urged Clare to eat and pointed at her stomach. Clare felt sick as though she were eating wet sliced vulva and clitoris.

Yani nodded reassuringly. 'Three pounds. I'll fix it. Eddie and I had many powers and a car and a house in Bomba. That was because we were not ashamed to turn back to our grandmothers' ways once your white god had let you down in Africa. For three pounds,' she held up three fingers and her husband nodded and held up three of his.

Clare looked at the jars and tins on the shelf and their Arabic labels. There was some graph paper pinned on the wall and the scrawls written down it seemed as menacing as the statuettes. Tar seemed to be running from their mouths and down the graph paper, as well. And thus anarchy had been loosed on the world. The Doctor of Sociology was asking three pounds for removal of foetus: 'Just *one* hair and some of your own excrems.'

Clare went out into Sacred Lane and the church again. It was still a cool and crystal white and smelt of incense. Some children were playing round Mr Hood's coffin lying in a side-chapel. The altar still wore its Whitsun scarlet and the Queen of Heaven lifted up her arms for all humanity to reach heaven through her. 'I wasn't at all a nice person either,' she seemed to be saying to Clare. 'I was a racist and regarded all this with distaste.'

The church smelt clean and Clare sat down again and dreamed again she was at a railway station waiting for the train. Then white deer and gazelles swarmed out of it, plunging down into frozen lakes. The priest was wanting to lock up his church and the click of his keys woke Clare. She stared ahead of her at the mosaic tiles on the floor. Pigeons were undulating up them and towards the high altar, while the priest was trying to prepare for the funeral and drive them back. But they only flew up on to the capitals of the piers and shat down while he turned to the children who were playing round Mr Hood's coffin, and tried to drive off two boys who were chanting at a girl with a skipping-rope, 'She's wearing towels again. I seen them up her panties on the swings.' The priest moved to drive a pigeon off the coffin but it only flew towards the high altar again.

Clare walked out into Sacred Lane again. It was evening. The stalls were being packed up and the barrows wheeled away. A few children were riding on them or trailing along behind. When she got in, Mr Toshidi was still leaning forward in his chair in pain, half falling on to the floor and complaining about the winds. The basketwork that the occupational therapy centre had given him was slowly unwinding beside him on the floor. Yani was in the bathroom bending over the huge and dirty bath. The squawk of a pigeon came from inside. It made a subdued noise as Yani cut its rashed red throat. A vein pulsed in and out on two beats, and blood pulsed as regularly in a stream along the inside of the bath. Yani took a breath and leaned further into it as though she were merely struggling with a piece of stubborn washing, pummelling and sighing 'Oh dear' as the bird kicked silently and struggled, its wings spread out for flight, its legs scraping the scratchy side of the bath, and its eye rolling round and round. 'You whites have lost your God, now.'

There was a noise downstairs. Two policemen stood there. They were looking for a Mr Ambrose de Bono.

'That's a lie,' Yani shouted down at them. 'Mr Hood just step under a car on a one-way street. He'd been drinking. I smelt it on him all the week. And it was his relatives, those white-kid ladies in furs who come and took the stuff from his room. I seen it with my own two eyes.'

The policemen stood there neutrally, then they went. Yani came back upstairs and pulled the bird out of the bath and thrust it down the lavatory where it went on pulsing. She tried to flush it away but it shot up, so she put a board over the pan and sat down on it, got up and poured bleach down, then sat down again till the bird silently capitulated underneath.

'I've fixed it for you,' she gestured at the bath which was still full of blood. 'Three pounds.'

Then Clare found she had started to menstruate. She gave Yani the money and prepared her white suitcase for Drawberry Road, praying that Ambrose wouldn't turn up there for cover. She was afraid too that Drawberry Road would read from her face what she had wanted. She must get away from London, not just from Slack Street anarchy. The Toshidis had broken rules. She packed her neat white suitcase. The little holiday parasols scattered over her sponge bag mocked her.

She made her way down to the granite viaduct that led from Sacred Lane towards the West End. It was heavy with trees. She could feel their weight as she stood at the bus stop, the garish green trick of May above. She half expected Ambrose to step out of it, as alien to Slack Street as he would have been to a Tory ladies' Bring-and-Buy. Her squeamish soul hoped this, but just then a number thirty-eight bus came along and took her back to the safety of Drawberry Road. But perhaps Ambrose would be waiting there with Miss Pugh? As the bus drew up she could imagine her father's voice addressing him, then her: 'Did you two make hay together, Clare-girl, while the two aged P's were away?'

After that, Clare made a little of Ambrose go a long way. But the trees remained slung with reminders. Clare wasn't pregnant, she told herself with relief. Things were just as they had been before. The view from the roof of the dry-cleaners in Slack Street was just a normal London cityscape. Nothing had happened and nothing paranormal hung in the trees. Yani was just a young married woman with studies to get on with, and a sick husband. Voodoo had no place here. Things only seemed to be falling apart, and she had only imagined that the Toshidis had broken rules.

But now, in Oxford, five years later, Clare often thought of that false alarm of hers. May was coming again and bringing with it, as it always did now, a glistening pagan reminder. Clare had got away from her parents. She had a room of her own now, and was grateful. But when she looked at the picture postcards from all over the world that the Fellows of Sanctus Spiritus College sent her, and the little toilet bag that she carried to the office each day which nearly matched the curtains at the bathroom window, and the wooden clip someone had given her to fix on her handbag, the Bambi deer's face that peered at her every day when she put her bag down, seeming to say, 'Are you having fun now you're safe from Slack Street?' – when Clare had these reminders she felt the ambiguities of her escape. Oxford was a place where people decide very quickly who is going to be useful to them and who not. Clare had settled for usefulness and the things round her seemed to nod and confirm this. 'Things didn't fall apart after all, thanks to your prompt action.' She still sometimes felt a slim satisfaction in the certainties of her Oxford world. She could see Grace Plasket down below wandering through Sanctus's Long Quad, passing her hand in and out of the fountain, then drifting on through Great Quad and looking up at the window where Clare sat at her typewriter, then telling her about the May Morning picnic she was planning.

'That will be gorgeous, Grace,' Clare could hear her certainty voice call as Mrs Plasket went on to tell her about her ex-lover, Anil, from Bombay, and his son Hari who was arriving soon. Next week in fact, and just in time for her May Day picnic.

'That would be super, Grace.' Anarchy would not be loosed upon the world, Clare felt sure, in Oxford, as she walked home under its brag of green.

IV

And so Clare sat at her desk in the College office of Sanctus, safely
writing out a birthday-card for Dr Pyecraft's wife, and another for
. . .? Whose card was it she still had to do? She stared at the picture
of the sleepy owl in his nightcap dozing over his Latin texts.

It was late April, nearly May, and the trees had a trick brightness,
as they unburdened themselves, that reminded Clare she hadn't
exorcised Slack Street yet. She was sad, not so much because of
the things she might have done as because of the things we do not
know we can do or want to do, till it's too late. So she filled in the
next sad little greetings-card 'Congratulations', sitting in her cotton
dress with the discreet white cardigan over it and pastel slippers,
then recorded dates for cake-sales for 'Feed The Minds' in her
little pocket diary.

But the card she was holding up was a get-well one. Dr Joseph
Conroy, the Music Fellow, had been beaten up by a gang near his
home in Judasland and he was in hospital. Dr Conroy hadn't been
near Sanctus for over two years and there were hints from his
colleagues. Perhaps the gang of thugs had been his students?

Clare had finished typing the last chapter of Alec Smale's book.
His dog was sniffing round the wainscot, waiting for her to exercise
him. As she packed up to leave, she could hear music from the
maze behind Long Quad. The college band was again rehearsing
for Bishop's Benediction Night in early July. Voices from its choir
floated at her, then stopped. They were supposed to be practising
Joe Conroy's 'Guga Motet' – a Swedish industrial saga, everyone
thought, his most recent composition. But the choir would hover
restlessly over his staccato G-flats, then float happily away on an
elastic string back into their Handel.

Endless pleasure, endless love . . .

As Clare packed her bag and washed her coffee cup and powdered her nose, she could hear Grace Plasket's slight American drawl again outside. Her greying hair flew over her face and the trug on her arm was loaded with stuff she must have taken from the Master's garden.

'He's been overplanting again, you see,' she laughed faintly. 'When I knew him in Lahore, of course there were no real gardens. He came to me first with this physical loneliness and longing in Istanbul where I was on a dig and happened to be pining for a German Jew from Indonesia with a spiky beard that prickled me each time we made love. But then he left for the Nile, and I heard last week', she sighed, 'that he died in Chicago last month. I've only just been sent his obituary from *Le Monde*. His body has been flown back to me. He looked rather like Einstein in his death, and it was sad that we never really said goodbye.'

> . . . Endless love
> Semele enjoys above . . .

came from the choir rehearsing in the maze.

'It was Anil who wrote and told me. I told you, didn't I, about Hari's book. The Press is interested in it. It's about witchcraft and the way Indian psychiatry looks at it. He's looking for a job, Hari is, thinks he might get this NHS one, in Judasland, in Dr Mally's practice. Anil is unhappy about Hari's English though, and wants me to give him some lessons. On a strictly professional basis, of course. I've never met Hari, though his father writes tenderly. Big things are promised for him, back in Bombay . . .'

There was a hissing sound from the maze beyond Long Quad. The choir seemed to be gargling then spitting as they raced through the last sequence of Conroy's 'Guga Motet', then sprang back suddenly and without warning into Handel and 'Endless Pleasure Endless Love . . .'

Clare said goodbye to Mrs Plasket, then heard the Master's wife calling her as she unwrapped her sandwich supper over her office typewriter. 'Clare, we've had such guilty consciences about you. We keep meaning to invite you . . .'

'Please stop keep meaning to . . .' This didn't sound grammatical though, and Clare more often than not took refuge behind good grammar as well as crisp white dresses with blue piping; or peach. 'Oh not to worry,' she cried back instead, 'we all know what busy people you and the Master are.' The cuckoo clock in her must have called the right hour or the right part of the hour because the Master's wife was telling her now about La Jolla. The bell rang in the quad for Second Hall and the fountain rose and lapsed peacefully in Long Quad.

'We're all so much looking forward to the Master's next book,' she sang out, and folded her sandwich-paper away, carefully disposed of the few crumbs she had made, rinsed out the cup she had made her instant coffee in, unplugged her typewriter, looked for her lipstick, locked up the files for the night, put the unwholesome dog on his lead and cried, 'Walkies, chum,' then added, 'Too true . . . How kind . . . Simply gorgeous . . . Such a blessing . . . That's a promise . . .' Then she left the office and Great Quad and crossed Long Quad with Alec's dog on its lead, and tugged it away from the gentle fountain. Long Quad had four storeys on all four of its sides and that made it echo like a cistern full of water every time the fountain dripped. And when the wind came running down the green tunnel that led out to the maze, the fountain was flung out over the dry yellow sand path that would suddenly smell of quenching.

Clare went down the broad and shallow steps worn with centuries of student feet and out into the college maze.

The maze at Sanctus wasn't a maze at all. Before the Reformation there had been a monastery here and the monks had kept bees and supplied the University with honey, apples, quinces and fish. But after the Dissolution, the supplies of fruit and honey and fish from the monastic stewponds had been withdrawn and harsh reformers had planted box hedges instead in crooked rows, and yews to remind youth of mortality. After the Restoration of the Monarchy however, the maze had been judiciously abandoned and over the years had become overgrown and turned into a pleasant melancholy wood where people from the nearby streets could wander. Clare liked going back to her digs along this magical tongue of green curling stealthily with the pressure of a tide into the heart of the city. She left the maze and stepped through the gate into Inkerman Street and peaceful Judasland.

No one really knew the origin of the name 'Judasland', though it had been discussed in learned journals. Some thought a hostel for pilgrim penitents and flagellants had stood here before the Reformation. Pilgrims in hair shirts, it had been asserted, stopped here on their way to the Shrine of St Frideswide calling, '*Me Judas miserere, O Virgo Turris Aurea.*'

But most scholars, however, thought that the name must simply be a corruption of 'Jude's Land'. Perhaps some monastic clerk with a grudge against the venality of the place had maliciously misspelt the name and 'Judas' had stuck.

'We hate it. It sounds so poor and common,' the older people of Judasland would complain. There had been petitions to the City Council to get the name changed to 'Rivermead', 'Flowerville' or even simply 'St James' after its parish church. But the City Council always turned down the request. In fact, the inhabitants of the grid of red and blue brick terraced streets had always just referred to the place as 'The Land'. The only people who stuck scrupulously to the old name were the new middle classes, who loudly, at their parties, praised their new discovery, 'a real working community with deep roots', and tried to revive old customs like Beating the Bounds and the May Day procession down to the river.

It was twilight and the japonica on the walls seemed almost to blacken and the voices of children came loudly among the birds, as though they were the true participants of this half-life of the day. Then the voices of the University would interrupt: 'It was lovely to see you at Margot and Teddy's last night. Will you be at Sir Jimmy's?'

'We hate the name "Judasland" and we hate them Varsity people too,' an old woman watering her flowerbox in Candid Street would add. 'We call them the "Busy Lizzies" the way they keeps on interfering.' Mrs Gage loved to stop Clare on her way home. 'And now they wants to start reviving the old May Day and the Beating of the Bounds, too. And the Man of Green ... Wouldn't be surprised if they tried to revive the sackcloth aprons we children went out scrubbing in before we went to school, or the Bishop's Certificate we could leave school with before we was twelve. But they stays on coming *here* ...' She would gaze out over the streets of checkerboard brick.

Most of the terraced houses had thin walls, two rooms downstairs and two above and no inside lavatories. So the college servants, compositors, railway workers, tallow-candle workers and sempstresses who had traditionally lived there had been enticed away to new council estates on the ring roads of the city where land was cheaper. Those who remained were bitter. The arrival of the middle classes had put house prices up and so their children and grandchildren had to take the same route to the ring roads. Clare was often buttonholed by people like Mrs Gage, and she had

46

taken to visiting one or two of the housebound, or shopping for them.

'We'd run straight out of St Jim's School and down to the river to play in the piles of sand the boats brought up ... But before school there was the doorsteps of Inkerman Street to be done. And they never gave you hot water. There was many a tear I shed on cold mornings out there at six ... I went there cleaning till last year. A Professor's house, Professor Boden's.' This was Clare's landlord so she pricked up her ears. 'Worked for Mrs Boden twenty years, till I got the telly. But when I saw what lovely houses there was on the TV I knew she wasn't rich at all,' she repeated. 'So now I stays at home ... Yes, I was in domestic service all my life ... My mum took in washing from the colleges, surplices and ladies' underwear and the house smelt all week of starch ...' Clare could still see the long lines running the lengths of the Judasland yards where women who took in college washing would hang out sheets and surplices ...

'The whole place reeked of soda and starch all week, and now these Varsity people comes down here to live. What *do* they be thinking of? I just don't understand. And you should hear the typewriters. My niece lives out at Hook and they've even got the typewriters out there if you please, where my uncle didn't even have an outside toilet. They don't ever stop. And what do they all keep typing about? And that food they eat. It turns your teeth yellow and your stomach too, I wouldn't be surprised. It's a disgrace ...'

Then voices would drop as Nellie Grainger appeared at the furry green mouth of the maze and stumbled blindly away down Candid Street 'looking for the horses'. They would frown and touch their sleeves and purse their lips and hint as Nellie stood there pinning Clare down with her husky voice and scanning her face with her white half-blind eyes.

'I'm nearly ninety now and I still love to see the sparks fly from the horses. And I was in the Boer War too. Sewing men's shrouds and making up their death warrants. Ninety and I've still got no husband. But I've seen three wars and six death-warrants of my own, and that was it.'

Nellie would disappear. She never dawdled in the Land. The other women smelt her in her dirty green pinafore-dress and the shiny yellow dressing-gown tied tightly round it, and got out Air Wick. Clare didn't like that look in her boiled white eyes either.

'It's a bad eye,' an old man whose pension Clare collected each week seemed to agree, waving Nellie away when he saw her hovering outside his front-room window. 'And she do seem to return to the old ways now these newcomers be around. They war bad days,' he would sigh, and then Clare could hear sounds from a newly bought house next door: 'No, no no. You must try to vomit it all out much more,' a woman's voice was calling. 'Keith, try and vomit up "The Arts" . . .'

"I could not decided', a tenor voice started to sing again, '"whether to make a career in theology or whether to devote myself entirely to the Arts."'

'Right from the pit of your stomach, Keith. Right from your pelvic floor. Try again, "Persecution was rampant in the land . . . I could not decide . . ."' Then a fast procession of demi-semitones came from the open window.

'"Persecution was rampant . . ."' the tenor tried again.

'No, no Keith. You're still not vomiting it out enough . . .' the woman's voice interrupted.

'"The saints were forced to flee . . ."'

'Let's go.'

'It don't be right somehow,' the old man was murmuring, listening, puzzled. Not long ago there had been plans to turn Judasland into a light-industrial estate. But the outcry against destroying a closely knit community where the old values still held had been so vociferous that the plans had been withdrawn, and each evening now as Clare walked home she could hear voices like this tenor's endlessly rehearsing, '"Or to devote myself entirely to the Arts."'

The old inhabitants would stare as they saw baths being carried into houses, new Georgian-style sash-windows being fitted back in, shutters, decorative fanlights and panel-doors. Someone had even gone so far as to repaint the faded advertisements down the brick sides of houses in Balaclava Road: WALKER'S TEAS ARE BEST. TRY THEM TODAY; and J. UPMINSTER SACRISTAN AND UNDERTAKER. PLEASE RING BELL ONCE. NO COALS SOLD AFTER DARK. And from the newly established St James's Arts Centre, more music floated out. The old man swore at Nellie Grainger and sighed as the new community tugged in various directions. At one house a burglar alarm had just been fitted over E.JUMP.BED TICKINGS. QUILTINGS. WOOLLEN CLOTHIER. And by the river that ran at the end of

Parnassus Street there was a faded notice: 'Ring bell once for ferry. One half-penny.' But instead of a syphilitic ferryman dragging himself out of a shed beside the worn rope of the bell, a huge bald American in a backwoods shirt and Wild West hat sat there on the wooden bench reading the *Principia Mathematica*, and teaching a group of American children to play poker.

'Gim Smallstein does watercolours of Judasland at any time of the day or night'; Clare was staring at the notice in the window of a re-Georgianised house.

'I've heard of etchings and French lessons twenty-four hours a day,' Grace Plasket stood beside her and laughed, 'but surely twenty-four-hour-a-day *water colours* is carrying the gentrification of Judasland just a bit too far. Thank God I've left the place,' she drawled on. 'You must come and see me out at Hedgencote.'

'Grace, I'd love to,' Clare said. 'Simply super.'

'I'll be in touch,' Mrs Plasket waved and lagged behind to examine the succulents in someone's garden, stole some herbs, threw water from a bottle at Alec's dog and called back at Clare, 'Hari's book is about magic and placebo in South Bombay villages. There was something lonely about his father. Rather like the Master. Needing me just a bit too much. Men always demand this. But I've never met Hari. His father says he'll be here in three days. The Judasland doctors have split up. Haven't you heard? Dr Mally is setting up alone. He really wants a woman doctor to run gyne clinics etc. But in the meantime Hari is going to help out. I'm going to invite father and son out to Hedgencote. You've never seen my cottage out there? An old blacksmith's. You must come out. Hari must be nearly thirty by now; even more. Fortunately his father is progressive and hasn't arranged a marriage, or anything along those lines, though his mother is more traditional. Cheers. Goodbye.'

A youth in a pink shirt swerved past on a bicycle riding no-handed, steering with his knees and calling out to someone invisible upstairs, 'Charles and Gerda say they'll meet us at six at the Dragon.' Gerda in a scarlet cap with long black hair drawn into a thick glossy tail behind her was pushing out her serious dark face at a young man with a bucket and brush who was leaning over a wall splashing up a poster about a Judasland gig.

Clare felt a pang at the normality of this joint effort and the easy relationship they seemed to have, as easy and as neutral as picking up a bus ticket or a packet in a transaction that had no overtones or bias. Clare could imagine Hari Sharma casually leaning over her and saying, 'Just a little more to the right. I'm afraid India must be out until next June.' And she was replying, 'Yes, I can't make it either till then ... Is it just the four of us? ...' 'The four of us.' Such partnership. Such a casual celebration of at homeness in the world. 'The four of us' set her in her rightful place along with Gerda in her red beret and boys riding no-handed down the street with rolls of posters under their arms to fly-stick at nights.

But Hari Sharma could hardly fit into such an English fantasy so Clare let him jump down two stairs, calling instead, 'Clare, what do you think? India is two-fifty-seven not out.' But that still made Hari seem too English, and in any case, Clare's knowledge of cricket was as weak as her enthusiasm for it, so she put Hari in a punt on a glorious afternoon when the lime-trees were spreading out their sweet heady heats and the tower of Magdalen loomed over them. He stood up in the punt and saluted its white beauty: 'I did not know your buildings shone, or that you had such glorious springs.'

He was smiling into the sun and warming himself as he tentatively lowered his punt-pole into the water, avoided its drip on his neat ankles and went on: 'Clare, tell me, which is more correct, con*trov*ersy or *con*troversy? ... I must get this pole down parallel, you say? ...' And Clare who had never been out in a punt was telling him to let it just drop as she spread out the red tablecloth her parents had sent her over the buttercup-laden meadows beside the river where Hari had stabbed the punt to a halt and pinned it, 'So here is our faithful steed,' while the water lapped and lifted the great chimes from the tower and spread them too across their afternoon meadow like a celestial apparel ...

Clare let him go on: 'Clare, Roderick says will we be at the Habbertons tomorrow night. Can we make it?' The gentle drip-drip sound came of punts being paced, then stopped. The chimes of the bells spread again over the water. But the great trees overhead were carrying such aggressive white shiny wares, like white condoms shining up there. They suddenly made her think of Slack Street again. Hari's book, Grace Plasket had said, was about witchcraft. But Hari was a doctor and not an out-of-work coin-op launderette attendant, so she let him still stand there by the moored punt and answer his own question: 'No doubt we shall be seeing them at Anne and Tarquin's, so the explanations can wait till then.'

But by this time Clare had reached the house in Inkerman Street where she had her bedsitter. She always dreaded this approach to the front door each night, climbing the six steps up, with her key clutched in her hand so that she could get the door opened and herself inside the house before the door was sprung open from the inside and an undergraduate leaped out, stepped back, stared and cried back, 'Tell them to bring at least a dozen glasses. And which car, do you think? Hell. *Which* car?' Oh what enviable 'whichness'. The arrogance of Oxford as the voices went on: 'I'd always thought there was something silly about the Greeks . . .'

'. . . nice Jewish South Africans, but they've turned the old farm into a post-mortem room . . .'

'. . . and said they needed three more Tuesdays to complete . . .'

But tonight it was only Clare's landlady greeting her at the door. 'Miss Bonnard,' she called. 'Is that you, Miss Bonnard? My dentist won't let me spit.'

Clare always dreaded the business of coming to a standstill opposite Mrs Boden. She would warn her landlady of her arrival home by clearing her throat as she started to climb the steps up to the front door, then clearing it again as she fumbled with her key in the lock, already having got it out of her purse at the turn in Candid Street, as she rehearsed some remark about the weather, or, 'Did Mrs Masters get her new gate?' Or, 'Did your daughter ring with the news about the baby?'

Clare hated being found on the landing too, caught out of her room like the snail out of its shell, naked and exposed with a Snug hot-water bottle in one hand and wet nylons or a minute egg saucepan in the other.

Now the evening ritual made her smile at her landlady who stood with her brown woollen legs planted wide apart in their sandals. But Mrs Boden was grim: 'Good evening, Miss Bonnard, I've just been to the dentist.' She faced Clare angrily and repeated, 'He wouldn't let me spit.'

She looked at Clare almost accusingly, her white face staring behind enormous black-rimmed spectacles that covered almost all the upper part of her face. Her expression grew even angrier as she repeated, 'It was a new dentist, and I *like* a good spit.' This was so apparent to Clare that she was always obliged to stand a little to the left as her landlady cried in outrage, 'And I like my food hot. Really hot. But my daughter gave me *cold* beans and tepid fish, and greens that were . . . By the way, there was a telephone call for you and I left the message on the jumbly-jim.' The jumbly-jim was an old climbing frame that had once belonged to the Boden young. Now their parents hung clothes on it and pinned messages on the warped wood of its frame.

'Just look at that cherry tree over there. Atrocious.' Mrs Boden's anger rose again. 'I *do* dislike such brightly coloured trees, especially if they are propped up with such staring stakes. If you *must* choose a flowering cherry . . . There was a telephone message for you, Miss Bonnard. Someone called Mardi.'

Once, soon after Clare first moved here, the telephone message had been from an old childhood friend, Nick De Berry. They had played together as children at Curley Hill and pretended to be cousins, at least Clare had suggested this relationship and Nick had agreed with the cool politeness of a boy who knew he had only temporarily to play with girls.

When Clare 'came up to Oxford', as her father put it, Mr Bonnard had urged her to get in touch with her 'cousin' again. He was a college bod, Dad said, an academic up-and-comer, a medic working in one of the local hospitals, so he had read in the correspondence column of his daily newspaper. Clare had sent a tentative note to Dr Nicholas De Berry at the hospital suggesting a drink and a chat about old times. She had got out Mardi's Christmas present, *Adventurous Cookery for One Person*. But the reply had come from St Martyrs' College and the invitation had been turned. Nick was inviting her to drinks at his college, and she went there not expecting a party and not dressed for one.

She was greeted by Nick, who was now a polished smiling bearded dwarf with large dark laughing eyes that almost reached his sideburns, and a long impish mouth. His eyes flashed at his pupils as he introduced them, twenty undergraduates and a dozen women from Lady Margaret Hall. Clare stood there in her tweed skirt and white woolly, smiling and nodding at each of them each time they called across her.

'. . . his tutor goes to Moscow each summer to chat up his spies.'
'. . . as spies to wanted boys . . .'

Clare stepped out into a rainy little courtyard where trees held out their leaves like playing-cards waiting to fall back into their rightful order when the rain and wind stopped. Someone gave her a drink and asked her about her dog and her garden. Before she had time to reply he had added, 'Or is it something else you do?'

'I'm fond of poetry.'

'Bak's writing porn.' There was laughter.

'Darling, he'd need me for that,' a girl in a white silk dress with a slit all the way up the back called over Clare's tweed self.

'. . . went to a solicitor to be hypnotised.'

'. . . in a class of her own . . . because she smelt wrong.'

'No Queen Victoria was the only one who did that.'

'Did what? What did she do apart from *not* getting VD?'

Clare giggled sheepishly, then she suddenly heard a familiar voice. Alec Smale from Sanctus was having a good grumble to a band of attentive students because his publisher had signed him up for another book, '*and* for the editorship of the whole damn series.' He was under threat, wasn't he? He turned to Clare for support. He'd thought of becoming a Catholic and going into retreat. But in fact he'd been invited by the CIA to Bellagio. He sighed, watching himself being watched. Then he introduced Clare as the girl who danced the Farandole each year with five thousand other girls at the Albert Hall. There was another burst of merriment and Clare managed to escape.

The air was heavy with the smell of limes and cottonwood and the university bells were clogging the evening air. The rain had stopped and she could hear Magdalen's bells again hitting the water again and again, and spreading along it till they faded. It was the water that kept up the myth, Clare thought as the talk went on round her: 'Fortunately Grania doesn't mean anything. Ever. That's the best thing about LMH women.'

'Terribly political but he didn't hesitate to use public money to fly between the Apac chimneys . . .'

'Is that how you broke your leg? eh?'

'No. I was a cheerleader.'

'Who were you a cheerleader with?'

'Wendy Crocker and Julie Nixon. Know them? Back home?'

'Sure, in primatology.'

Clare walked stiffly away. Nick De Berry called, 'Marvellous to see you again, another survivor of all the changes in our day and age.' Nick had blown her a kiss as she crept away. Her legs felt waterlogged. Her shoes felt like skis. She felt as though she had a heavy leaden scooter helmet on her head. She hadn't seen Nick again, since then. These days it was always Mardi or her father on the phone.

'We should have frozen their assets and seized their lands,'

Clare could hear Professor Boden calling from the conservatory he had built behind his sitting-room, to house the rows and rows of index boxes he used to emend his vast *Dictionary of Medieval Armour*. He had been imprisoned by the Anarchists in the Spanish Civil War, but now in retrospect he did not think even they had been revolutionary enough. 'It wasn't just the Communists who sold the pass,' he would grumble to Clare on the few occasions when the Bodens invited her down for a glass of sherry. 'What? Whah Wha?'

But tonight he was at work in his conservatory feeding more evidence into his boxes that the watershed in medieval warfare had been far earlier than even the most revolutionary thought had ever claimed.

It was said that his wife could never forgive the University for not giving her an Honorary Doctorate. She had attended Evensong in the cathedral each evening in her black cap and gown for the last forty years, sweeping up the aisle just before the canons and choirboys came in, genuflecting deeply and then taking a seat in the choir and watching with a stern eye for choir boys who misbehaved; and leading the congregation's responses and inserting bits of muttered Latin in between which she had located in some very early draft of the Book of Common Prayer. She had sailed back from the cathedral, her black gown swelling out behind her bike, and she stood there now with her little black bun of a female academic cap still on her head as she called to Clare:

'There's been a call for you. How I do dislike low ceilings. My daughter took me out to William Morris's house at Kelmscott, but it was so dark and poky. They say it's only had two owners since the sixteenth century, but I can't think why either of them didn't do anything about those bleak little windows. I'm afraid that spoilt my day. And the trees round about. I've left your message for you on the jumbly-jim. It was Mrs Bonnard, I think.'

Clare thought that perhaps Mardi wanted to know whether she had received the little porous wallet she had sent her. It was made of some spongy material and you put all your waste scraps of soap inside. Then you soaked the bag in your bath and used it as a sponge. It made a lovely lather and none of the dog-ends of soap were wasted, Mardi had explained. She had bought it in 'Feed the Minds' Clare supposed, not having plucked up the courage yet to enthuse about the gift.

Or perhaps Mardi was hinting again that the Bonnards hadn't

been seeing enough of their daughter lately. 'Your father says you haven't been all that generous with handouts for a visit to the city of dreaming spires, or is it screaming tyres, eh?' Clare could hear her father chuckle at the other end of the line. But if they came for a week-end, whom could Clare invite to meet them? And how soon would they discover that her life had more connections with banging pipes and toilet-roll invoices than with *Brideshead Revisited*?

'What lovely fun you must have at Oxford, Clare, in that fab Varsity job. And think of all the distinguished people I shall have to be bobbing curtseys to up there. And all the reverend and illustrious Profs we shall have to get our best bibs and tuckers out for. What shall I wear for college functions and river do's? Your father and I shall have to learn to take a back-seat and not feel too *de trop*,' Mardi had gone on when Clare had accepted the post at Sanctus. 'When you hive off to dances and punt-suppers on the river and big parties in big Georgian rooms looking out on to . . . But first you'll have to learn how to cook. I mean proper *haute cuisine*.'

Mr Bonnard had agreed and offered to pay for Clare to do a course at a smart school off Bond Street that normally catered for debs. But so far no one had come to dinner. Mardi had written cheerfully with more recipes and cookery tips and Clare had written back trying to sound convincing: 'We enjoyed the chocolate mousse tremendously. The orange sauce with it was just the thing to cut up its sweetness, we all felt.' Then she had looked at the scarlet tablecloth her parents had sent her. Mardi was saying, 'Such a glorious colour and good tempered too, so that if things get too hilarious and you start chucking chicken bones around or some swains spill their wine . . . What fun *we* all had. Are *you* getting enough? Of the fun?'

Clare looked at the little presents that consequently decorated her room: pottery mugs that had been personalised for her, muddles-and-mendables bags; ear muffs and warm winter footees with a big red eye at each ankle and grinning white tigers' teeth along the toes. She supposed the prizes could at a pinch be sent back. But in a city where men so vastly outnumbered women it was strange to have no respite from the one-egg saucepan, the one-cup coffee percolator, and the late-night niblet tin for the biscuit to be eaten last thing after the egg-cup and egg-spoon had been washed up and put away, the niblet broken carefully for fear of mice, and carried to the mouth like a medicine before she brushed her hair and took out the little bag decorated with yachts that held her cotton night gloves. Would she stay here for ever eating these secret guilty meals on her bed, ryvitas and triangles of soft cheese, marmite and spaghetti hoops, worrying in case another mouse found its way into the waste-paper basket? Then creeping noise-lessly to the lavatory with her kettle behind her back so that she could kill two birds with one stone and not be caught twice in the semi-criminal act of living in someone else's house.

'Dear Mardi,' she had started to write, 'Thank you for Fun with Soap-Bits-and-Bobs . . .' Then she saw the trees again, hung with their votive offerings and here below, her room hung with other votive offerings that made her panic. She noticed again how the pattern of her dress seemed to match the pattern of her sponge-bag and now it seemed also to match the pattern on the 'Bits-and-Bobs' sponge. She started to wrap up Alec Smale's book to send off to his publisher, then thought of the totem-pole brooch he might add to her current certificates of achievement, and the big kiss he would give her as he said, 'Bless you, Clare. I'll give you a signed copy when it comes out too. And you shall come to the launch. I promise you that. I won't let you down.'

'Done. That's a promise Alec,' the floral patterns all agreed. 'Big deal!' a coarser voice added. 'And I'm booking the Albert Hall for your next lecture on "The Role of Extended Diphthong Neutrality in North Icelandic Saga".'

But the yellow plastic milk-bottle to collect bottle tops for blind dogs took no heed of these threats and the giant clothes-peg to hold coupons for Fourpence Off Big Value Coffee and Bio-Cleansers was as relentless. Had she been walled up in these little necessities as a punishment for her craven life? She suddenly panicked at these rewards given for daughterliness and for 'not jumping the gun'. She picked up the big green foot with blue footprints that were supposed to hold memos and shopping lists together, and the red kitchen blackboard with pink chalk entitled 'My Forgettery'. Mardi had a good eye for a career woman's needs at Clare's time of life.

Clare picked the kitchen blackboard up and threw it across the room, but it only bounced on to her bed and relaxed there. She picked up the little bedside radio with the snooze-buzzer on its alarm and threw it on the floor, but it only gave out the first few bars of 'Jesu Joy . . .' She threw the big tramp's foot memo-jotter at the window but it only hit a glazing-bar and bounced back at her. And all the time the voices came louder from the streets below: 'Ally, shall we bike or car? . . . And what about Dickon at the squash-courts? . . . We didn't pick up the Hendricks in the end . . .'

Undergraduates sauntered past on the other side of the grey wall that bounded Sanctus. The plump knock of tennis balls against rackets and asphalt came, and more leisurely voices called down from windows parallel with Clare's, 'Which wines? . . . Whose tutor? . . . Whose girl? . . . Which part of Rome? . . .' The whichness of it all was again its magnetic arrogant richness. There seemed to have been so few 'whiches' in Clare's life. The Swiss souvenir doll that her parents had brought back for her the time she didn't go on holiday with them seemed to nod, sitting in its cantonal costume on a pile of clean linen, and the arrogant voices still came from the open windows all round: 'Beate can only count up to sixteen, judging by the Picasso numbering in the Hermitage.'

Maybe when Clare died, the floral tributes sent to her funeral would be shaped like small crochet tea-cosies and chintz cases for holding nutcrackers in and these smiling Swiss dolls. She panicked again as she thought of the Swiss doll now guardian of her clothes cupboard. Her sewing-box seemed to be lined with the same floral rewards as her blouses, and matched her eyes; and gayly fencing angels presided over by archangel-umpires had been liberally stamped over the new summer dress her parents had sent 'for her round of summer parties and do's'. Women, she supposed, never ran on their husband's swords. Instead they became the linings of picnic-baskets or accessory-bags, enclosed in there by the same female self-discipline they so doggedly professed.

Clare thought again of Yani at Slack Street. Yani now wore a brightly-striped Chewa dress, not a fizzy green C & A and split tights. Her room smelt of joss-sticks not cheap scent and hair tint. Ambrose was there too, working in a path. lab.

The voices still came from the windows of houses opposite in Inkerman Street, and still seemed to dance out as joyfully as the last movement of a Mozart piano concerto: 'They both know food inside out . . . insisted she was pregnant by a Pathan . . . She'd sign her own death-warrant . . . Jesus said it would have to be the bell-tent delivery . . .'

Then the evening bells started up. The day had been clear and warm for late April and the great bells had stood out against the waters round them and had spread for miles, first the great sad bell of St Mary's with its chain of hope and suggestion, slow, halting, then turning to doubt. Then came Magdalen's chime and the two rivers picked it up and sent it up the old stone streets and into quads and round bends into sad corners that no one laughing in gardens or in punts on the rivers had found out yet as they danced out calling, '... went to the Palace to collect his K. But she still didn't come out ... Sir Denny Hillbright, but she still ... I always thought there was something funny about the way he insisted on paying for you.' Then the voices were silenced by the massy proliferation of the late spring.

V

'Yes,' Mrs Grace Plasket sighed as she bent over the Master's flowerbeds again, 'I was there in Amman with the British Mission when American agents were planning to blow up the Palace where we were all living. It was there that the Master of Sanctus took me under his wing, and I loved his hard white body for three months. Out there, he's always been guilty of love.' She whisked flowers out of the bed and into her big wooden trug. 'Clare, are you lunching today?'

The Fellows of Sanctus lunched in the old Exemption Room just off Long Quad where the fountain played. The domestics ate in the kitchen. The college ancillaries, clerical staff, librarians and secretaries lunched in the Cruet Room, a long cold half-underground room, at a long table presided over by the Steward and the Cellarer, one at each end. Sometimes Mrs Plasket would join them and gaze across the table at a junior typist and call in her dreamy, half-intoxicated voice, 'That's a nice blouse you've got.'

'I got it in Rome. At Rinascente.'

'No you didn't, darling. You got it in UPIM. I've seen them all hanging up there, in long rows. But still, "Rinascente" . . .' she dwelled lovingly on the word, 'it rolls so well round the tongue. Italy is a wonderful place to get a feel of life. I once had this Italian guy in the Cantonment in Delhi. He took me under his wing, knowing it would jeopardise his reputation, knowing Italians are the most wonderful lovers. You've got to be joking if you think the French know anything about underwear.'

The Steward cleared his throat and said to the Cellarer,

'The wife was taken bad last night and we had to call in the doctor.'

'Dr Courtland?'

'No. Dr Mally. The new one.'

Mrs Plasket laughed. 'Mally put me on his Chippendale chair to examine me and my breasts just popped out at him. You see, I'd known him in London. Someone threatened me with a knife and he came to my rescue.'

But the men were directing the conversation towards the college bowls club, so Mrs Plasket turned back to Clare and told her about the row in Judasland betweeen Dr Charles Mally and Dr Courtland. Till recently they had been partners in a healthy practice, and no one knew what their quarrel had been about, simply that the practice was to be split and Dr Mally, the junior of the partnership, was to open his own surgery in an old warehouse in Spide Street where a gunsmith, a bookbinder, an upholsterer, a dentist and the girl who did the Judasland watercolours had set up their workshops. Patients from the old practice were given six months to decide which of the two doctors to re-register with, and while people were still discussing the merits of the two, Dr Courtland put up a huge finger-board at the Parnassus Street crossroads 'To The Surgery', and a large notice by its entrance inviting over-forties to come for heart check-ups on the latest and most advanced form of electroencardiograph he had just acquired.

Dr Mally replied by setting up a Well Woman clinic and advertising for a woman partner. Dr Courtland then sent his two children to a smart North Oxford prep school used by a lot of University people and Dr Mally enrolled in beer-brewing classes and furniture renovating. Dr Courtland then opened the gardens of his large house in Balaclava Road for the Conservative Party's annual fete, and Dr Mally responded by giving sermons on sexual love in the Methodist Hall, and taking walkabouts round Judasland, rosy and boyish and smiling at all his patients, dropping in on old people for cups of tea, visiting the Scout Hut, or joining in Parish Lunches. He joined the local choir too, and often ate at the Community Centre in Spide Street, while Dr Courtland dined at the High Tables of the colleges. Clare had seen him in tux going towards the Hall of Sanctus as the dinner-bell went on guest-nights, and it had been rumoured that he was to be made an Honorary Fellow, while Dr Mally was made Chairman of 'Fiddlers We' and the skittles club. So social status jousted in Judasland with the common touch, and so far the two doctors were running neck-to-neck in their war for patients. Dr Hari Sharma, it appeared, was to join Charles Mally's side in this.

'How did the move to the Dental Centre go?' Mrs Plasket asked Mally one day as they sat side-by-side in the Community Centre. It reeked of hot fat and they battled with burger and chips. 'I hope the stomach pumps didn't get mixed up with the dental drills?'

Charles Mally gave a loud guffaw, much louder than the poor little joke merited. His youthful face was red as Grace went on, 'These psycho-analyst guys at the Devonshire, the first one was only interested in extra-marital sex and the second only in masturbation. And the third one asked me if I always wore my husband's shoes. Now I thought that one was *damn* rude. After all, you wouldn't like it if your doctor asked you if you always wore your wife's pants and bra!'

Charles Mally guffawed again and bent over his greasy chips, and skidded them from side to side on the plate, wiped the grease off his chin and shook his head vehemently as if to dissociate himself. 'No. I haven't got a wife yet, fortunately or unfortunately, but I wouldn't care for a showdown like that.'

'You mean you would have jumped on your stethoscope in your anger and tipped your blood-pressure machine out of the window, or sent it to be recycled, if anyone asked you . . . ?' Mally grew rosy again. It was surprisingly easy to tickle him.

Somehow Clare had got lost in this exchange, and she was surprised when Grace turned to her and said, 'We'd love to have Charles with us on May Day, wouldn't we? These guys and us, on our May Morning picnic.'

Charles Mally laughed louder, grew rosier, gave a hiccup and said, 'Pardon me.'

'Charles and Hari Sharma and Clare and me. Hari wouldn't like to miss it. He's interested in pagan rites. He's written this book on witchcraft in South India. Medical Aspects of.'

After Charles Mally had gone Mrs Plasket told Clare that Hari was living in Parnassus Street, and that he was depressed because his book had just been turned down by the Press. 'I told him we'd help him. It's just his English that's a bit stilted. Maybe between us, maybe you could help him rewrite in a more fluent style? He's doing the morning surgery at Spide Street tomorrow. If you'd like to come along, we could collect the book and have coffee and see what repairs need doing . . .' Clare knew by now that Mrs Plasket was a complete fantasist, but she agreed.

'Was there ever a Mr Plasket?' she suddenly found herself asking, surprised at her new voice.

Mrs Plasket just smiled as though the question were beneath her and did some yoga, saluting the sun on the floor and sighing, 'My skeleton is going to pot!'

Clare exercised her new voice again: 'It sounds rather improbable. Mr Grigor Plasket ... Mr Jacques Plasket ... Mr Moses Plasket ... Mr Thunder Drum ...'

Clare had a sudden feeling of space round her as she ribbed Mrs Plasket. She remembered running between broad fields as a child with a wind in her ears and the sky a distant drum and new space everywhere. 'Let's be cousins,' she had said to Nick De Berry. Now she laughed as Mrs Plasket stretched up towards the greasy ceiling saluting the sun.

'Have you never been in love, Clare? Have you never discovered you've got VD? Who was the guy?'

A little of Rome or Delhi or Slack Street could be made to go a long way, and Clare replied, 'Ambrose was black and our relatives made difficulties. His as well as mine.'

Mrs Plasket laughed. 'I know. "*Rinascente*" is a much more romantic word than "UPIM". He was UPIM, Ambrose was. From Brixton or Peckham or Handsworth, and got chippy and had tantrums and cried, "It's a lie due to the colour of my pigmentation. Blood is on all your hands ..."'

'No,' Clare began, but Mrs Plasket went on, 'I know because I had one from Tooting in Bahrain. In the oil. I'm sure Hari Sharma is more *Rinascente* than UPIM, so let's all go out to my cottage at Hedgencote afterwards, for breakfast. It's a Saturday, May Day, so both doctors will probably be free. In any case, Charles Mally has still only got a tiny practice in spite of all his pilgrimages to the various wayside pulpits in Judasland. Even if it were a Monday, his surgery wouldn't be swamped with people wanting their carbuncles swabbed or their motivation tested. I doubt if Hari would be any good at testing anyone's motivation if he's at all like his father who never ever really understood my needs.'

Mrs Plasket sighed. They walked back to Sanctus together. Dr Pyecraft saw Mrs Plasket on the stairs and stopped dead in his tracks. Grace saw and tactfully withdrew. 'See you tomorrow, Clare.'

Clare went back to her desk. Dr Pyecraft was leafing through some correspondence. He was Tutor for Admissions and an old member of Sanctus was offering to give a large donation to the Library Fund on the understanding that his son would be admitted next year. A delicate reply had to be sent. Another delicately worded letter had to be written to the mother of a student who had failed in two successive years to get himself a place. The mother was suggesting that she and the Tutor for Admissions should meet at an idyllic and very out-of-the-way Country Club Hotel in the Welsh Marches to discuss her son's needs.

'And her own needs too, I should think,' Clare said, then felt surprised at what she had said.

Dr Pyecraft smiled. The student's mother might not have been all that pleased when she reached the rendez-vous at Llantynerch. Pyecraft had eyes like little warts and such a large space inside each of his nostrils that one began to think unpleasantly about the draughtier side of eternity. He gave Clare a ghost of a smile and started on the next letter to an American student who had majored in 'Freud, Jung, Marshall McLuhan and Demographic Contracture'. He proposed to live not in college but at the Holiday Inn that stood on the ring road, and had written to Pyecraft for information about its heating, plumbing and saunas. Finally Dr Pyecraft asked Clare to put an advertisement in *The Times* and in the *University Gazette*. His wife had left him so he needed a secretary to carry on the mammoth task of his *Dictionary of the Bulgarian Churches*, known in college as *Oh Bulgaria*.

'She must be attractive enough,' Pyecraft outlined the advertisement, 'for me to want to work with her, but not so attractive that she's likely to have a very full social life, leave early at night or run off and get married. She must dress well enough to please, but not well enough to be a distraction. She must be discreet enough to be invisible when she's not needed, but intelligent enough to adapt quickly to *Oh Bulgaria* and my standards of scholarship. But she must not be intelligent enough to get bored or restless ...' Dr Pyecraft smiled. Clare smiled back at this happy summary of her own person and its sunny reflection on the men she worked for. 'In fact,' Dr Pyecraft drew in a deep breath and summed up as Clare fashioned the advertisement, 'my new secretary must be like a small but seaworthy craft plying in and out between the great ships of a great river.' Clare nodded and smiled and the advertisement sped ahead.

'Pompous, meticulous and boring old don who smells of tea-cake and warm margarine and damp old clothes, seeks some silly girl who loves mothering men and sitting in their damp gardens clasping cups of weak tea, and beaming as they explain the Oxford

63

system to her and how it is that no Fellow can ever be dismissed except for "gross indecency" ... And that is thought to mean in Great Quad, and with someone of the same sex. We've been doing things the same way, I should say, in this outfit, since about 1356 or thereabouts.'

The band in the maze was rehearsing again:

How vain is man again I say how vain ...

Clare wasn't sure whether it was the music outside or the idea of 'gross indecency' that brought the conversation round to Joe Conroy, the absentee Music Fellow. Dr Pyecraft looked at a student poster on the wall. It announced a talk on 'Cultural and Linguistic Aspects of North Cornwall'. Next to it there was a picture of a hand being stabbed by a great iron bolt being driven into a wide vein in its palm. Then a white dove emerged from the palm's artery. 'Peace' it proclaimed; 'Peace through Christ', it announced venomously.

'Do you think it was students who mugged him?'

'I sincerely hope not. No, Joe Conroy has been a good friend of ours,' Dr Pyecraft ticked Clare gently off. She had heard college gossip when she ate her lunch in the Cruet Room. She knew it was very hard to get a Fellow ousted from his job. Along with stories about left-wing plots to get scouts to go on strike, the embezzlement of Junior Common Room funds or the move to deconsecrate the Chapel, she had heard talk of dons who spent all their time in Zurich or the States. But Joe Conroy came into a different category. He only lived in Spide Street, in Judasland, a few hundred yards away. Other dons covered his absence as best they could and protected him from bitter students. It was said that Conroy's wife and children had left him and that he spent his days doing jigsaw puzzles, playing a pianola and constructing multi-lingual crossword puzzles. Now, as a few more Fellows drifted in to Clare's office hoping to be offered coffee, she heard one of them say to another, 'Did they discover who it was that mugged him?'

The other Fellow had laughed. 'It was his own pretty bovver boys, Jason and Orlando, who got fed up when no more money was forthcoming.' They had beaten Conroy up badly, with cricket bats draped with barbed wire.

Clare reassured the Fellows that she had sent flowers and

messages from them all. 'Do you think he'll be back for Benediction Night?' everyone asked her, as though she visited Conroy daily. 'Do you think we ought to look out for a substitute conductor for his Motet?'

The 'Guga Motet', the Swedish Industrial Saga, was being rehearsed out in the maze again, but again the chorus seemed to have a way of floating off his top staccato G flats and bouncing back into the Handel they were to sing later like a frisky dog always bounding after the wrong rubber ball:

> A Public Monument Ordained
> Of Victories as Yet Ungained

'I don't expect Conroy will be here on Benediction Night to notice whether a bit of Jupiter gets mixed up with his laundry workers breast-feeding their babies on Clapham Common,' one of the Fellows observed as the voice of Jupiter sang out again,

> Cool gales shall fan the glade.

'I feel we should all be standing to attention.' But a hard wind suddenly blew, and the music backed unexpectedly away down Long Quad. Then the choir bounced back, singing about a wholefood co-operative.

'Choirs seem to be autonomous these days. This seems to be a very eager one. If you asked them to go a mile with you it seems they'd go five.' Joe Conroy in his good years would have gone ten or fifteen with you. If you had asked him the date of J. S. Bach, he would have told you the dates of J. S. and C. P. E. as well, not to mention the dates of Mach, Buther and Tornheider. Clare had once told him she was going to try a Dutch recipe from her *Adventurous Cookery* and he had been pleased to give her a rundown on food in East Germany, where he had spent most of his vacations in his productive days, collaborating with a poet on the score of a folk opera about the canteen workers in an elastic-band factory near Dresden. Or so Fellows reported.

The wind came again and the music was snapped off. Clare at last got down to writing to her parents.

'Let's hope this wind doesn't interfere with Benediction Night in July,' she had written. 'I've been coaching Mark Tulley, our Junior Fellow, in the long Latin prayer he has to chant to the Vice-Regent, standing with a sort of soap-dish thing in his hand, offering five eggs on behalf of the Bishop. No one is quite clear what these eggs mean. The prayers, though, are for the soul of Richard II. He died unshriven it is believed, and gave Henry IV a guilty conscience. Later, bishops . . . it is thought . . .'

But Clare didn't tell her parents that the Benediction was really just a game of trying to secure the most distinguished guests to dine at High Table. The guest-list went up at least two months before Benediction Night and evolved in different directions from week to week, changing shape like an amoeba. Fellows could scan the chart from day to day and see who was in the lead: Dr Pyecraft with his controversial brain surgeon, or Professor Peary with his equally controversial food king. The *premier danseur* at Covent Garden might trump the Director of the Open-Air Theatre, but where did the editor of a quality porn magazine fit in? And the agony aunt of a women's magazine?

So far the guest-list wasn't electrifying, the Fellows agreed. Clare told her parents, however, that 'we shall be having fun . . . wish you could be here to see us all . . .' Then she tore this up as insincere and just went on, 'It would be lovely to see you some week-end. But at the moment I'm terribly booked. Next Saturday is May Day, and May Morning is a high day and holiday here in Oxford. Each takes to his or her punt, plus a champagne breakfast usually provided by the men. Our particular men include two of the local medical bods so that if any of us develop pleurisy on the Cherwell or swallow too much cold river and tadpoles . . .'

But this extent of falsity wasn't to her taste either and she tried again: 'It can be heavenly on May Morning, even when it's cold . . . This year, our particular little foursome . . . Grace and Charles and Hari and . . .' She was going to write 'yours truly', but instead she just wrote 'me'. 'We are having breakfast on a punt and then are off to a small Cotswold village where Grace has a cottage. It should be fun. Charles is the Judasland GP and we usually have fun when we get together . . .' Then she scrubbed this out equally ashamed, and tried again: 'The red tablecloth you sent me is much appreciated by the mob, and the cookery classes you gave me at that smart place in Bond Street were certainly a good investment. I've got to make pâté and spice cake and garlic bread for the four of us . . .'

'The four of us' . . . the daring arrogance that set her in her rightful place beside girls in scarlet berets with long hair trailing behind as they helped their boy-friends fly-stick and crept laughing down the midnight streets. The four of them would all drive to

Normandy later on perhaps, or to Rome. 'On down to Rome', that was the right phrase. 'We've been lent a flat near the Via . . .' But at this point Clare's invention gave out.

One or two of the Fellows were washing their coffee cups. The rest had just drifted away. She could hear Alec Smale down below in the quad say to Mark Tulley, 'Clare seemed slightly cool and preoccupied. Do you think she's reached a certain age? Maybe it's time to take her out to another cream tea at Ellistons. Or cinnamon toast even, at the Randolph.'

'Once more into the breach, dear friends . . . Did she charge you for that index?'

'Not yet, I don't think. Maybe I could give her a dog instead. Then she wouldn't feel so lonely and conspicuous on those long Sunday walks on Port Meadow that every woman *d'un certain age* has to endure. I don't know whether she'd enjoy it, but she'd get to know other shoulders to have a weep on if she had an object of regard at the end of a slender silk cord . . .'

The men separated and Clare could hear their individual voices echoing round the quads. Then they were muffled by the garish spring green that trickled off the walls or broke out of it like green sweat. She could hear Somnus in *Semele* being charmed out of his deep sleep, and the green too seemed also to be being charmed out of an ancient sullen dead stone sleep.

Clare walked home. The green seemed almost to be undermining the city, as though the Lord of Misrule had spread his nets over the walls and spires and towers to trap them, then bring them down. The stone nymphs on the urns at the college gates were entwined in damp green too, soft and slipping round the stone as the earth abandoned its gravity.

She left the sad and crumbling stone gates to the maze and went down the narrow lane with its beech hedges that led to Judasland. At Parnassus Street she was trying to decide which was Dr Sharma's flat, then making mental notes of what to buy as her share of the picnic food. This time she wouldn't panic, nor would she be forced into any part.

Judasland was quiet now, like the pause between two centuries, the gap between two worlds, the interval between two acts. From time immemorial there had been a right-of-way for the people of Judasland through the maze. Some of them were college servants. Some did vacation work in the kitchens. Some were just children from the local school on holiday who had the right to play cricket there, fish in the river, and climb the huge cedars that screened the college from the great military barracks beyond, and the coke stacks. But now children dropped litter and tore up plants and hacked at the stone of ancient columns and the right-of-way had been quietly suppressed. Few people now knew the way behind the old piggeries and the water-purifying apparatus and the sheds where old beds and desks were stacked. Clare would often see Nellie Grainger there, or occasionally another elderly person from Judasland, but never anyone young.

She could see a few bluebells in the verges, and a young foxglove. Alec Smale had wanted her to get a dog. In fact, in her loneliness she had taken to going to St James's Church in Parnassus Street and had enjoyed some of their activities. It was there that she had met Charles Mally, and there also Polly Ives, a great bundle of a Pastorate worker with a great bundle of books under one arm and under the other a big plastic handbag stuffed with papers: 'Cartesian Doubts Resolved', or big illustrations of the Arguments From Design. Clare would hear Polly Ives explaining to Charles Mally why an 'ought' can sometimes follow from as 'is'. She could hear his great squawks of laughter as though a pheasant had been disturbed in the bracken. Then Polly would look at the big watch that was slung from her waist beside what looked very much like a large rosary: 'I must start thinking of homing in on the big city.' She would fumble with her piles of books. 'A guy hath need of me. And some student childer . . . as we God-slot folks see things . . .'

Mrs Plasket would watch Charles Mally as he made a date with Polly for a brush-up or a teach-in on the Communion of Saints. 'Oh for a real pioneering male from the outback or the Sind.' Charles would give his laugh as though Mrs Plasket had said something funnier than she in fact had. Polly would stack 'Great Thoughts and Their Thinkers' on the back of her bicycle, make a few notes on her wrist, then lower her long purple serge habit round her bicycle, drape it carefully, then sail away crying, 'Praise be.' And yet Clare had grown to love the church in Parnassus Street, if not Polly.

St James's Church, Judasland, wasn't old but it was beautiful with that softly recessed look of a much-loved place. But money was needed to rewire it and to stop the damp pushing up the brown parquet blocks off the floor and the water from dripping down Our Lady's cloak. A steeplejack was also needed to put wire-netting

68

round the top of the *campanile* to stop pigeons nesting there and disturbing High Mass. And the great gold-and-rose starred interior of the baldacchino over the High Altar badly needed restoring.

The Vicar had invited his parishioners to coffee in the church hall. After they had discussed plans for money-raising they were to visit the church for vespers and then see the extent of the damage last year's floods had caused. The church seemed to float round Clare as she walked up the side aisle peering where the Vicar was pointing at the damp. It seemed to lift her up into a generosity she rarely had on her own. It had been built in this poor part of the city at a time when the Tractarian movement was appealing to beauty as a form of transcendence. Clare felt another sudden lift, and then, as the Vicar's group stopped in front of a box full of ugly loose escaped electrical wires, she saw a plaque she had never seen before. It commemorated three boys who had been drowned in the river on the annual Beating of the Bounds in 1923. There was a sudden hush in the church.

'That's why we never beats the bounds now,' an elderly woman standing beside Clare smiled.

'How did it happen?'

The old lady shrugged. 'I wouldn't care to say.' She looked behind as they went back to the church hall. Nellie Grainger from Spide Street stood behind them in her dirty pinafore-dress and shiny dressing-gown. She had never got the manner of other regular college servants or acquired their funereal deadpan look, the habit of melting into the background or disappearing like a mist. On the contrary Nellie had this way of buttonholing celebrities so that respectable working-class women all shuffled on and away, embarrassed. Nellie often worked in the Sanctus kitchens when they were busy with conferences.

The Vicar had showed them the extent of their financial problems as church members, and they had all met for tea and cakes in the church hall. Nellie drifted in too, to eat, and picked on Clare: 'Five men I've had and five death warrants, but number six, he come to me every morning for his breakfast. Bacon clangers I gives him every year for ten years when he comes off night shift on the tracks. But then one morning he doesn't come so I goes up to the hospital . . .' Clare knew the rest by heart: '. . . and there he war, just set there with a big S pinned on the end of the bed for paralysed . . .'

Clare could hear Mrs Plasket's voice almost as clearly. She

wasn't a churchgoer but she had been invited to give advice about the restoration of some flower paintings in the vestry. Charles Mally was shaking his head at her vehemently and Polly Ives from the University Pastorate had arrived back and was listening to Nellie: '. . . Then it war his eye gone as well . . .'

Sometimes the women of Judasland carried aerosol sprays after Nellie, 'English Rose' or 'Gold Chiffon'. But Nellie was always undeterred, telling them calmly of the green monkeys at Bristol Zoo or the secret springs under her house in Spide Street. 'But his good eye shone out beautiful under that "paralysed" in the hospital,' she ended.

'Nellie, Clare, have you tried one of these what-nots?' Polly Ives called back. 'We call them Father's What-Nots, don't we Father? Because he loves them all gooey-goo, don't you Father?' The priest nodded briefly and disappeared. 'Don't we Mrs Maisey?' Polly Ives went on, 'Mrs Maisey has embroidered us such a beautiful peace-panel, haven't you, Mrs Maisey? Ah, Mrs Maisey is asleep, bless her. So you come from the University too, do you? Like poor Joe Conroy and our Nellie here. We are praying for both of them like mad. St James's is to have a reconciliation week. Could you give me a briefing?'

'A briefing?' Clare stiffened.

'The latest rundown on Joe Conroy. The state of play. You *are* at Sanctus?'

'I met him in Ankara,' Clare could hear Mrs Plasket. 'He was outside the hospital after the CIA had stopped tailing me there. But he was bleeding like a . . .'

Polly stood there swinging her rosary and challenging orthodox medicine on the subject of Conroy, depression and mental illness as a whole. 'How is he? Our fellow Judaslandite, Joe Conroy? Has he been able to make *the link-up?*'

'S for paralysed,' Nellie's voice came from the refreshment table, 'all down one side. But his one good eye said . . .'

'Yes, Nellie dear. He was a good man to you. But to get back to the subject of Oxford academics, it seems to me,' Polly turned back to Clare, 'that the cleverer our dons become, the more difficulty they seem to find in seeing that two plus two make four. Nothing more and nothing less . . . Simple as say "sin",' Polly went on, swinging her rosary meaningfully. 'Has Joe got his act together, do you think?' she added in a firmly lowered voice as though she were discussing some medical verdict. 'Has Joe Conroy got the spiritual jigsaw puzzle fitted together in all its rainbow glory?' Clare felt slightly menaced, as Polly persisted, pulling her long damp blond hair out of her huge questing eyes, 'We had a stiff session together last week, Joe and I did. A really stiff sesh, getting down to basics. Is that what we all secretly need and want?'

Clare felt even more menaced by this public intimacy, but she was growing to like Judasland and enjoy her walks home after Evensong or choir rehearsals. Judasland no longer belonged merely to the very poor and it did not yet belong to the professional classes. This pause in its history was the best escape Clare had from the business of being a college treasure. Here she no longer felt she was on heavy skis, with a heavy helmet and leaden lips that spoke the words other people thought she ought to be saying. It might still be good here, she thought, picturing Hari and Charles Mally sitting at the table with the red tablecloth in her bedsitter. She had baked them stuffed aubergines, or courgette and tomato pancake, and Hari was to be her guest on Benediction Night. She could already see him in the college maze while the white-coated servants carried the drinks round and the band played Handel.

But in fact Polly was accompanying Clare home, asking about Benediction Night, and Clare was explaining how prayers had been said ever since the Wars of the Roses, for the repose of the soul of the murdered and unshriven Richard II. Polly was nodding and saying they would have *her* prayers as well that night, and Clare was explaining why very few prayers would be said before the evening was given over to eating, drinking and music.

'Sure. Sure. Oxford's ways,' Polly was agreeing liberally. Then she was launching into her ideas about Trinitarianism in *Finnegan's Wake*, offering to lend Clare Morpeth-Watkin on *The Long Haul to God*. 'Maybe that should be prescribed reading for Joe Conroy and all people in a mess. The real challenge as we Christian bods see it . . . But goodness, I'll have to come back to you on that million dollar question . . .'

They had reached the door of Clare's digs. Polly stood there in the night as though she could dismantle the starry heavens. She stood there with one foot in at Clare's front door. 'You haven't, by any chance, got a copy of Thomas Hardy's poems? I feel I really must come to terms with his arrant pessimism. It's a must. Have you got to grips with it yet?'

Clare said firmly that she hadn't. She smiled goodnight. Polly nodded and grinned. It was just that she was keeping her 'Prayer-eye' on Joe Conroy and Nellie Grainger and thought Thomas Hardy might help her try and understand Conroy's gloom. Polly pressed her lips together and nodded her determination to come to terms with the 'two errants' of Judasland. She was getting up a prayer-workshop. Praise be. Had Clare heard of it? Clare shook her head.

'Come round,' Polly went on. 'Come round to the clergyhouse one night and we'll have bangers-and-mash and bang out a correct theory of the Resurrection of the Dead. I have a small workshop too, over in the new Community Centre in Spide Street where the doctor hangs out and the dentist and the whole bang-shoot of us in the caring professions. We'll be putting together a new theory of women's liberation too, based on the huge fact of who happened to be standing at the foot of the Cross. In some way, you and I seem to have chosen the better part. Spinster-bods like you and me . . .'

Clare was annoyed to be linked in this way with the Pastorate worker, especially as Polly seemed at least ten years older than Clare as she planted her large feet apart in their tiny hot slippers and reminded her that singles like them had different parameters and insights.

Clare could see Hari sitting on the college lawns clasping his neat legs beside him. Then they were dancing in a great striped marquee. Or he was standing by the fountain in Long Quad waiting for her to lock her office and come out to Wittenham Clumps with him. But instead Polly Ives stood there with her at the front door of the Bodens' house in Inkerman Street, and Mrs Boden was shouting from the hall inside, 'In or out?' Clare could picture Polly laying muddy parsnips on her volume of Thomas Hardy as her jolly and determined voice called out at Hari, and she shook his hand, then squeezed it in sympathy: 'From Bombay, ah that must be exciting and rewarding.'

However, just then, as Clare stood at the front door warding Polly off, Mrs Boden called out again from inside, 'Who's that at the door at this hour? Tell them in. Or out.'

'Right,' Polly grinned and saluted. 'Out and about.' She fumbled in the Bodens' decaying privet hedge and behind their dustbin, then pulled out an ancient bike, hitched up her purple habit, hoiked herself over the crossbar and pedalled away to her night workshop, while Mrs Boden went on angrily, 'My daughter took me to Renderick Castle today, Miss Bonnard. Oh those shameful Tudor barley-sugar chimneys. And those pokey courtyards. Worse than Sanctus even. And there were bees that got in your way when you tried to chew. I do like to chew in peace. And I don't care whether Renderick Castle has had two owners or fifty since that unsavoury go-getter William I built it, or rather jerry-built it, in ten sixty whatever-it-was. And I must speak to the organist at the Cathedral about the choirboys' teeth. Those Mars Bars. And not nearly enough fibre. And the canons don't eat enough fibre, either, judging by their complexions. I must have a word with Canon Mardon about their fibre up at the Cathedral . . .'

Clare could see a light go up in the Community Centre and assumed that Polly Ives had begun her night-shift with God. She also noticed from her top room in Inkerman Street that Joe Conroy's lights were on too, in Spide Street beyond the Community Centre. The hospital he had been taken to after the street attack must have discharged him. She had better make enquiries next day and find out if the college knew that the college rat-bag was back.

The small red and blue chequerboard bricks that most of Judasland was built of were made by hand before the industrial revolution had come to Oxford, moulded in sheds in the winter when other outdoor work was hard to find. Spide Street was taller and darker than the rest though, and built of chilly grey cement-like industrial bricks, as though a stony façade had been clamped on to stopper up what lay behind. It was said that Spide Street had once been Oxford's Mount Pleasant, and that until well into the present century policemen only went there in pairs, and never went there at night. But now as Clare stared over at the tall houses that overshadowed Candid Street and Parnassus Street, she could only see Conroy's white and eyebrowless face, smooth as a moon floating in the night. She decided after all not to say anything to the Vice Provost about his return.

VI

'My last analyst used to ask me,' Grace Plasket turned to the man sitting next to her in Dr Mally's waiting room, 'whether I were afraid of death. Of course I wasn't, but I wanted his love. So I used to say . . .'

The patient sitting next to her turned his face away. Joe Conroy from Sanctus was an albino. His pink eyes shone under his sheaf of chemical white hair. His lips creaked as though he used them and his long pink ears for seeing with. The savage scoring of his face had left shiny white tissue that matched his hair. His lower face was swollen by drugs and his cheeks shook as he stared at Grace. Then he stood up abruptly and went to the corner of the waiting-room and fiddled with the tandem bicycle he had leaned carefully there, touching its handlebars and adjusting the two children's tub seats on its back mudguard. Mrs Plasket gazed at the red and green chariot. Someone had fixed plastic dragon's wings on behind.

'Of course, I couldn't say that about death in Accra though,' Mrs Plasket added.

There was silence for a moment as the waiting-room digested this. 'Vindaloo, if you please,' a woman in a feather hat broke in, 'and all in a row along the table . . . as if we war cattle. And the cheeky so-and-so came up and said it was his daughter in the photo in his wallet. Now what would he be doing, I'd like to ask, carrying a snap of his daughter in her birthday-suit around? In Inkerman Street? In the Land? Not with all those details. Too many details these days if you ask me . . . Everywhere it's the details.'

The surgery door opened and the new doctor stood there.

'Dr Conroy, please,' Dr Sharma called.

The man with the white scars got up, stood still for a moment, then went in. A youth murmured to his friend, 'They should've put the bomb by the other door, if they wanted the maximum body-count. By the cosmetics counter . . . eh?'

Voices came from outside in the street and the spurting of the dental drill upstairs. A group in the hall next door were doing keep-fit and singing, 'When your hips feel small and your spine's all tall . . .'

'Been bumping into the Ministry of Defence then, Dr Conroy has eh?' The woman in the feathered hat offered her friend an Opal Fruit and nodded to the doctor's door.

After the vicious mugging Conroy had dragged all his furniture out into Spide Street and put price tags on it. The street was narrow and it was soon blocked by tables, chairs, beds, and a Blüthner piano. Conroy had stood on a Pembroke table and put the whole barricade including his own manuscripts under the hammer. Traffic had to be diverted into Candid Street, Salvation Street and Balaclava Road. A warden arrived and then the police. Finally the Master of Sanctus had appeared. He had invited Dr Conroy to come and discuss his future with him several times. Now he demanded that Conroy either see a doctor or resign his Fellowship.

There had been a series of bad summers when the sun hung like a cold dead animal in the sky behind thick layers of lint, and icy winds blew round corners and tore petals off young flowers, leaves off young trees, and even took great oaks and chestnuts in the college maze. Most people in the Land put this down to nuclear power, or nuclear testing, or to the amount of hardware being thrown into the sky. But Joe Conroy had begun, as cold grey day followed cold wet one and there was no love in the sun, to feel that it was a moral fault. 'We get the weather we deserve,' he told his wife. 'The weather reflects the degeneracy of the time. Like a mirror.'

His wife, who had been planning to leave him ever since the birth of their twins, shrugged. She was tired of trying to persuade him that he had no effect on the dead grey sky, and that pacing round and round the garden all day wouldn't exorcise any thing. But the garden had become Conroy's treadmill, and he spent all his time walking round it, trying to pump away all that damp air, and siphon that grey cloud of hopelessness from above his head. His attackers must have watched him at it for some time, perhaps from the Community Centre. Conroy had told the police the youths had banged at his door late at night asking for Rod. He had never seen them before. They must have mistaken him for someone else because they kept calling him Laurie.

'We've heard that one before,' the Fellows of Sanctus had commented. 'He's played I spy once too often in Spide Street, I suspect.'

Dr Joseph Conroy had never sat easily at Oxford. He had taken both his degrees at Birmingham University and knew very little about the ancient one. Once in the Senior Common Room of Sanctus he had innocently admitted that he didn't know which college was called 'The House' and he had blithely referred to New College as simply 'New', and didn't know about All Souls, didn't know where most colleges stood financially, or even geographically. His alienation, along with his preference for Birmingham, was so breathtaking that he had been accused of making a cult of not knowing Oxford, apart from its railway station and its Woolworths and Golden Eggs. He would boast that he had encouraged American students to turn an honest penny selling hot-dogs along the tow-path in Eights Week and in the Broad Walk.

There had been a genuinely more amused laugh when he announced he had been invited to Moose Jaw, Ontario to be its composer-in-residence and conduct the Moose Jaw Orchestra in his latest work which most Fellows suspected was about a jam factory near Leipzig in East Germany. The laughter had been colder though when Conroy announced that he had never heard of the many University dispensing committees for over-riding University rules and statutes, and that he never intended to use any of them. Consequently valuable students and precious money had been lost to the college. Conroy would ostentatiously read the *Daily Worker* at college meetings and volumes of Esperanto at High Table. Some Fellows thought it was *War and Peace* he was so deeply into over the *poulet farci*. Others thought it was his East German opera. One Fellow who knew some Esperanto maliciously declared that the High Table volume was entitled *What To Spread On Your Bread*.

'If the students bayed for a pound of poor Joe's flesh, he would give them ten pints of his urine.'

Conroy always dressed in a shiny pinstriped city suit and waistcoat and an open-necked shirt. His ankles were always bare and white, and no one knew whether his dress and his jokes were genuinely meant as confrontation and subversion or whether he just didn't know he should be wearing evening-dress at guest nights and Bishop's Benediction.

Then there were his guests at High Table when he couldn't bring Prince Kropotkin on Liberty or his book on bread-spreads. He would peer short-sightedly over at a food magnate or a press baron, shake his sagging jaws, and peer through his cracked glasses: 'We all know by now that wealth trickles down from the rich to poor as easily as water down a mountainside. It's harder to find a better example of the First Law of Hydrodynamics than modern finance.' Then he sneezed. The baron, who was about to make a large donation for the library fund or the new Fives courts, had smiled and agreed.

Then there were other High Table occasions, Benediction Nights when Conroy would invite as his distinguished guest a young dentist from Black Pill, Swansea, a piano-tuner he had met at Blackbird Leys, or a local-authority rent-collector from his Birmingham days. The rent-collector had been unhappily placed next to a celebrated American conductor and had eaten very slowly, chopping up all his food carefully and methodically while he talked about its mastication, then breathed very heavily over it and examined his knife and explained to the celebrated conductor that Georgian glass was warm, and urged him to feel the glass decanter that was on display. He then explained why the Birmingham branch of the War Resisters League had not been able to see their way to providing transport to the Bull Ring for the City Council's Shrove Tuesday Pancake Race in aid of its new toy-library for the under-fives.

The American conductor had sat there very tall and upright as the local-authority official explained why he had not sung in the church choir as a boy, and why, after he had had his tonsils out, he had suddenly started to want to sing. The conductor lowered his head civilly. He too had sung as a boy. In fact at Tanglewood when he first went there . . . 'Talking of Tanglewood, they say there's a maze here.'

Conroy's guest had stopped his slow mastications to squeeze mustard he had chosen from an array of about five different tubes he had produced before him, then pecked at the college grouse and asked, 'What kind of slaughtered beast meat is this?' He pushed the half grouse to the side of his plate, and went on with more satisfaction, 'In Birmingham there are plans to start up a little Greek food shop near the book binders' co-op. From my mother's bedroom window you can get a nice view of it and the whole of Smethwick, come to that. What do you do for a living?' Then he gazed again at the name written on the card in front of his neighbour's dessert spoon.

The whole of High Table was listening in on this conversation as they waited for their guests to finish and the waiters to be given the signal to withdraw the plates. Everyone held his breath and the college servants hovered impeccably till the Fellow on the celebrated conductor's other side had interrupted,

'How do you like our poor man's David Hockney?' and directed his attention to the latest acquisition on the wall of the Hall. Then the servants had moved in and the plates clattered and it was clear that Conroy did these things deliberately to subvert High Table.

Next guest-night Conroy had invited the pilot of a Viscount he had travelled to Dresden on.

'You *do* like to lasso people,' his wife remarked. 'Greek stamp-collectors, Spanish vegetarian bike-dealers, East African ... you are growing like Mrs Plasket.'

'Who's she?' her husband had replied; then added, 'At least I don't lasso them because they'll be useful to me.'

'And these Arvac Bookbinders,' he would say to his neighbour at High Table, 'are so intolerant,' the remark made apropos nothing just to see if his neighbour could – blindfold, so to speak – pin anything appropriately on this particular donkey's tail. Though the phrase 'freezing out' was never used at Sanctus, the Fellows would mentally wash their hands in self-exoneration like Pilate every time they ended an encounter with Conroy.

In fact, the Senior Common Room conspired at Conroy's exclusion only in the way that we do when we instinctively move to shut out cold and rain, or close our eyes when we see rased orchards, shiny bald fields, or streams high with artificial foam. Conroy sounded a knell on all friendships, as his first wife had discovered, and brought a chill wind in summer and killed all joy with black frost and no dew. It wasn't pessimism he created around him but something more fixed and dead, like flowers turned to concrete, meadows to waste lots and gardens poisoned by doses of gas and lime.

Conroy's first wife had suffered more than his second, in the places which were barred to her as well. She had studied at Oxford and now on marriage found herself excluded by the same unspoken and unwritten rules that excluded her husband from the social life of a world that refuses to be bored or chilled. As most of her friends had been at Oxford, and her first tastes formed there, and as she had once associated the city and the University with happiness rather than threat, she had felt deeply about being turned into an outsider, and had disappeared from the place that had no longer any place for her. At first she took up work in the city – teaching at the prison and making tea at the outpatients of the big hospitals nearby.

But she only met other dons' wives there, and they reminded her about their husbands' latest books and latest TV appearances and latest trips abroad, or compared Greek coffee with Turkish in Ankara and Athens Universities, and recounted how quickly they made friends with Arabs when a terrible storm started up in the desert and they were miles from civilisation.

'Everyone welcomed us in, even though we all had to talk in finger language. We all got completely colour-blind too, and it didn't strike us till afterwards what a memorable or indeed outstanding historic occasion it had been for our rather dry central Oxford academic world, meeting up like this with simple but marvellous people who saw us for what we were. Yes, we responded with as much awe for them as they had of us. Multi-racial all evening without knowing it, and even when that terrible cyclone stopped we just went on being, being, being together with them, and loving every single moment of it.'

Then, in the pause before the volunteers had to start regathering the lily-cups of tepid tea from the outpatients or prisoners, the other volunteers would turn to Mrs Conroy: 'What does *your* husband do, what? You know, you are lucky belonging in the real world. Oxford can be a terribly Ivory Tower place for dons' wives like me. We out here need constant reminders of you in there – in with it all. I do envy you. It's fun to have a bike instead of the worry of where to park. I'm not a materialist but I do think two loos are very useful. I'm not a materialist, but we do appreciate our second home after the awful publicness and hassle of Oxford. Though I'm sure life in the tower blocks could be fun if you put your heart into it and really got the tenants organised and going . . . in weird places like Brixton and Lambeth. . . . Yes, I envy you and all other timely reminders of other ways of life that make us feel small and useless and very humble here at the top of the very muddy and very obscure little river called the Thames . . .' they would end menacingly.

'Do you think? . . .' Conroy would look at his wife with cold anger in the evenings when she got in from the prison. His face was as white as his hair and his loose mouth was screwed up. 'Do you expect me to make a name for myself by settings of Christopher Robin and *The Wind in the Willows?* It's a pity Oxford's pursuit of excellence by its very definition automatically excludes it from accepting strangers, the foreigner, the other.'

Childless Mrs Conroy had seemed less happy each time Clare had taken mail and college salary down to their house in Spide Street. She seemed to have been making the same rabbit-hutch ever since Clare had got to know their cold colourless house. She was always sloshing coats of red paint on the hutch, red then yellow then blue, till it was almost a Union Jack, then buying a rabbit and then another because she had let the first one die, standing there staring at it. Then she had got a job at South Lambeth hospital, and Sanctus Fellows thought when Conroy's second wife was pregnant that things would go better. His new wife would cycle around the Land with the twins like white shining scar-tissue strapped into the cheerful dragon tub seats on the back of their tandem.

'We're both has-beens, I suppose,' she had once sighed.

Conroy had frowned. 'I didn't know *you* ever made claim to have been anything.'

Carey had played the violin and he had met her at a rehearsal of his most famous work, 'A Folk Mass'. He had sprung to fame with it in the fifties. 'Pa's Pop' had been sung in churches up and down the country and had even been a hit in the States and West Germany. And CND had borrowed several of its verses, and tunes. An early reviewer had dubbed it 'Pa's Pop' because it was the kind of pop music that even the parents of its adherents found themselves humming as they drove to work or waited for the tube on crowded underground platforms at night. It was the music of hope and vigour. It was music that could be sung by professional choristers in a cathedral, or equally well by handicapped children in a Special School.

But then Conroy had blithely, and with the strength of more and more serious work in the pipeline, applied for a Fellowship at Sanctus and had been given one. But after that, the only creative work he did was in the summer of each year when he went to East

Germany for three months, to Dresden and Leipzig where, it was said, his works filled the opera houses – though Fellows visiting these cities had only once ever seen a poster billing the first night of a Conroy opera and hadn't bothered to go to it. 'It was about ball-bearings, I think.'

And now even Conroy's Folk Mass was only very occasionally revived. His *Asperge Me* was sometimes sung in the Cathedral, and his *Qui Venis* in Sanctus chapel, and from time to time schools would sing other parts written in the vernacular, particularly one beginning 'With hands I take . . .'

But recently, after Conroy had withdrawn to Spide Street and spent his time pacing round and round his garden trying to work the bad weather away, one of the Fellows had suggested that they should get the college choir and band to present his 'Guga Motet' at Benediction Night. Perhaps this might give him the green light to go on with his work. But their hearts sank as the shrill frying sound of electronic modules came from the maze where the rehearsals were taking place. This was not even the rousing canteen music of East Germany that more amiable dons ascribed to him, about truck and tractor driver communes. This suggested lack of integrity and *bona fides*. Conroy chose never to perform his East German works here. 'Maybe there was a grim poetic justice in the mugging,' Joe told his wife. 'I'd never set eyes on them before in all my life. Those lads. They just climbed into our garden to smash it up.'

His wife stared sceptically; then she softened. 'Twigs, will you please go and see a doctor? The Master has asked you to, so many times. There's a good Twigs.' She hadn't called him Twigs for a long time. His first wife, ominously, had called him that too. The hospital outpatients that he visited consequently was anxious to see Conroy transferred to the Herber Institute. He had been referred to the Herber two years ago to consult a doctor who was supposed to be helpful to creative people. The doctor, however, had advised him to take up clay modelling. Or pipe-cleaner modelling. Conroy couldn't remember which. The doctor had sniffed his breath and written on his notes, 'Alcoholism???' Now, two years later, Carey Conroy and the Master between them had persuaded Joe to be admitted to the Herber Institute.

The Herber Institute had originally been the Herber Asylum, founded in the eighteenth century by a Quaker philanthropist on low-lying ground by the river, where it was thought the dampness of the air would still the ravings of dementia. The land was fertile and trees planted that ran in great colonnades now along the banks of the Thames. The hospital buildings were a soft golden stone that had weathered well, and the great pediment over the main doors that led into the huge domed entrance-hall bore the legend: *Sicut Lilia. . . .Imp.Rege. George II.*

The Institute was run on the strict behavioural principles of its founder though, and had no time for psycho-analysis or even for psychotherapy. The Professor in charge belonged to the moral Boy-Scout movement. He believed in the reinforcement of productive habits and useful ways of thinking and the discouragement of negative ones. Once, this had been done by physical coercion. Now the instruments were drugs, then simple social coldness towards anyone who desired obsessively to wash his hair or talk about his 'voices'. The daily 'cold showers' advocated by the founder to discourage unsocial behaviour now varied from the denial of food, freedom and companionship, to the application of caustic soda to the lavatory seats. There was no evidence on philosophical, economic, clinical, or even statistical grounds that any other method of psychiatry worked.

The houseman who had admitted Joe Conroy had taken a careful history. But it was a long one, and the consultant, when the notes were presented to him, hadn't much time to do more than glance through them. Dr Nick De Berry from St Martyrs' College, sitting in his office under the great glass dome of the Herber Institute, had a lecture to prepare for his students, a supervision to give. Then he was due to lunch with his publisher in London at one, and in the afternoon – every afternoon this week it seemed – he had a long string of private patients for whom, co-incidentally, behavioural therapy did not seem relevant. Then, as with most academics, there was the editorship of 'a whole damn series' to think about.

Consequently De Berry was obliged to use the lucky-dip method of diagnosis as he looked through the notes the junior doctor had carefully prepared. In any case, he held no brief for prolonged history-taking. It only encouraged patients to dwell on painful thoughts and feelings and inevitably to reinforce them. And after all, psychiatry itself was in doubt. Oxford philosophy had taught him that though the word 'subconscious' might have a function in the language, there was no logic belonging to the word 'unconscious'. Psychiatry must be an exercise in getting the nation back on its feet, and the government, by its new policy of returning the mentally ill to the community, was only too ready to help in this.

So the lucky-dip method of diagnosis was brought into play. The patient's painstakingly compiled case-notes were opened. De Berry read the statement about Conroy's recent mugging. Then he flipped back and saw the query 'alcoholic?' He looked at his patient. He trusted his own intuitions more than a thousand pages of case-notes. In any case, alcoholism wasn't a disease but an obsessional habit that could be mastered. De Berry passionately believed in human freedom, so he smiled over at Conroy and swung a neat white-socked ankle up and down. His dark shiny dwarf face was freshly polished for London, his cheeks held angel's eyes which he rolled up and down and flashed as he asked Conroy, his laughing eyes almost reaching his dark sideburns and his wide grinning mouth, 'So you've had a bad time? Have the police been at all helpful?'

Conroy looked at his protector and suddenly cheered up as he pictured him in a corsair's costume, or even dressed in black dinner jacket and black tie – lassoed as Conroy's maverick guest at High Table.

De Berry sat there with his long slender legs elegantly crossed and his biro tapping. He smiled in a way that made Conroy feel a kind of weakness. The doctor's long arms swung down past his knees and his long-fingered hands twisted round and round and almost touched the floor as he smiled at him with his large and shining eyes and asked in sympathy, 'And the muggers. . . . That's what brought things to a head?'

'. . . Yes, I suppose so. And the weather. I feel as though I've committed a terrible crime and that it's upset the weather.' Conroy could never breathe through his nose so his mouth always hung open. De Berry nodded and swung his foot up and down and watched himself swinging it, then suspending one ankle. 'I suppose it's partly such a feeling of failure. I haven't lived up to my early promise.'

'Which of us has? You're a . . .' De Berry took another lucky dip, 'you're a musician? My niece learns the flute,' he went on, trying to cheer Conroy up and thinking of music teachers clapping in three-four time as though Conroy were a woman he were trying to put at her ease. 'She hopes to take it up in a big way. Which is your instrument?'

The author of 'Pa's Pop' was rather taken aback. 'I play several instruments and', he said modestly as though he were confessing to writing verse on the sly or square-dancing, 'I compose.'

'Good. Keep it up. So, on the whole, you've got over this,' De Berry gestured at his wounded face, 'you'll get back to life and feel that, er, on the whole life, is worth living? Etc. Etc.' He grinned. 'On balance?'

'Living in the city of screaming tyres and streaming noses hasn't really helped my self-esteem.'

'Quite so. Quite so.' The doctor woggled his foot again and pressed his fingertips together and pushed them at his nose as Conroy went on, 'Oxford's softened me. Once I was strong but now I'm weak and compliant. But I blame Oxford when I should be blaming *myself*.'

'Quite so. Quite so.' The doctor's little Japanese watch ticked on the inside of the file.

'Maybe what I'm feeling guilty about isn't really the weather at all. Not the waste up there,' Conroy pointed up at the ceiling, 'but the waste in here,' he tapped his head.

'Quite so.' The doctor wondered whether to fight his publisher about the diagrams clause in his contract. 'But you've got over that unpleasant business? The students' attack?' He jogged up and down.

'Oh they weren't students,' Conroy protested innocently. 'I met them out at Blackbird Leys. I picked them up near the M4 and they lived in a cockroach infested high-rise at . . .' Conroy bit his tongue and broke out in sweat.

De Berry nodded with understanding and encouraged him to blurt on: 'Yes, I suppose I *did* invite them. My wife . . . I . . . I suppose . . . my marriage has been a mess, and I've never faced up to my . . .' He gestured and De Berry nodded sympathetically.

'You must try not to be too hard on yourself. After all, it takes two to make an impossible domestic situation. Right? But not two to cause a mugging. Or does it? I see you've been a patient here before.' De Berry flipped back through the medical records. 'Many moons ago.'

'Just an outpatient. I get such bad creative block . . .'

'Don't we all. The child you adopted,' De Berry went on, plunging into his bran-tub dip, 'must be growing up by now.'

'No, we never adopted her. You advised us not to. You thought we wouldn't be good parents.'

'Quite so.'

'So I married again and have twins.'

The doctor plunged again: 'Have you ever tried to get any of your work published? You know. . . .written the odd letter to the BBC and the Arts Council. I've just got into the publishing racket a bit myself. It's not all that difficlt.' De Berry looked at his invisible watch again.

'That's part of my problem,' Conroy edged forward shyly. '"Pa's Pop" was a top of the pops for over a year. My Folk Mass. But that was back in the fifties, and since then I'm only appreciated in East Germany.'

This was beyond the fathoming of the medical records so De Berry closed them and said, 'Why not go on trying to write a bit while you're here? Get some of the patients to their feet with a good tune, what?'

'My trouble is that I didn't want to stay in the "Pa's Pop" vein. But no one accepted my other self. They just wanted more Pa's Pop.'

It was then that De Berry remembered singing in the school choir, that roar of '*Blessed is He*', that guitar hammering out 'Hosannah.' 'Pa's Pop'! It came back to him.

'Maybe,' he said, to terminate the thought of his choirboy days, 'you'll find a new vein while you're up here. I don't expect we'll keep you for long. Go away and enjoy yourself. Get down to some work.'

Conroy's confession about the youths from Blackbird Leys had put him in De Berry's keeping and now he was grateful to him for this little jerk back to life, this small permission to live again. He was so grateful that he smiled at the young corsair and said, 'You must come and dine at Sanctus sometime, when I get back. I am beginning to feel sure I shall get back . . .' Conroy spoke shyly, in his mind already back at Sanctus, telling his wife in the confiding way he had of the new chap he had lassoed; not a Youth-Hostel leader this time, or a chap who made reeds for oboes, but a young corsair of a doctor . . .

De Berry sat very still as Conroy lassoed. The patient looked so much like a British Leyland car worker or a traffic warden that it hadn't dawned on him that he was talking to a colleague from another college. To make matters worse, De Berry had been short-listed for a Fellowship at Sanctus and had observed all the shibboleths when he dined there, had discussed Alban Berg's *Altenberglieder* with the Maths Fellow, had shown his grasp of the present University admissions system, and talked incisively about cuts in research grants. But in fact the college had announced that none of its short-list candidates had been satisfactory, and the Fellowship had not been filled. De Berry at thirty-three was still only a lecturer attached to St Martyrs', and one of the rejecting Fellows – and the author of 'Pa's Pop' – sat there smugly opposite him, hugging a piece of manuscript paper and blowing his nose, then letting it dribble.

De Berry looked at the big heavy pale sweaty face. 'I've started writing a Requiem,' Conroy was boyishly confiding, clutching his small piece of manuscript paper ... De Berry stared at his own almost gaitered legs as Conroy tried to 'secure' him. The face was swollen by drugs and under the chemical white hair the long scars shone.

'This is interesting,' De Berry said, in the voice he used when he wanted to get rid of his pupils. 'Look, can we meet again and go on with this?' He remembered his two long sessions with private patients this afternoon, the unfolding layers of Sally Bellchamber's early experiences of males. 'Look, let's meet again, shall we say in a day or two? When you've had time to settle down here? You're an unusual sort of person, you must know, and I feel sure we can sort things out ...' Sally Bellchamber's fees should be raised a bit perhaps, to ease her away from her obsession with elderly academics.

They both stared at the unread case-notes. 'I'll be seeing you again in a few days. OK? OK? Take it easy till then. And not to worry about the ...' De Berry paused and touched his face, then went out to his car. He had just under an hour to get to London and find somewhere to park.

The patients at the Herber had all been lying in rows when Clare had arrived at the Institute to take Conroy his college mail. She was surprised at the sudden rosiness of his face, as he joined happily in a rather Western style of yoga. They were doing it to loud music and talking even more loudly above it: 'Now a stone-mason's in a different class from a brick-layer,' a wiry middle-aged man wearing a black waistcoat was explaining. 'A stone mason's a real craftsman ... I was a monumental mason, too. Did all the tombstones and carried the corpses in a black suit and a top hat.'

'Feel your pelvic wall,' the therapist interrupted.

'Is that what got you down then, the corpses, and brought you in here, Mr Bell?' the patients called across as they struggled to raise themselves on to their shoulders, or hung upside down.

'Oh no, my word!' the stone mason replied indignantly, as he thrashed the air with his legs, and the therapist cried, 'Let them go all mushie and feel your pelvic wall . . .'

'Oh no, my word. Of course not. The fault was all that Do-it-Yourself our Joan made me do. Not the monumental trade. Oh no. It was the DIY.'

'Let's do the eagle now,' the therapist called.

'No, I was always out and about and seeing the world when I was in my blacks. Twice buried a professor . . . Black coat . . . black hat . . . black car always at the ready because there was no chill rooms in those days. No, it was all the DIY. That was my downfall . . .'

And there was Joe Conroy, lying on his back, his face flushed and grinning. To Clare it was a pitiful sight, but Conroy seemed to be enjoying himself. He seemed horribly integrated in this *danse macabre*, twining his left leg round his right arm and lowering himself to the ground as the undertaker's mate called indignantly, 'All that DIY. That was my downfall.'

Afterwards Conroy took Clare down the gardens to the broad fertile meadows beside the river where buttercups grew. As they strolled between the great colonnades of trees he told her that at last he thought he was getting back to work again. It was a new Requiem Mass. He gazed over the Thames where a few scullers were at work. Clare expressed surprise that an asylum had been built so near a river where patients might try to drown themselves.

'No one tries to commit suicide here,' Conroy protested solemnly. 'This is far too much of a healing, caring place. A great community.'

They left the great oaks and elms and chestnuts and he took her across the walled garden where the patients once exercised. There was a sundial here and a fountain paced evenly. He showed her the little lean-to built on to the inside of a great Corinthian column that he had been given to work in. He had laid out his manuscript papers and seemed to have completed quite a lot of his new Mass. He was at the *Qui tollis peccata mundi*.

'I call it Pevensey Bay,' he spread his arms round the golden column and called cheerfully, 'this little shack. This place is my new freedom. I no longer feel the need to sell off my home and my manuscripts. This new space is for music. And as for these "scratches",' he grinned as he stroked his face, 'I'm growing up enough to see those thugs in their right perspective.'

'What a wise idea, Joe,' Clare heard her old office voice say. Conroy's mis-shapen face, his white overblown moon on a cold eyeless night, grinned suddenly, almost a wink, and she was forced to look away, as she said painfully, 'You're looking much better too.'

'That's the new life-style,' he winked again. 'My new way of seeing things. For the first time for ten years my impulse to write has come back. I'm no longer threatened by the need to put on an act before the Fellows of Sanctus.'

Clare had been charged to find out his plans for the future but just as she was about to ask him about next term, another patient came in. He said he was a Fellow of St Martyrs' and recognised Conroy.

'Whom are you under?'

'Nick De Berry. A decent guy. Very helpful.'

'I'm under the Professor. I'd met him once or twice at High Table, and I see now why they call him "the blue denim ghost". He just sits there pressing his fingertips together and saying "Quite so. Quite so. Is there anything you would like to ask?" If the Virgin Mary appeared in a vision he'd just say to her, "Quite so. Is there anything you'd like to ask me about your son . . .'"

Conroy didn't normally see much in this kind of humour, but now he burst out laughing. 'Good man.' He patted the other patient's arm. 'Nick De Berry, thank God, is spot on.'

'I suppose I got rid of my wives instead of my job,' he added when the other patient had gone.

'You mean, you feel – ' Clare began delicately, but suddenly Conroy seemed to grow more excited.

'I mean to invite Nick De Berry to dine at Sanctus some time.' Conroy hadn't deigned to dine at Sanctus for over two years and now suddenly he was talking proprietorially about showing his distinguished guest round the maze. 'Ours is an arts-man college, isn't it? Music. Eng.Lit. Maybe a scientist's presence, a distinguished psychiatrist . . .'

Conroy went back to his work-table. Ideas sprang at him again like nice children who have been mischievously hiding for too long and who now dancingly reappear, springing up dressed in funny clothes. He scribbled and smiled and laughed. 'We also learn cookery,' he told Clare, 'and badminton, and I'm in with the young set who seem quite interested in my type of music.'

Clare stared at two women in a corner, two very sad young women who sat side by side there with heads lowered. 'Shall we shut our eyes for a moment?' one of them was asking.

'Are you going to shut yours?' They looked at each other and then slowly lowered their eyelids and stuffed their mouths with Opal Fruits. 'Are yours still shut?'

Clare watched the slow exchange of sweets. 'Joe,' she asked, 'are you sure you're all right here? The Master was asking after you . . . wants you to let him know as soon as you're ready for a visitor . . .'

'My future is re-emerging. Thanks to this set-up where I've actualised my real inner space,' Conroy reported sententiously.

After Clare had gone, Dr De Berry swung on the door handle of the room and gave his simian smile. 'Working? You find you can concentrate? Can we talk again?'

They walked together down a corridor, Conroy mentally making a note to put in his diary, 'Nick De Berry for Benediction Night?'

At the door of the room, De Berry paused. 'I've got one or two people in here, if you don't mind.' He gestured round the room where six students were sitting and three occupational therapists: 'Jill, James, Sue, John, Ted . . .'

'Hi!'

'Hi!'

'So, how are you feeling now, Dr Conroy?' Dr De Berry sat down and asked with ostentatious courtesy.

'I'm beginning to feel far less distressed about . . .'

'Good. You feel . . . ?' The doctor put his head on one side and revealed his earnestness and sincerity by a slight cocking of his eye that one or two of his students were meant to pick up. They replied with the same look of exaggerated seriousness.

Conroy, unaware of the eye-journeys, went on, 'Of course I've been far too long on the alienation-ticket for my good, or for music's.'

De Berry moved as though to dust down his elegant drainpipe trousers. His students watched.

Behavioural therapy at the Herber Institute was based on the belief that if you discouraged a patient from expressing his distressing thoughts and feelings you could also discourage him from thinking about them, and so disqualify him from feeling them and even having them. Consequently when Conroy started to talk swiftly and confessionally to De Berry about the terrible feelings of inadequacy he had at Oxford, the drying up of his art, the failure of his two marriages, the effect of the bad summers on his moods, De Berry just crossed his legs, recrossed them, shuffled his papers noisily wagging his slender ankle up and down, then interrupted, 'Why do you still think, after three days here, that you too are a maddy or a saddy? You're not like the other people here. Or do you want to be?' The students eyed the doctor and smiled. 'Why do you feel the need to lean on us so? To escape? We'd like you to leave here tomorrow.'

'But I'm still feeling rather jaded.' Crestfallen, Conroy tried to maintain his dignity.

'You don't look it.' They all stared at his fleshy swollen face.

'I'm still feeling I may do something to those boys who . . .' Conroy stroked his scars.

De Berry reproached him gently, 'You told me last time that you *invited* those youths . . . Perhaps you're not a maddy or a saddy but a glad baddy.' Conroy's hand still faltered at the scars on his face. 'Those scratches are taking a long time to heal. Maybe they'd do better at home with wife and twins. You'll weigh-out tomorrow? Right? I'll tell the charge-nurse.'

'But suppose my vengeful feelings come back?' Conroy said feebly, still stroking his face. 'I often feel I might . . .'

'You're as capable of dealing with that as you always have been. We believe the patient's place is in the home, so why not go home and practise a little free will? Lots of people recommend it.'

The doctor cocked his eye again at his students. They tittered as De Berry applied his aversion therapy, enjoying the special relationship with his students that it brought. His lectures and demonstrations were always well attended and he was happy in his rapport with his students now, so happy that he forgot he was treating a colleague, another man, and not demonstrating his well attested techniques for detaching over-dependent female neurotics who grew too attached to him for anyone's safety.

The junior doctor who had taken the case-history so painstakingly was uneasy now. De Berry had forgotten that members of the University weren't supposed to be seen in front of students without their consent. And also, De Berry had obviously not delved far enough into the notes to discover that Conroy had been raped as well as mugged by the gang. He hadn't even told his wife of this fact, so that De Berry, not being able to take the unconscious very seriously, gave it wings to escape on a night flight because he only saw a vain middle-aged man in front of him.

He extended his eye-beam to his expectant students again. 'In this hospital we cater for saddies and maddies. Only for them. Not for daddies in paddies. What was it you were telling me about Oxford's self-infatuated people?'

The students breathed out heavily through their noses and shuffled a little. 'Isn't it time you got back to some more of "Pa's Pop?"' A student gave a sudden popping sneeze and they all tittered again. It was all being videoed too, Conroy suddenly felt sure. 'We don't want this place to get a reputation for being a free bed-and-breakfast.'

But De Berry must have thought he was still at High Table or in Common Room because he went on in his slightly reproachful way, 'And anyway, a lot of boysies and girlsies are coming on to the ward next week so we want you gone.' Conroy rose stiffly, staring round for the video cameras. 'Give us a ring sometime, if you feel like a session. We could have one or two seshes. Not more, I'm afraid. I haven't the time.' De Berry closed his palms.

Behind the fixed students the consulting-room walls were equally still and white and fixed, and staring as the students videoed. De Berry had overdone the aversion therapy. Conroy didn't care whether it was aversion, or deconditioning techniques that were being demonstrated, or some form of moral shock treatment. He suddenly felt sick. They had videoed the rape and were showing it on a school-bus or on rag-day. He shivered and felt sick as the sound of the students' laughter spread through him. It seemed to irradiate him. Was the doctor demonstrating how to deal with gays? Or was he demonstrating how to deal with failed but self-infatuated composers? Or was he demonstrating, at the request of the Master of Sanctus, how to get rid of the University's deadwood?

Whatever it was, it seemed to be done by irradiation, and Conroy felt sick again as he felt waves of it rolling up him from the water meadows and the city and the University. The Fellows of Sanctus, too, were all smiling as they watched the video. His youthful rapists were grinning as they turned it on. Even that cold unripe fruit from the college office, Clare Bonnard, was watching. Even the people waiting in the doctor's surgery in Judasland were watching. Everyone was at it, discovering what happened to the vain and overtrusting man who had eagerly tried to tell the youths of Blackbird Leys and the doctors at the hospital about his music, his loves, his hopes, his failures, and his self-disgust.

Conroy quickly packed up his belongings and cleared out the little lean-to the hospital had lent him and cleared out of the Institute. Then it occurred to him that they were right to video him so. He had deserved every inch of it. The sky was hard and cold, and grey rain came down every now and again like an accusing message, a button pressed to record more self-condemnation. That buggered self could have no end. He walked quickly away from the hospital, down the colonnaded walks and along the river bank trying to avert his eyes from its weak grey recording flood.

But after Conroy had fled from the Institute, his ward had rung Carey Conroy and Charles Mally's surgery in Spide Street to tell them that Conroy had walked out in a fit of anger. As he wasn't under a section, they had no powers to recall him. Perhaps De Berry had already forgotten the technique he had proudly demonstrated on his patient, or perhaps the Institute's right hand simply did not know what its left hand did. At any rate, the hospital had washed its hands of Joe Conroy and returned him to Judasland. The Master of Sanctus had, however, been informed that Conroy had walked out, and now invited him to hand in his resignation and vacate his college house within three months.

When Conroy faced his wife again fevered with his humiliation and distress, she just curled up her lips in a rueful smile. 'For years you've been complaining about your depression and it's not surprising you don't like it when it's diagnosed at last as mere constipation and you're publicly purged with your students standing round and then sent home with your clothes under your arm.' Carey was suddenly full of bitter laughter. 'So now you know what it feels like to be female. Women just have to get used to being treated with studied seriousness till they've actually been taken.' She went on slowly, 'You always were a sucker for seduction, eh Twigs? Always so compliant, and then so angry with yourself for being so compliant ... so angry at your own vanity and yet so much more angry when it's someone else's turn to point it out to you.'

Conroy hadn't told his wife had been raped. He hadn't told anyone except the junior doctor at the Institute. Only Clare Bonnard had noticed how flushed he was as he pursued his over-assiduous yoga on the ward and fell in with such earnest devotion to the routine of the hospital.

Carey Conroy only saw her husband's puffy and sulky expression. She knew only too well what happened every time he confided in someone and tried to 'secure' them to himself. Now she rang her father who taught in Cambridge and told her husband she was going over there for a few days. The twins were staying with friends down the road. They had been there since Conroy's attack. Carey had wanted them out of the way. They were happy with friends, and she too wanted, she thought, the chance to be alone for a few days. 'We poor silly women,' she kissed him goodbye, 'we women always have been treated like this.'

It was only then that Conroy experienced the full horror of his rape, penetration, and despatch. He was suddenly sick over the kitchen table. The car drove off and he was sick again. He wandered out into Spide Street and down the road to the comfort of the church. He wandered in and sat down. It smelt pleasantly of incense and he tried to pray. Then his eye caught the plaque on the wall that recorded the death by drowning of the three Tyler boys in 1923. He suddenly envied them their purity, by the meadows. Their deaths were good ones. Among the white flowers they had found a hood to shelter themselves in. His twins were innocent too, and they too needed to be protected . . . But he heard footsteps and the swish of heavy serge cloth and heard Polly Ives from the Pastorate coming and went quickly away.

Next day Dr Hari Sharma was also obliged to use the lucky-dip method of family practice, when Joe Conroy settled his tandem bicycle with the dragon child-seats at its back against the wall of the waiting-room and went in to see him. But Dr Sharma had picked out the fact that Conroy was a composer and not a piano teacher and he was pleased with the first client in his new career in a prestigiously cultured city like Oxford.

VII

'I see you have discharged yourself from the Herber Institute.' Dr
Hari Sharma tried to look into Conroy's face.

'Let none escape the whipping,' Conroy replied with a grotesque
grin. Sharma's English was good, but he wasn't familiar with
biblical references and he frowned as Conroy went on, 'And ye
after the manner of ye, thy forefathers be damned. Unto such
generations as shall know thy seed.'

Hari Sharma was tall and slender and elegantly dressed in a
grey-blue hand-tailored suit with hand stitching round the lapels.
He hoped to make his career in the West and was secretly delighted
in his first patient. Symptomatic or asymptomatic depression? he
asked himself as Conroy sat there, his puffy face and shiny hair
making a grin seem even more grotesque.

'What mischance had caused your face . . . ?' Sharma gestured
at Conroy's scars.

'An angel once gave me a kiss. But now I'm *manqué* every bliss.
Sans the lot except the Sanskrit writing on the wall. Thy twin wells
shall be purified.'

Sharma smiled at Conroy who sat there in baggy pin-striped
trousers with greasy stains down them, and bits of scrap paper and
fluff caught in their turn-ups. He blinked through his small pink
eyes. He was wearing his wife's embroidered sweater and his
plimsolls were held together with bits of sellotape.

'You are a musician,' Dr Sharma reminded him gently, 'and that
means basically a dutiful artist's soul. But with a duty to society.
And it is necessary to eat. Bowels? Sleep? Relationship with your
wife? I am not married myself. Though I have plans in that
direction, I am a little too much of the Freudian,' he laid down his
pen and confessed shyly, then stopped when he saw the expression

on Conroy's face. 'Do you feel that friendships you have made are no longer seen as valid by other people? I will prescribe this well tried and well attested drug. Solverin D. Six tablets each night before you go to bed. That will ease your depression, and return you to your creative course. And sir, there is a very sympathetic University and culturally oriented environment for artistic temperaments such as yours.'

He looked at the notes. No letter from the Herber had arrived yet. The long English weekend was probably responsible for this lack of liaison. The medical notes only recorded Conroy's depression and the muggers' attack in the back yard of his house. 'It might be a correct decision for you to return to the hospital ward for a few weeks. The patients at the Herber Institute do many interesting and artistic projects, so I am told.' He leaned over his patient tenderly. 'They do crosswords for mental alertness and also quizzes. Then there are ancient places to visit. Ancient palaces to be seen. Many excursions. They sometimes paint while musicians play to them. Then they plan, a joint project, the running of the ward. All this is done democratically and on a friendly basis. But I stress, being a University branch, the orientation is toward culture. Maybe you did not give the Institute a fair trial. It is basically a community caring for the needs of those who carry the burden of advanced consciousness.'

But Conroy just stood up. For a moment Sharma thought he was going to attack him, but he just grinned again and said slowly, 'They've taken away the *mysterium tremendum*. They've taken away my lord and lady . . .'

Sharma carefully wrote down the unfamiliar words. '*Mysterium tremendum*.' He looked up and asked, 'Is that from the Latin?'

'It's from pure wells.'

Sharma nodded and crossed the 'as' off the front of the 'asymptomatic depression', and added 'Psychotic episode?'

'And how is your wife? Please?'

'She went with the rest of the rapists.'

Sharma nodded. 'So you experience great weariness of the spirit?' He leaned over again and tried to comfort him. 'You imagine these bad things. You are too sensitive. I have been hearing good things about the celebrations for May Morning. Can you perhaps as a resident of both town and gown explain the ancient ceremonies to me?'

Conroy shook his head. He hadn't shaved and pinkish hair grew on his chin and sprouted from his ears.

'You will find these tablets will lift your mood if you are patient. You may also find perspiration, dryness of the mouth and constipation, but please eat plenty of brown bread and be patient. Thanks to the modern science of pharmacology you will, I assure you, see the sun rise again on your creative talents and your peace of mind. Please come and see me again in one week's time. It is good to see the *literati* back on their chosen roads of academic and artistic attainment.'

He held out his hand to Conroy, glad to meet him and glad he had broken in the new word 'literati'. Conroy however just took the prescription form and was gone.

Someone brought Dr Sharma a cup of weak tepid coffee and he went to the window to tip it away and stared out at an ugly sight. A tall bearded man was standing in the car-park behind the Community Centre. There were ribbons tied in his straw hat and he was jumping up and down on one spot calling, 'Ri-fol-lattety-oh.' Bells jingled on his ankles.

In the waiting-room Sharma could hear Mrs Plasket's voice. 'Come to the REAL Greek Islands.' She was reading a cheerful poster on the doctor's waiting-room wall, beside the ones about Immunisation and Smoking.

'Ah, the REAL Greek Island.' Grace stared at it and sighed, and turned to Clare who had also come to register at Dr Mally's new practice. 'I thought the Greek Islands I went to last time seemed a bit phoney, what with all those soggy chips and paper caps. That Greek accent sounded so reprovingly Welsh. Perhaps the coach driver, Archimedes, didn't take us quite far enough.'

Grace rose to her feet as Sharma stood in the surgery door. 'Hari. Anil got in touch with me. And this is Clare, who's willing to help you touch up your manuscript a bit.'

Dr Sharma looked around the waiting-room. Most of the patients seemed to be over sixty, and welded into their seats like candles into candlesticks.

'Perhaps they weren't the real Greek Islands at all,' Mrs Plasket was still sighing. 'At the ones the Brits always get sent to, you're only allowed the one scoop of beans and you have to queue for it beside the toilets . . . Perhaps Anil and I missed the real Himalayas too, and the real Ganges, and the real Taj Mahal. Such is British life.'

'My daughter went to Barry,' another patient interrupted, 'and they said the liquid comes with the beans, and the vindaloo repeated on her all the time she was queuing for the sun-burn at the hospital.'

Dr Sharma shrugged and called in his next patient. Outside his consulting-room more morris men were rehearsing for May Morning, and the man in ribbons with bells on his ankles was now bobbing up and down under some ivy that was being tied on his straw hat, and darting a long wooden pole at a washing-line, as a girl's voice called, 'Try to get the swordstick-play a bit better, Keith, and don't forget that the ivy has to be struck down in three motions, to conquer evil.'

Then another man appeared in the yard, entirely wrapped in green leaves, head and face, hands, neck and feet. He danced round blindly in wider and wider circles, then he hit a car in the car-park and fell, and protested, 'My eyeholes have slipped again.'

'And you've lost your nose hole too. Don't forget you are the apotheosis of the negative zone, so start again – '

'"Dibby-dibby dandy."'

'A bit more ferocity in that "dibby".'

Dr Sharma was anxious to develop a more fluid English style and get the *entrée* into university circles, but he wasn't sure what aspect of the scenes taking place outside he would be expected to participate in.

He could hear the women in the waiting-room as they stared out at the Man-of-Green bobbing up and down with a whistle between his teeth and his hands tied behind his back. 'Do you remember how it warn when the Man-of-Green come down to the Land on May Days? I was more scared of him than the spiders. I wer. He was that black I skit in the cubby.'

'Yes, that Man-of-Green. Don't ask me who he war. But he comes each year and we girls war pushed in the cupboard. Our mother said, "Don't let me see you looking at him." Though the boys war all following him down the street.'

Hari Sharma looked out with boredom and distaste, then with some satisfaction at his now crowded waiting-room. Grace called to him again, 'Clare looked at your manuscript, Hari.' Clare sat up as Mrs Plasket added, 'She thinks it doesn't need more than a little stiffening here and there. A bit of tightening up. Nothing basic, just a slight stylistic re-tuning.' Hari beamed and ushered Mrs

Plasket in. But she was too eager to practise her Bombay dialect on him for him to be more than minimally interested in her enlarged toe.

Clare Bonnard waited for her turn to register and look out into the Judasland yards. The maze at Sanctus was compensation for the lack of reward she felt at the college itself. It was like a pipe or a leat that led into the echoing cistern of Judasland. Gradually she was beginning to learn about the past of the people who had served the colleges for centuries. Sometimes the dripping of the tank was sad and sonorous.

She had heard the stories of women who had gone out into domestic service at twelve; of those who had served University families for fifty years; of the seamstresses who had made their clothes, the cellarers and stewards who had sampled the High Table wines. She had heard stories of loyalty and devotion rewarded and unrewarded; of college servants who spat in their masters' soups and those who fawned or name-dropped. She had heard the story of the scout who had committed suicide after 'overstepping the mark': he had presumed to attend the funeral of the professor he had served for fifty years. She had heard of other suicides of this kind, and the waters that re-echoed in the cisterns of Judasland recorded thousands of unnamed griefs and neglected offerings as well as the ribald laughter from college kitchens.

It was a far cry from what was going on out there in the yard now. A student dressed entirely in thick black serge was carrying an animal's snout under his arm and had started to sing

Green a green doddy
The sod and the croddy

Another student was practising a one-man band: drum, mouth organ, foot-harmonium and nose-flute. Two girls came out carrying a huge cross of more green leaves shaped like a woman with breasts and hips and a neat waist they were trimming with nail scissors. Once these activities had been 'real'. The people of Judasland had taken part in them. Now the women stared sullenly out and repeated in the local monotone, 'The Man-of-Green. Every May Day he came down the Land. All covered in green leaves. You couldn't see his face. We girls were always just pushed away in the cubbies, but the boys used to follow him all the way down the street. Hop, hop he goes. May Day's still a bad day for the Land.'

The women dropped their voices as Nellie Grainger stood in the waiting-room doorway for a moment, and hovered.

'She still don't go showing her face round here in a hurry. Not yet. But he – ' Mrs Gage lowered her voice as Joe Conroy fidgeted with his tandem bicycle, then left the surgery, ' – Now he's from one of the colleges, but he's all right. Keeps himself to himself. Not like some of them. Forever on about this and that, and we won't have the other either. And the fancy cheeses they sell in the shops! On my word! But,' Mrs Gage leaned over to her friend and dropped her voice, 'Dr Conroy's all right. But he feels he's done something very, very wrong. It's a pity someone else around here never had a thought that way round what she done wrong.'

They were eyeing the corner of the room by the reception desk. Nellie Grainger stood there for a moment, then she went out.

'I even saw her in Littlewoods. You should see the stuff she was feeding her face with. And the stuff she brings back from the colleges! Don't dare to show her face down here, and yet she don't mind snuggling and hugging round the back way into the colleges.'

Mrs Gage brought out an aerosol spray and puffed it once or twice round the room. They stared out at the dazzling green trees heavy with May's presence in the yards at the back of the streets.

'We all feel just as bad each year when May comes round.' Mrs Gage turned to Clare 'Not since 1923 she hasn't shown her face. We'd made the wreath to lay on the river as we always done on May Day . . .'

Clare looked puzzled, so Mrs Gage explained: 'You've seen the tablet in the church about the three boys? The three boys drowned in the river in 1923?' Clare nodded. 'They were lovely boys. They was all three of them Tyler boys, the altar boys at St James's then. Then it was a pride to be called up to the High Altar, Jim was boat boy, Peter was thurifer . . . In those days the whole parish went over the river in May to bless the waters. The boundaries went as far as the sand by the mill stream and we all used to go in a boat. Mr Paley it was . . . used to row us over to the bounds down by sandtips, with the wreath. We used to pick the flowers from the riverbanks and we'd carry them all round the Parish boundaries. Then at the Salter's Arms they used to come out with a tray of the pudding and drinks. I don't know but what the drinks were much other than ale or cider. But a certain person had already took too much. They said she took it from the Vestry before it was, you know, 'done'. Lived with a certain gentleman who had the keys. . . . Anyway.'

Mrs Gage leaned over and whispered to Clare, 'We got into that punt on May Day in 1923. We was all very young then and liked a bit of fun. But she was different. Usherette in the cinema. Then a dresser at the theatre. Then at the bindery.'

Mrs Gage had told this story so many times that her voice had become stylised in the telling and she would pause just where her audiences had made her pause two, three, four decades ago in her tellings. 'But no one wanted Nellie for long. Too lively she was. And when we was all sat there in that boat and Mr Paley rowing us over . . . He's gone now. . . . Went last year, used to come to me every day for fifty years for his dinner. But they all gorn now and it's all almost forgot.

'But I can remember it as though it was yesterday, the way a certain she lifted her skirts in that boat and started up with her 'Ta-ra-ra-boomp-te-ay, It is my wedding day.' And she'd had too much of the drinks in the Arms as well and she tottered over sideways and the boat overturned and we all clung hard. But the three boys never come up again and when we got to the bank the water was, well, it was quite still as though it hadn't seen nothing and wouldn't tell. As though it was innocent as break of day. And it rained all day.

'But no one ever forgot what she done. Nellie Grainger, for years she was just sat there at her window. Never set foot in the Land for thirty years. Always crept out round quiet-like by the maze door of the college. After that day in May, we petitioned the Council again and again to change the name from Judasland. It always made us seem so poor and crude and rough. We wanted it "Meadowcroft" or "Thamesville". We even got the priest to raise the matter with the nobs, but they were hard men then, and now the women ones is even worse. I mean, even "St James" would've done better as a name. "Many waters do not quench love." Indeed.'

Mrs Gage went on, 'Nellie Grainger wrote that out, got someone who wrote nice to do it for her, and pinned it on her front door if you please. Sometimes you could see her at night with her pencil out in the street when it was dark, going over it: "Many Waters . . ." again and again.'

Dr Sharma stood in the doorway asking who his next patient was. Clare stood up and went in. He looked at her rosy, snub-nosed face, her impeccably clear skin, and her clothes like other neat skins round her. Her accent was good. She was obviously from the educated classes, and she was willing to turn his rejected manuscript into a bright morning for Third World psychiatric medicine.

'You are a university student?' he asked eagerly. 'A postgraduate perhaps?' He opened his delicate plum-coloured lips and filled in Clare's medical card. He had a way of lifting one thick eyebrow when he was interested, and smiling with half his mouth.

Clare smiled. 'No such luck. I'm a secretary at Sanctus Spiritus College.'

'That is Latin,' Dr Sharma said with lowered head, still smiling and writing. 'What does it mean? Please?'

'The College of the Holy Ghost.'

'In India,' Hari replied neutrally, 'ghosts are not holy and we discourage them. It is only the mentally sick and the uneducated who talk about ghosts and spirits. To the rest these are normally regarded as paranoid ideas. In medicine, however, we see a certain placebo value in exorcising ghosts. Exorcism, as I have explained in my book – but you have read it? Did you get the gist of my argument about the treatment of spirit-possession through placebo witchcraft, and the extent to which the psychiatric forces can morally use the sorcerers? . . .'

Dr Sharma returned to Clare's record. 'Please, have you ever been in hospital? And do you take any medication?'

She stared at him, tall and dark and delicate in build. His eyebrows were silky and thick, but under them his eyelids were heavy and full and his eyes, dark like deep clean wells, suggested an eagerness to reach out to all people and wash them in serenity and happiness. His upper lip trembled. He lowered his eyelids as if in prayer, then lowered his dark and glossy head. Then with newly drawn-up strength he asked her, 'Is there anything you would like to ask me? Is there anything you would like me to do for you?'

Clare wanted to ask him what Hindus felt about evolution if they believed in the recycling of bodies as well as of souls. She wanted to ask him if it were true that he was single and planning to settle in Oxford. She wanted to ask him if he were ever racially insulted or exploited. She wanted to ask him if he believed in happiness. She wanted to ask him if he would be happy in Slack Street as he lifted his thick eyebrow and smiled with one corner of his bloom of a mouth. He looked satisfied as he filled in her medical card, then he looked at something he had written down previously and asked her, 'Tell me, Miss Bonnard, what does *Mysterium Tremendum* mean? And is that pronunciation the correct one? And does the thought express a Bible thought to you, or a particular Latin text? Or is it Greek culture it brings to mind? Maybe a mythological analysis could best clarify the thought? Do you feel I have made my point quite clear in my book, namely the extent of the problem of a culture not yet oriented into the Western high-technology culture? Its pre-industrial symbols which paranoia naturally picks upon . . .'

But Grace Plasket had been fabricating when she had told Hari about Clare's enthusiasm for his book. Clare hadn't even seen it till now, the manuscript lying on a chair, and beside it a new straw hat for the river picnic with the price-tag still fixed to the black ribbon. Hari's right eyebrow had curved up again as Clare said she needed more time to work on the book. He indicated the manuscript, they gazed out of the window into the car park and the yard where the undergraduates were still knocking sticks at washing-lines and chanting to penny whistles, 'Green the green doddy . . .'

'It is clear to me,' Hari sighed, 'that though in the West, magical practices have all but ceased, there is still a sense of the *Mysterium Tremendum* that the Christian religion ignores at its peril . . .' He opened his eyelids very wide and his liquid dark eyes were very full. His delicate lips parted as he redelivered the phrase. But how was it spelt?

Then he smiled and, to Clare's relief, looked out of the window. 'Do you think the weather will bid fair for our May Morning picnic?' The straw hat beside the manuscript made a similar appeal. Hari's smile was suddenly jolly. Clare noticed his tie was as pink and neat as a child's tongue.

He sighed and opened his mouth slightly. 'I am relieved that you think my brain-baby', he gestured to the manuscript, 'needs only minor adjustments. As I have said, English is my second language. Naturally I long to be fluent in it, but, alas, it seems that this destiny is not to be so. We could perhaps meet some time for a cup of coffee to discuss such alterations as may be necessary. In a coffee bar or at my flat?' He smiled and held out his hand. 'But we shall be meeting again before then on our celebratory picnic to which I am very much looking forward.' He smiled.

'That will be lovely,' Clare smiled back, still surprised at the college treasure.

But Dr Sharma seemed delighted at her Englishness, good manners and accent. 'I will let you have another copy of my brain-child.'

When Clare got back to her lodgings that evening, Mrs Boden said there was a guest upstairs for her. Clare leaped up to her room, thinking that Hari Sharma had brought his manuscript round. She hadn't liked to ask him for it in case Grace Plasket had invented the whole story of its rejection and resurrection.

So now she bounded up the stairs to her room, but when she got there she could see the purple habit and chunky-knit jumper of Polly Ives from the University Pastorate. She was munching one of Mardi's home-bakes and flipping through Clare's bookshelf. It was she, she explained, who had brought Joe Conroy to the surgery this morning. He wouldn't have come otherwise. It was problem-atic, she fingered her neck where her dog-collar should have been. Joe hadn't yet seemed to make the link-up and Judasland was essentially the caring community where link-ups could be made.

She explained this in her clear and joyful voice. She appealed to Clare: 'What is our next move to be? Our prayer-workshop is particularly concerned with Joe and Nellie Grainger. We've had our prayer-eye on both of those two spiritual wanderers for many moons now.' She tipped some leaflets onto Clare's bed. They were about the Resurrection, and there was a diagram clarifying it, together with one on the Holy Spirit. Clare was annoyed because Polly in her eagerness to erect a large arrow leading from time to eternity, and explain both to Clare, had knocked a Chagal print off her wall.

'Whither?' Polly drew a lot of lines and circles on a piece of paper, then made them intersect. This was somehow supposed to prove other intersections too: 'i.e. God is that circle because he is infinite. We are straight lines because we are poor and mortal. But, but but, but wait.' She pushed her tongue out and advanced her arguments till her straight lines curved and touched the completed circle. 'We can still be touched by the good Lord, praise be ... Just like that.' She grinned as she brought about the triumphant union of line and circle, and of time. 'Time as seen by man,' she advanced, 'and time as it exists in the eye of a wise and loving God. If only we could help Joe Conroy make the link-up it'd be clear as the blessed day.'

She got out a yellow biro and added, 'Yellow for His Son bringing light and life and hope and forgiveness ... Perhaps you know Joe Conroy better than I do. "To be or not to be." Shall we go ahead with the rescue operation? What the tactics? And what the strategy?'

'He's ill. He's in the hands of doctors,' Clare protested.

'True.' Polly leaned over. 'But don't you think, Clare, that all healing depends on a true co-operation of soul, mind and body and if the soul is in the right place, the mind and the body come more easily to heel? No one asks us to torment ourselves. I believe,' she lowered her head and dropped her voice, 'I believe we are sometimes called on to intervene.'

Polly knelt down on Clare's bedroom slippers. Clare could see a scrap of paper that had got caught on the wool of her bright orange home-made sweater: 'Bring to the boil and stir till thickened.'

'Let's get weaving then.' Polly crossed herself and rose to her feet. 'What do you think?' She rolled a table-mat tentatively along her chunky-knit sleeve, then pressed some cheese to her ear as if to check its pulse. 'Perhaps it's time we ordinary folks intervened. I mean, with oodles of prayer. It could effect the right miracle. After all, you can't learn to swim till you've jolly well jumped into the pond. So, now Dr Sharma (*Deo gratia*) has done *his* good thing, I feel it's time for us to do ours.'

Polly's big bulk started up under her clerical robe: 'Get the ball rolling . . . We here in the Land want to help Joe Conroy face the truth four-square bang-on, that evil is a fact. We women are its first victims, so we must be right here waiting to catch. We women are the arms of the community into which the bleeding sufferer falls back trusting. Joe Conroy and Nellie Grainger . . . But we are strong and we won't rest till both the wanderers are back four-square in the community where they belong.'

Polly's lips were moist and parted, but her eyes were glaucous as she went on, 'Step number one in reconciliation: get his children back to him. We can't bring back the three poor Tyler boys from May Day 1923, but we can make other home-comings viable. Joe Conroy must see that God didn't just stamp out two sexes, male and female, like cups and saucers. He made plates and dishes and glorious concoctions for holding flowers and leaves in, and Conroy's twins are proof that God didn't mean him to end in some dreary backwater of squalor and grot.'

'Polly,' Clare said, only her voice was the well bred voice of the college office and lacked imperatives, 'Polly, I think we should leave Joe's children out of this. I think Mrs Conroy means to take them over to Cambridge. Perhaps we should go round to Spide Street and see if he's got food and . . .'

But Polly's glaucous eyes had cleared and she was singing almost to herself, 'Shall be done. Shall be. These things shall be. Some day I really mean to get down to the problem of evil.'

Then as she ran downstairs and draped her habit round her bicycle, Clare could hear her singing:

> 'Two little podlings,
> Two little oddlings,
> Two little portions of rhubarb pie . . .

He who shall offend against one of these . . .'

VIII

The May Morning picnic began badly. It wasn't actually raining, but the wind was cold and wet, tore the trees and sent blossoms spitting off them. Clare stood where they had arranged to meet at the top of the Broad. But half past five came and people streamed down towards Magdalen Bridge – thousands of them, it seemed – and no one from her party had turned up.

Finally Mrs Plasket appeared on a bicycle, but the crowd was so dense that she had to abandon it. They could see Charles Mally wedged in his car. Some youths were trying to lift it up. Then he disappeared into the crowd streaming down Longwall to the tower and the bridge. But Grace and Clare couldn't get near the water. A boy tried to play his electric guitar and was cheered by the crowd. Another set up a transistor and began to play his clarinet to the background of Mozart.

It was still freezing when the great moment came and the clock in the college tower started to chime. But someone had fainted and an ambulance siren drowned the slow strikes of the bell. Then there was silence and each strike seemed to press the previous one further and further into this silence. A bird cheeped, then abruptly stopped. The whole world seemed to have stopped. The sixth chime came, then silence; then the hymn came down from the top of the tower.

Clare shivered. She could see the tiny white petals of the choirboys' surplices fluttering between the battlements of the tower, as the hymn came: 'Te Deum Patrem', small and pure and faint and shattering. She had never seen so many silent people before, white-faced, blue-lipped, while these small neutral voices from above seemed secure in something that had existed long before God.

They sang what was supposed to be a hymn, but it was more primitive and more chilling. Green trees hung all round the grey college. Green was draped off the city walls. Green anguish, halting, retreating, then advancing. Green joy spilling out of a sudden green flush-flood, while clouds hung there filled with icy water. Oxford had always been a place that received few and only small contributions from women, but this hymn spoke of a place to which men did not contribute either. Of an earth that was not man's friend; of a place unmarked by human entry and ends; of a destiny that had no common point with the destiny of humans and their history . . .

Then the hymn was interrupted by a noise of shouting and punts being knocked together. 'Someone's fallen in,' she heard a call. 'They've. . . . I can't see, but Marigold is on Jim's shoulders and she says . . .' The wind tore at the leaves and the flowers and turned the clouds into engines of war. Clare thought of the three Judasland boys drowned when the water rose, and the Toshidis at Slack Street and how terrified Eddie had been of winds. She stood miserably still in the dense damp crowd till the hymn was over.

The choir in the tower had started an affected catch, 'My Bonny Lass She Smileth', while champagne corks popped. May Morning had arrived, and Grace had found Dr Sharma. He stood there pale with chattering teeth, looking miserably round him. Then he recognised Grace and nodded – just gave a methodical nod, as if he too felt that humans were a mere impediment in nature's processes.

May stood even more heavily on Clare than it had ever done before. The carols were over and the bells in Magdalen tower were pealing out over the water and the water was giving them back. People were peering over the bridge and policemen were walking across a bridge made of punts and peering down into the water. Someone, it was repeated, had fallen in. Clare thought again of the Judasland boys in 1923.

Morris men were already in formation waiting for their one-man band to appear. More bottles were opened. Cans were sucked. The ambulance men lifted a youth on to a stretcher. May had such a gloating touch. The morris men were stooping now and dancing near the ground while the Man-of-Green appeared, a girl leading him because his eye-holes had slipped again. He was more black than green now and he made pathetic noises as he twirled, so that Hari looked at him with distaste and asked politely when they reached him, 'Is the aim of this ceremony to cast out evil spirits? Is there still lurking in the English consciousness a nostalgia for the old days of mystique and empire? You wish to conjure up times that were perhaps better for you as a nation?'

'Possibly.' Mrs Plasket took a puff from her cigarette. 'Your father told me that if I had gone to Peshawar with his brother I should have improved the conditions of his other wives no end.'

Polly Ives from the Pastorate had cycled up gayly and interrupted, turning to Hari, 'No, this spring ceremony has always existed, and it is still as relevant as it has ever been. You see,' she leaned over to explain to Hari, whose teeth were still chattering: 'Purification of the water and fertility of the land. To make the seed grow and multiply and then, praise be,' she took a deep breath, 'the Lord was there in His Own body, so these rites become a memorandum – to remind us that there is no longer any need for us to make cruel sacrifice. God got there first, do you see? That's what May Day is really telling us.'

There was another chilly silence, then a morris man came over and hit Hari with a bladder. He frowned and sniffed and fingered his nose and edged away. 'I see,' he said again, impatiently. He was wearing a mustard-brown jacket and an ochre shirt and tie, and he looked slightly bad-tempered, and less ingenuous than in his blue bespoke jacket with the neat collar stitching. He turned to Polly: 'You are trying to revive pagan rituals and magical practices as warnings and reminders?'

'Bang on. By the way, I think I met your brother in the Mission Field in Bombay,' she smiled again at Hari. His frown deepened.

'Oh no. Most certainly not,' he replied firmly. 'My brother is Congress Party and a surgeon in New Delhi.'

'*Salut* then, all the same.' Polly shook his hand happily. 'Have you ever come across the Burley Fathers – Burley in name and burly in nature – in Delhi then, by any chance?'

'No. Most definitely not,' Hari replied, his accent growing less English all of a sudden.

'Or Father Edwards?'

'No, definitely, that I have not done.'

'His wife did all the creative work on our peace panels. Peace is a must these days and you Indians seems to understand it so well. I seem to have lost my Sea Scouts and Youth Rangers. They seem to have hived off on their own. More power to their elbows. Are you having a picnic? What fun. Could I share my viands with you? If we pitch in together . . .'

'We're driving out for a picnic,' Mrs Plasket said firmly, but Polly was delighted: 'Oh what fun. Where shall it be?'

'I'm afraid we wouldn't all fit into the car.'

But Charles Mally, who had found them at last, called out, 'It's all right. Hari and I will drive out in my car, on your tail.'

They drove out past large flat fields, then came to smaller, more crooked ones with hedges and narrow lanes running round, stone bridges over streams, a canal, then a river, a saw-mill, then some woods. They ran over a railway bridge and passed a stile standing alone in the middle of a field like a horse-fly. Polly had finished telling them about her thesis and how it was to reposition marriage in the time-place continuum.

But its reinstatements didn't seem to impress Grace Plasket, who started up again: 'Hari's father was the first Hindu I ever made love with. Of course, I'd been in Karachi, but Islam had different ideas on women as you know . . .'

Clare felt attached suddenly to Grace Plasket by a thread that led out of Slack Street to Bombay, Dahomey, the Sind. Bombay was as far as the vicarious life would allow her. But then the chill of May Morning and its shiny gloating spread over her again and she was silent. She could see Hari and Charles Mally in the car behind, on their tail as Polly and Grace discussed Muslim married life from a Christian and a Hindu point of view.

Then Grace was talking about Hedgencote, the small town they were heading for where she had her cottage: 'Polly, you should be living out at Hedgencote because one has to have strong opinions out there, even about the shape of the church tower and the flowering cherries beside the Jubilee Hall. I suppose it's fear of letting their minds go, out among all that green. Like Victorian ladies wearing corsets to prevent their figures from going to pot. We don't let ourselves go to pot at Hedgencote, even though there are no shops and buses and library and no music except Stainer's 'Crucifixion' with the Parish Clerk as soloist and the dentist at the harmonium. You'd be in your element, Polly, at not going to pot.' Then they arrived at Hedgencote.

The cottage was old and small and damp, but Grace threw some twigs and fir-cones and wood on the small fire which warmed the room, and it heated up the two small ovens on either side of the grate where she put bread rolls. She pumped the Primus stove up and put a kettle on it, and undid the jar of coffee. 'If you want to wash your hands,' she said, 'it's right up at the top. But mind your heads,' she added.

'Right,' they all said and started to climb.

The coffee steamed in its large blue-and-white cups. They hugged them between their hands, to get warm. Grace had put some brandy in the jug and it cheered them all up. They choked with laughter when Polly Ives cried, suddenly putting down the slice of bread with thick peanut butter on it that she had quarried out of Grace's food-store to build herself up with: 'The Lord, praise be! must be having a good secret chuckle of quiet fun as he gazes at that drop of water on the window-sill that he has just turned into a spectrum of all the colours of the rainbow as a witness to his love for us.'

Clare looked at the drops of water condensed on the lid of the coffee pot. There was silence. The brandy was unexpected and Clare wasn't used to it, so she suddenly laughed as Hari murmured, 'Yes, and the Table of Elements would also be another good witness.'

'And the Oxford-to-London train timetable. Or the list of boat sailings from Bombay and all the Mayors of Brixton.' Hari laughed too. Polly munched. Charles wandered round while Mrs Plasket lit a cigarette, 'And the bus timetable to Land's End.'

In the lane outside they could hear two old men calling to each other over an old stone wall: 'What do these newcomers be thinking on, buying up all those pig-pens and them skemmy old barns when they could've got themselves a nice Council with a belly-garden? What do they be thinking on?'

'Ah, and they say some of these houses do be very old.'

'Ah, and they war here before my grandma war and before the old queen.'

'Ah, but I don't hold with all them old houses. They should've been knocked into the ground with the foot-and-mouth.'

'Ah, but they do say the ground be too damp.'

'Ah, and they could have them old barns if they didn't take all the trade away from the Old Plough. And there war five shops here once.'

'And they do be such a wind these days, since the old days went. They was never these winds before the newcomers war set down here.'

Mrs Plasket sighed, as the old men fell back into silence, 'This is where my life started.'

'You mean you were born here?' Charles asked.

'Oh, no. I mean this is where I used to bring Anil.' Hari frowned. 'Yes, I suppose I failed your father too. There was always something intangible between us. And I fell in love with him simply because of his dark sensitive doe-eyes and his sweet body smell. But he was never more than a good father and a good husband, so when we were together in the Algarve . . .'

Hari cleared his throat. 'To which period of history does this house belong?' he asked coldly, peering at the damp plaster peeling off the walls.

'All right. I'll show you round. But first let's get out with our picnic. Before it rains.'

They walked in single file along the main road till they came to a turn by a pub which let them into the quietness of high hedges and wet banks and bluebells. There was a smell of warm road and stinging-nettles and lime-trees. They talked in a desultory way and then fell silent. The road narrowed and the hedges grew higher, and then they were in a green tunnel with windows here and there that looked over a thick forest of oak and chestnut where deer like white-grey tree trunks grazed very still.

'How are you settling down in Oxford?' Clare asked, falling into step with Hari. 'Are you finding your way about all right, in your Judasland "parish"? And how are you liking our English climate?'

Hari lowered his eyelids. 'My father warned me of what I should expect. And I am beginning to grasp the working of the National Health Service.'

'And are you kept very busy in the Land?'

'Fairly busy. There are many elderly to attend to, and the waiting-lists are very long. But soon, I hope, when my duties in the practice have settled into a routine, I shall be able to get down to the revision of my once-rejected book that you have so kindly volunteered to monitor for me.'

'I'll do my best. As far as I can see, it's only a question of style.' Clare had received the manuscript and glanced at it. Now she searched for a euphemism for the word 'stilted'. 'We are beginning in this country to use a much more relaxed style. Do you think you'll stay in Judasland?'

'My plans are fluid. My real interest is in the geography of psychosis. But I have worries at the moment which make me question whether I am the right personality type ... You work inside the University?'

'Oh yes. But I'm only the secretary to the academics. I try to keep the lines open between the scholars. That's all.'

Hari nodded. 'I do not yet know many *cognoscenti* or academic philosophers, though I am deeply committed to an Enlightenment way of life and thinking.' He laughed, slightly puzzled at Clare's embarrassed response. 'I don't think I have fathomed the British yet. Are there perhaps some University worthies, musicians and composers for example, who are *persona non grata* for some reason connected with their social class?'

'There are loners,' Clare replied discreetly.

'I am worried.' Hari looked as miserable again as he had done during the May Morning ceremony. 'Maybe in your capacity as college secretary you come into close contact with all the academics?'

'You must come to our Bishop's Benediction Night when term is over, and meet some of them.'

'Thank you. That would be a good introduction to the university medium for me.'

They walked on in silence till they came to a stile, and the green tunnel opened on to a hillside where cows grazed and kingcups reflected a golden day, and the larks rose. They went down and down till they came to the river and walked along its hard mud-caked banks. Black cows clustered together in a sulky haze below them in a dip of the green meadow. It grew very warm all of a sudden. A train rattled along on the other side of the hill and a single lamb bleated. A stoat raced ahead of them into a wood. A broad glade appeared and they were walking on grass to a place on a bend in the river where it widened and deepened.

'Let's sit down for a bit,' Grace said.

They sat and looked at the water and the sun rose high in the sky. 'We want to get to the White Hart by midday,' she went on. But they all lay down on the bank and listened to the water slurping in the reeds and the creakings of young animals in its havens.

Grace suddenly kicked her shoes off and started to paddle. The sun grew warmer as she lowered herself into its deepest spot and splashed out across the river. Polly went over and started to paddle too. Charles was exploring some hedges, and Clare and Hari were left alone.

'Have you ever been to India? You would like it, I know. Here a doctor prescribes tranquillisers and pain-killers and gives blood-transfusions to the ninety-year-olds. Once I was called out in the night because a child's eye lacked lustre. Is this the land of Shakespeare?' Hari smiled ruefully as he watched the water. The only time he had seen a breath of life, he said, was once when an accident had taken place and he had gone forward in his capacity as a doctor, and people had rallied round him with a light in their eyes as though this were the one red-letter day in their lives. Something for once was real, because someone was sick or dead.

They had offered him tea afterwards and had thanked him. 'You are', they said, 'one of us now.' As though this were the highest tribute that could be paid to an Indian.

'Where is the language of Shakespeare and where is the metaphysical consciousness . . . his optimism? his pessimism . . .' Hari was asking.

'I read Hamlet at school,' Charles Mally was replying. 'We had such fun with those ghosts. On the battlements. One of us had a whoopee cushion.'

'I like it,' grinned Polly, nibbling her lips with satisfaction as she dried her feet after her paddle. They wandered on.

'No, I suppose we're not a very lively, vigorous or life-enhancing nation,' Clare agreed. 'Perhaps I'm like a lot of people, I had a rather inhibiting childhood. My mother was ill and I felt I had to make it up to my father by being a very good daughter.' She told Hari about life at Drawberry Road and how she was always being told to keep it up and congratulated for merely staying alive and cosily at home.

'My father and his second wife used to send me flowers to the theatre when I had bit parts; when I was an extra. That made me feel so old. And as though the flowers were there to put a lid on a well for good.'

'My father served with the British in World War Two. He was decorated for services. Have you still got your parents, Clare?'

Clare told him about them. 'They keep hinting that they'd like an invitation to Oxford, and I can't help being a dutiful daughter. I'm like a Swiss doll in national costume.'

'You do not seem like that to me,' Hari replied politely. 'My parents, too, are very possessive. My mother manages the farm. She is the one who rules in our household. This I have always tended to resent and so tend to assert my male superiority and become a little too authoritarian and aggressive.'

'I haven't noticed that,' Clare reciprocated dutifully.

'Well, it is there,' he sighed. 'A patient came to see me the other day and I feel I behaved in such a high-handed fashion that now he may do some harm. Bad damage to his health or to his domestic life, or to his professional situation. Oh dear,' he added ruefully, 'I must try to recapture the professional detachment that I set out with when I made my graduation vows. It is a very bad thing to become empathically involved.' Clare lowered her head with college discreetness.

'"It Is Good To Be Out on the Road,"' Polly sang as she went on ahead.

'I still do not fathom the English,' Hari repeated to Clare. 'And I have never found a Hamlet among you so far.' They laughed. He said he had drawn strong impressions from his study of Shakespeare at Senior College in Bombay. From Shakespeare he had drawn the impression that the British were strong and energetic and full of laughter and love and anger, and very fond of strongly reacting and never tolerating inertia. And he assumed the poor were full of vigour too and fought back against an oppressor as they had done in the Second World War. 'Instead, you seem to be worried by this word "to cope". You seem to spend so much time setting up agencies to help each other "to cope". "Can she cope?" I am always being asked. Divorce. Death. Falling hair. Ingrowing toenails. Broken toys. Each is a challenge to the British ability to cope. Is life like this?' Hari lifted his thick eyebrow and smiled. 'So you were young when your mother died?' he changed the subject.

'I was twelve.'

'Was it a long and painful illness to leave such a sad residue with you?'

'She had difficulty in walking and I was only allowed to see her in the hospital gardens. They were beautiful gardens. But frightening. You could hear the flowers clashing together like nasty girls in satin dresses at a party.'

'Your mother was there because the air was fresh? ... No doubt.'

'Well, really because children weren't allowed in the wards.'

'And was she well enough to enjoy all this strange beauty?'

Clare cleared her throat and said at last, 'She was away from it. Far away.'

She could see the grounds of High Lodge Hospital where she was allowed to visit her mother once a week if the weather were fine enough for sitting out. A bird's song in the plushy trees above them as they walked reminded her of how it had been, how everything seemed to gloat at her mother's sickness. She could see in the walled garden, could see the flowerbeds behind her all grinning and showing their teeth, huge and bloated blossoms, as her mother said in her slow blurred voice, jerking her head up and down with the effort to get the words out: 'Dear me. I must take it easy. The doctor says I'm a bit run down at the moment.' Her voice was pitched like a little girl's or like a young woman of the thirties, bored and talking over the phone to a friend about her 'specialist', as the river rose and gained a kind of sick brimming, its lips thick and greedy and not to be satisfied. The flowers clicked in their throats, swallowed and set out to swallow Clare.

A black cloud approached like a battleship across a dulled and surly sky. The wind was colder. Hari looked at his watch.

'It may be necessary for me to leave soon. A patient I am worried about. Do you know all the academics at Sanctus College? Do you find any that are. . . .' His right eyebrow rose as it did when he was concentrating, and he looked unhappy again.

There had been a big greenhouse in the walled garden of High Lodge Hospital, behind the wooden sun house where Mrs Bonnard used to sit.

'My mother,' she would contort her face and try to get the words out, 'gave - me - a - very - good - and - very - expensive - education . . .' Behind her in the great hot tent, the callous blooms thrust their insolent cheeks out at her like the *grandes dames* of a decadent age, dresses, perfumes and jewellery keeping them all enclosed in their domestic hot-houses. They flaunted themselves behind Mrs Bonnard in her different kind of closed-off life beside the nurse with a spotty white face as though wasps had been at it. The other patient beside Mrs Bonnard sat very upright, cool and white like a unicorn, and the beds of Scavis Mitior, Rastum and Graecia in the locked tropical hothouse tittered and whispered behind her as well.

Triune Deus, hominum
Salutis auctor optime.

Clare could hear the singing from Magdalen tower again and the two rivers sucking it up, and the streets picking it up, and the students in their punts more alone than they thought as they slid under the willows. The huge and ancient trees round them too suddenly seemed to have been sucked out and upwards from a prehistoric world as the choir ended: *'Ovante lingua canimus.'*

'Hari, doesn't this remind you of spring in Kashmir?' Grace was calling as she unpacked the lunch.

'Oh yes,' said Hari without much accord.

Charles Mally and Polly Ives had come up and they had all stopped where the river suddenly bent away and disappeared. They stared across a field of long grasses full of buttercups and Queen Anne's lace. Ahead of them they could see a May Day Man-of-Green creeping and dancing and hopping about among the long grasses and making towards some woods almost as dark as he was, as though he belonged in there with spiders and dirty black privet and stained ground and fouled wells. May stood heavily on Clare again.

'We'll forget the White Hart then,' said Grace, uncorking wine and unpacking the rolls and cheese and salad. Hari produced some curry patties, cakes and bananas, and Clare some apples. Polly produced an enormous box of papadums, but Hari shook his head and said they were unrepresentative.

Charles had brought a big box of chocolates with an ostentatious velvet ribbon. They all stared at it. 'It looks as though you were taking us to the cinema.' Charles gave his great guffaw.

Hari was talking to Clare. 'You will see my moral dilemma when you have fully understood my book. Whether the medical profession should acknowledge and exploit popular beliefs. To effect valid cures by kow-towing to popular spirit beliefs? How to make the patient realise the nature of these placebo cures ... I myself have been forced at times to resort to the pretence of calling the witch doctor to drive evil spirits away ...'

And there Clare sat in her neat white pleated crimplene dress decorated with yachts and lanyards, now guardian of the ordered life. She smiled at Slack Street now.

Hari smiled, lowered his eyelids over the beautiful deep wells of his eyes and shook his head. 'It may be that my mother will come on a short visit in the autumn, and she will bring me real tea.' He roused himself at the prospect of real tea, opened one eye wide and then half-closed it again. 'It is not possible to get the best quality here. It is not fresh. It is not the best. It does not travel. When my mother comes I will invite you to taste real tea.' He sighed. 'I have not travelled well, either, I am afraid I am in trouble.' He looked at his watch. 'How long will it take us to get home? I am anxious to make a phone call concerning one of my patients . . .'

A hard gust of wind came and blew their food wrappings away. It grew cold suddenly and they stood up and started to walk again towards the White Hart. The wind grew stronger. In the thick forest ahead of them, the wind suddenly raced through the trees.

They reached the White Hart. It was nearly three and it had closed, but they sat in its garden till the landlady came out and agreed to make them some tea. Polly had made herself a little kite with a cotton-reel and some paper refuse she had picked up. She launched it into the air but another sudden wind slapped it down. She launched it again and this time a more savage wind caught it up and twisted it and tore it in half and flung it on the ground again. The woods seemed even rustier.

'There's going to be a storm,' said Grace, as they sat down on beer-barrel seats at a beer-barrel table.

An Aunt Sally stood grinning at them at the end of the lawn by the hedge. 'What is it?' Hari had frowned back at the gaping and jeering wooden face. Sawdust was trickling from her belly and black tar seemed to be seeping from the lewd smile at her thick wooden lips.

Her leer reminded Clare of Slack Street again, the Toshidis' clay mannikins and the way she had escaped from her pregnancy and run back to Mardi and her father when she saw the steaming godlings Yani pulled from the oven, tar dribbling from their eyes and noses as the bird squawked from the lavatory pan. The wind blew savagely and the trees shook their heads. How afraid Eddie Toshidi had been of the competing winds, and how afraid she had been of their placatory rites.

Then, as the wind blew in the forest, Clare could see someone come out of it, hairy, with huge bells and fur round his eyes. He was carrying branches and the trees round him seemed to have ears and eyes and a more ancient threat than High Lodge Hospital.

Hari was staring as the Man-of-Green approached. He looked back at the Aunt Sally. 'It is strange to find these objects so close to the groves of Academe,' he tried to joke.

'We are still very close to the world of daemonia.' Polly sat cross-legged on the ground close to the ugly grinning Aunt Sally. 'We Christians believe that we are still very close to the powers of evil and that the devil is very much in the ball-game these days. To me, that Aunt Sally is the basic religious statement of our age about sin and how tawdry and grotty sex without commitment can be.'

The wind came again and the Aunt Sally's lips seemed to demur. She seemed to be licking the tar that had run from her eyes and nose. They could see the morris men at the mouth of the woods, advancing on their party, springing out of the forest that Grace called Cotnose, dancing out of it while Hari talked of spirit possession and Polly Ives talked of sin.

'Originally the hymns they sang were horribly profane,' Grace Plasket was saying. 'I don't know *when* they cleaned the songs up and turned them into hymns and handed them over to schoolboys, but that they did.'

Cotnose broke in a black sea in front of them and the sky was dark again. The Aunt Sally was licking her tarry lips, and the morris men were carrying the cross they had made out of leaves, which the women had pruned prudently until it became a woman with breasts and thighs and a waist they trimmed with scissors, before they hauled it upright.

Clare thought again of her mother at High Lodge Hospital, and the tall madonna-like woman who used to sit with her and smile when Mrs Bonnard gave her poor odd crooked smile. Clare had been told she had died of scarlet fever. There had been an epidemic in the hospital, and as children weren't allowed inside, she had never seen her mother after that summer of 1940 when she would struggle to lean over her daughter enough to jerk out, 'My mother . . . and my father – ' then after a long pause, ' – sent me to a very . . . expensive . . . school.' And Mrs Pax, the madonna who sat beside her, would smile briefly and go on working serenely at her Woolworth's tapestry of Trooping the Colour, and complaining mildly that she'd run out of matching wool for the horses' fetlocks, while the tapping sound of Rue, Coryliss and Distended Rhee knocking on the side of the hot-house seemed as though they were trying to get their attention and call them inside. The nurse sat there beside them, her white face still scarred by black wasps. She kept a tin teapot and a tin alarm-clock so that the staff would know when the time had come to fold their caps and aprons and clock off.

Clare's mother had struggled painfully to her feet when Clare came over to the summerhouse where they sat. There was something Mrs Bonnard wanted to say but she couldn't keep her balance and the nurse called, 'Topply girl. Got the wobbles again?

The garden's all locked up, my dear, so you can't run away even if you didn't have the wobbles. Come and tell me all about it instead.' Then the nurse went back to her tin teapot and emptied it out with a bang into a trench behind the glasshouse and fumbled in her big bag for her bicycle pump.

The trees rose huge above the patients' heads, great leaves pattered together, and the weeds and herbs that grew out of the crumbling stone urn with *Et Rei.Publ.* carved into it smelt sweet. The birds' voices rose like a children's party among the tittering blooms of Paeonia Rubra and rough Scavis Mitior. Clare had always hated the month of May and its yearly ritual sacrifice.

'In parts of India,' Hari was saying, 'there is still the magnetic theory of magic. Everything is conjoined with everything else. They are the same substance and the same tissue. If you kill a man by cutting up a stone ten or thirty miles from him, that is because they are both of the same spiritual substance. In my book I have carefully appraised the use of this belief in dealing with certain forms of possession or rather belief in possession . . .'

Clare nodded politely in her dress with the yachts stamped all over it. The winds shook the forest. More morris men were streaming out. Someone seemed to be stooped over the bushes stuffing food and blood into his mouth, then hiding the blood. The wind spread through the daisies and seedy grasses and tore at some washing on a clothes line and banged on the picnickers' tea-table and knocked the cups off their saucers and tipped the milk-jug over the table.

'There's going to be a storm,' Grace said. 'We ought perhaps to be getting back. If we go through the woods there'll be some shelter.' Charles gave a guffaw as though Grace were going to proposition him in there. Hari looked at his watch grimly.

Just then a car drove up to the White Hart and a figure was now half-walking and half-dancing across the lawn towards the kitchen door of the pub. He saw Hari and swung round.

'Dr Sharma,' he called out cheerfully, his sideburns moving slightly up as he smiled and shook his hand. 'What are you doing in these parts?' Nick De Berry was wearing a great yellow rose in his buttonhole and had the manner of a parliamentary candidate, dancing along and waving to his electorate as he did his walkabout.

'Oh, how do you do, Dr De Berry,' Hari smiled. His right eyebrow lifted up in the way Clare had liked when she first saw him and before High Lodge Hospital had intervened.

De Berry stood there waiting to be introduced, and then he vaguely remembered Clare . . . the friend of a friend whom he had met out at Stanton Harcourt? But he took both her hands and shook them in his. Then he shook Hari's again. He was the publisher's advisor who had rejected Hari's book. 'But do let's meet again,' he had said. 'You could give me a ring sometime and come over and have a chat about your way of doing things in Bombay.'

Now he smiled. 'Out for the day?'

'Miss Bonnard has kindly offered to help me set my book on its right course for posterity,' Hari tried to joke.

'Full steam ahead then. We need a good blood transfusion from the Third World into our medical canon. When can you come round and have drinks?'

'I am anxious to get back to Oxford now,' Hari explained. 'I am worried about a patient.'

'I'm on my way back now,' De Berry said genially. 'I could give you a lift. Don't I know you?' he repeated to Clare. 'Oughtn't I to know you? Weren't you the one who typed out my magnum opus on rat models in agoraphobia?'

'We used to call each other "cousins" at Curley Hill and you kindly invited me to a party . . .' Clare's voice came from a long way away.

'Of course. You must give me a ring some time and come round too.'

Nick De Berry ran a chicken-farm out beyond Hedgencote so Clare had to sit in the back of his car with the chicken feed while Hari and she were driven home, talking about publishers' contracts and take-overs.

Clare could see Charles and Grace and Polly Ives disappearing into the woods. It wasn't their fault, or Hari's, that the picnic hadn't been a success. The trees hung over the lanes they drove along as if to stifle her with their own boastful excesses. She would have liked to get out and walk alone with Hari and stop the trick of green. Her mother, after all, was dead, and the picnic had been broken off before its true end.

The bells from the tower of Magdalen as they arrived home chilled her more than they had done at six that morning. Someone had drowned at dawn.

IX

Hari Sharma hadn't read the part of Conroy's medical notes that referred to his rape until after the patient had left his surgery. And still no letter had been received at Dr Mally's surgery from the Herber. But he felt he hadn't given the patient nearly enough help, and during the picnic his thoughts had been no pleasanter than Clare's. He therefore asked Nick De Berry to set him down at the door of the surgery in Spide Street. Nick had been telling him jokingly about the colleague of his who had been researching into the long term effects of Solverin D, but he hadn't been able to make much headway with its side effects on patients over fifty: 'Most of them had got rid of themselves before symptoms, Parkinsonism etcetera, had set in'.

'I see,' said Dr Sharma, letting himself out of the car.

'Goodbye Sharma, and give us a ring sometime and we'll have a chat. We'll lay something on for you. We'll be in touch,' he called after the retreating figure in Oxford's inimitably magnanimous style.

Then he turned to Clare: 'Let me drive you home. Where did you say you lived? And what was it we used to call each other as children? Brothers and sisters?'

'Cousins.'

'Cousins, that's it,' he sighed. 'Still, there is a certain truth in these hoary old pieties. You're still at Jesus?'

'Sanctus.'

'Quite so. I suppose you know most of the Fellows? I used to sing in Conroy's "Folk Mass" when I was a boy: *Qui tollis*,' he hummed. 'What do you think of Sharma's book? Any hopes of salvaging it? Or helping a Woeful Oriental Gentleman?'

They had reached Inkerman Street and he opened the door of

his car for Clare, and then came round. 'You've still got it, have you? The MS? If I could have another look at Chapter . . . the one about Western norms and Hindu traditional medicine . . .'

'Sure,' said Clare in her best college voice, sliding her neat knees round to the pavement and stepping out. For once she didn't dread putting her key in the lock in case Sebastian or Will or any other student should leap out into her unlived life.

Professor Boden stood there however. He beamed at Nick. 'Old delinquent.' He turned to Clare: 'This is the room I come to when I want to be ordinary.' He waved them downstairs into the kitchen where his wife was trying to wash her hair in a small plastic basin from which two broken eggs had been displaced. 'Don't trust Nick De Berry, the old *roué*, for more than three minutes, Miss Bonnard'.

'Hullo, Nick,' said his wife from upside down. 'Did you enjoy yourself at Sir Eddy's last week? I thought the new colour of his lats was simply outrageous. And as for those tall blue delphiniums! – delphinia – ? I hate that shade of blue! And as for that rather Fascistic sculpture in his dressing-room! And there was his wife quarrelling about the accusative case. I mean you can't go treating Church Latin as though it were Vergil!' her voice trembled with anger, but the Professor chortled with laughter at women's tiffs.

'By the way, Miss Bonnard,' he called as Nick lowered himself into the great carving chair that stood in under the window in their basement kitchen, 'there was a phone call for you. Your father, I think.'

His wife raised her wet hair from the plastic basin. 'Yes, it was your father. Ugh. Just look at that evening sky.' She gazed up through the area window. 'What an ugly pink. I just can't accept evening skies that colour. They upset me as much as cold food. And modern religion.'

'No one cares what you feel about cold food or religion,' Professor Boden chortled, and so did she.

'Too true. Miss Bonnard, the drinks are over there on the dresser. A really nasty sherry that I can't touch. It brings me out in a rash. Or that rather pathetic little wine . . .'

But the Professor was already pouring drinks. Now that Clare had introduced a University friend to the Bodens, she was 'one of us' and they felt they could use her first name, and invited her to their part of the house for the first time.

The Professor hummed. 'When do we eat, then?' he interrupted

Clare's modest little story about her short life on the stage. 'Miss Bonnard, or rather,' he cleared his voice, 'Clare, your father was wondering if you were expecting them down for the weekend of Benediction Night.'

'I've been invited,' Nick grimaced and swung his legs over the side of the chair. 'And you, Tim?' he asked the professor.

'I don't like their chef. And in any case they allow their women into Hall afterwards, and to share some of the fruit and nuts. That is the thin end of the wedge I think, so I said so. But Pyecraft wouldn't take no for an answer. He's promised to let me out of the sub-musical offering, however, after the port's done the rounds.' The Professor drifted away to his conservatory to emend some entry on the long-bow constituency of East Cornwall, after the Battle of Crécy.

'Could I have another peep at Sharma's text?' Nick asked, when he had finished discussing the detestable Algarve with Mrs Boden.

The Professor and his wife both laughed from different ends of the house. 'Don't let him, Miss Bonnard . . . Clare.'

But Clare said, 'Sure, sure,' and took De Berry upstairs. 'The book's a bit like a cat's fur when it's wet and ruffled and all the hairs are lying in different directions, and all need to be stroked and put together again.'

Nick grinned and lowered himself on to her bed. 'Do you think *your* hairs are all matted and at odds with each other and all lying in different directions, needing to be set together, body and mind? To drive away bossy little college secretaries' needs to manage the Fellows of Sanctus? Eh?' He drew her on top of him. 'And be managed by them? You're not a virgin are you?'

'Oh no,' she said, as though he had got a wrong name or address; a kind of clerical error. 'Oh no.'

His eyes alighted on the tiger bootees Mardi had made for her with big white teeth over the toes, and the Swiss doll, and Clare's woollen 'thinking-cap', also a present from her parents.

'If you'll be nice to me, I'll recommend that we join forces and redo the book together. "Sharma and Bonnard on Cultural Weighting in Third World Psychiatry". "Sharma and Bonnard on Cultural Psychosis".'

Clare laughed nervously as he slid his hands up into her armpits, then brought them down under her breasts so that her bra snapped open and he called, 'One more river to cross. But you don't need a bra. Stand up and let me see what you look like without one.

Free as a bird.' Clare stood there sheepishly, dutifully, then crossed her hands over her breasts.

'I love to shake woman out of her smug little world of little things,' Nick grinned.

'Oh yes, I agree! Too true! Alas.'

'I've already made your breasts leap out of your prim little aviary like two birds.' Nick looked round at her gay little bedsitter, full of its jolly reminders of life for one. 'Oh the sadness of sardines on toast and spiced tea-cakes for one.' He drew her on to him.

'I suppose that's so.' Clare could hear her ridiculous laugh.

She could see over to Spide Street again tonight because the light was on again in Conroy's top room. She could picture his full lost face again like an egg broken into a tumbler of water, a large soft eye in water, watching unblinking. Then she remembered how she had found him at the Herber, his smooth pulpy face wrinkled into a terrible grin as he lay on the ward floor jerking his knees up and down as he had been told to do and saluting the sun when this was required by the yoga teacher. Then Clare thought of Mrs Pax up at High Lodge Hospital when she was a child, and how the other patients whispered that this madonna-like woman was really a poisoner. But the poisoner sat there serenely working at a tapestry of St Theresa in *petit point*, like a nun.

When Clare thought of them and herself, she consented to let Nick lean over her again and draw her on to him parting her arms and legs.

'I love unformed women . . . women like half-opened roses. Giggling beguiling girls surrounded by' he looked round her room, ' – teddies and hair-tidies and embroidered bags for curlers and – ' he ran his eyes along her bookcase, ' – *Adventurous Cookery for One*. And a cat to be fed and kept happy, and a planter on the windowsill to complete the secretary's world. Even when you were a girl you were always busy being nice to me, and I deserved it because I was a very vulnerable boy, and now,' he put on a child's mischievous voice, 'you must let me into your secret tree house . . .'

Clare felt surprise as well as pleasure after she had enclosed him. As she lay there, it was like the times in childhood when she had been kept from school for some reason, and had gone out and seen a world without children in it, the world of adults she hadn't even known about.

But then Nick grinned and got dressed. The Institute was on

take that night, he told her, and he would have to stick around in case one of the junior doctors lost his nerve. 'If you get an hour of need we could meet once or twice. Not more I'm afraid. I'm pretty tied up at the moment . . .'

Before Clare could think of any proper response to this bounty, she heard Professor Boden calling up the stairs: 'Miss Bonnard . . . Clare . . . you're wanted . . . a gentleman . . .'

She ran down, dishevelled, and saw Hari standing there anxiously. He wanted her to find out where Joseph Conroy was, where his wife could be found, and where his children were. She told him how the children had been staying with a neighbour and that Polly Ives had been anxious to see them restored to their father. But she could hear Nick moving about upstairs, so she simply promised to ring Hari from Sanctus as soon as she could tell him more.

Hari frowned and left. He had rung the Herber, but the ward-secretary simply said that as Dr Conroy had discharged himself, the responsibility was not theirs. So Hari rang Charles Mally but he was out.

Clare went back upstairs. 'That was Hari Sharma.'

'Himself. Worried Oriental Gentleman.'

'He wanted to know whose patient Joe Conroy was at the Herber.'

Nick was dressing. 'Clare, I can't discuss hospital affairs with you,' he reproached her, kissing her lightly on the forehead. 'I love your college-treasure manner. Do you do it just to be seduced by the Fellows? A sort of typewriter fetishism? . . . I must dash . . . College secretaries are my "thing". I really like to take them on the photocopier or on *Adventurous Cookery for One*. Or when they are telling you about the landscape of their minds, then lifting the college telephone receiver: "College Office . . . Yes, I'm working on my mind" . . .'

But Hari wanted Clare to find out what had happened to Conroy and his twins, so she had barely time to take this as it was meant. And now Hari had gone.

Conroy had told himself again and again after his stay at the Herber Institute that nothing additional had happened to him since he had been mugged and raped. A doctor as self-infatuated as himself had used him to show off to his students, but that was all. It hadn't happened to Conroy. He had just been an example to medical students of the type of man who invited buggery. To think that the students' mirth was an event in his own life was to be like the man whose country slides into dictatorship but who commits suicide because his mistress has discovered he dyes his hair.

Conroy had minded De Berry's refusal to be lassoed by him more than the loss of his wife. He had tried to lasso people once too often. But he minded that more than he minded his wife's departure and his children's. Three children had been sacrificed at the Beating of the Bounds in 1923, but he envied Nellie Grainger the finiteness of her part in the tragedy compared with his own sticky narcissism. He could still hear De Berry's laughter, his students' jeers, the Sanctus Fellows' lowered voices, the condemnation of Judasland, and his own complicity with Oxford's vanity. That would drag his children down.

He wasn't to know that the lucky-dip method of psychiatry had not allowed De Berry access to the fact of Conroy's rape, and that the consultant's main preoccupation, after his contract and pub- lisher's lunch, had been to keep the discharge rate on his wards at a healthy high level, and to keep a respectable balance between healing, research and private patients. Even if Conroy had known of the perfect insouciance of the Institute and understood its behavioural philosophy, he couldn't have reasoned himself out of what, by now, had become an obsession. A terrible anger at his rejection by De Berry rose in him. But worse – behind this rejection lurked a planned revenge: Sanctus College and the University had just used the Herber to pay off old scores. They were all kicking him in the teeth now because of his indifference to their celebrity.

He felt female again. His anger splashed back in his own face as self-disgust. He woke at four in the morning when the sky was white and accusing and the morning tribunal whispered with the dawn birds that he had deservedly been found out and judged. Ever since his youth he had done nothing but invite rape, and now he did nothing but watch himself being watched by the Institute's watchers who had been set round him now to accuse and damn.

Few people deliberately seek out the person who has seen through them and drawn attention to their Achilles' Heel. Yet some cultivate an uncannily close relationship, a sticky one like a mess of chewing gum you can't extricate yourself from. So Conroy got stuck in the image of the University jeering at his predicament. He could hear music coming from the maze at Sanctus, Handel's

Firework Music again being rehearsed for Benediction Night. But its stolid progress was innocence and only accused him further. Its drums rolled at him. Its trumpets were a white world that had condemned him to fly forever outside it in the limbo of those forever damned by self-infatuation.

Were his twins to fly round for ever too? Were they also to be contaminated? Was this an inheritable taint? This connivance with buggery? Polly Ives had sat on his kitchen table and munched and said no. His twins needed his love: 'Adult personality problems are a mere self-indulgence where the lives of children are concerned. And children are healers. Recovery, Joe, may come *through them*.'

Conroy wished her gone and she went. But as the day wore on, the corrupted in him once again became the injured. The whole world was set there to destroy him. There was no pause or meadowland between his anger with himself and anger with 'them'. The switch went relentlessly down, then up; on then off. There was no place of rest in between.

But sometimes a brief pause did come between cursing himself and cursing them, and he saw this pleasant watermeadow land clearly with a river running through it. He had a moment's peace and security. But then the sky came lower and darker again, and lower and more threatening, like hard carpeting to bind him down with more accusation. The pigeons stood alone, out in the garden and along the roof, scratching and dancing their hard little dances like the morris dancers practising all week. They banged about eerily all night and woke Conroy again at three when the morning tribunal summoned him. He told himself again and again that no one was watching, jeering and judging. He told himself again and again that the people out in the street were as likely to be directing their taunts at him as the clock ticking away on the dresser was likely to have caused his twins' pet mouse to die in its wheel.

And yet the connection remorselessly held like a strong dyke. Indeed, the more insight he seemed to acquire into the ludicrousness of his obsession and the outside world's innocence towards him, the more tightly the insight locked him in an unexpected but relentless grip ... Impotence to change! and the guilt which followed that impotence! If *nothing* could stop him feeling himself in the centre of their ribald attention, he must curse his own stupid rigidity, his congenital defect, his inability to believe the world was not centred on him. There wasn't a moment in his life when he hadn't been absorbed in the effect he was making on other people.

'Pa's Pop' itself had been an attempt to lasso life's De Berrys. His *Panis Angelorum* mocked him now.

He thought with a shudder of the little shanty room at the Institute where he had so blindly launched on another ego trip, a further search for rape in some other form. As he stood in his garden in the early morning looking out at the enormous mystery of the world and feeling how slight even the greatest humans problems must *sub specie* be, his own nagging self-obsession became more terrible because more trivial and more ignoble, till he saw he was permanently crippled by his soft weak white polyp self.

Finally, however, as he stood there, he calmed himself. Oxford was the world of seeming and appearance, not the world of being or of fact-based life. The life of an Oxford don was one of simple reaction to what had previously been said and done. Nothing was a solid or settled experience in itself, or rooted in the concrete world. Everything was just reflection, and the man who was safe was the man who acted unanswerably so that there could be no further spasms, and no further reflexes. It must be checkmate. The thought of the meadow's middle ground came to him again. Some childhood hymn. The green meadowland where the river ran and children played.

'Hosanna,' he said to himself, as he collected his Solverin D from the chemist. 'Come my beauties. Come my lovely ones of the meadows. Come my hosannah child favourites.'

Polly Ives had come back with his twins, his two little children. At first he wanted to keep his children at bay in case he tainted them too. But Polly was suggesting bringing them home from the neighbours. They were after all his joy, she pointed out. God did not do these things spitefully. God could hurt but not harm.

Conroy was still walking round and round his garden when Polly brought Sam and Jesse out to him. 'Here they are, Joe. Two nice little portions of meat-and-two-veg, and plum-crumble to follow.'

The twins were sitting on the shabby old settee in the bare house with their bare feet curled up under them. Conroy lifted his boys up but their thin white legs still curled up under them like dolls. 'Come, my hosannahs. Come, my lovely ones.' The meadows spread out like a mother's clothes in the middle ground he had suddenly found.

Polly Ives beamed. It was as she had hoped it would be. Joe Conroy was at last making the link-up. Here was the Christian commitment beyond male and female. Hetero or queer, life goes on.

'I could lend you G. Tamasy,' she said softly and in awe. 'Shall I bring him around? And there's another very relevant pamphlet on the crucifixion and its message for . . .'

But Conroy was hugging his children, and seemed wrapped up in them so she just said softly: 'You're at the right door, Joe, so keep hammering on. And remember, the Land is a very caring and supporting community. Goodbye, you two little podlings,' she smiled at the children. 'You know, Joe, you are helping Nellie Grainger too, to redeem herself. By facing the horror, then the return of man . . .'

But the thought of Nellie Grainger only made Conroy think of wreaths of flowers being lowered gently into streams of pure water, unpoisoned by self.

As he still stood there she decided to put the twins to bed for him, and carried them upstairs singing:

> Two little pods and two little oddlings.
> Not very bad but not yet godlings.

Joe followed her upstairs to where the twins were whispering and giggling together in their big shiny Heals bunks, among their big wooden Heals toys bought for the children Conroy and his first wife had never had; simple polished wooden shapes and big wooden bunks that seemed far too big and shiny for the skinny twins.

'Oodles and oodles of prayer,' Polly was saluting Conroy and saying goodbye. 'I want to give other people a little of what I've had. And Joe, you've got a lot to give too . . . The world needs your music . . .'

Conroy smiled faintly. He could hear De Berry and his students bawling out the *Et in Resurrexionem* of his 'Credo'. Then he could hear his children giggling and wriggling on their bunks, then the water in the river running between the quiet neutral banks of the childrens' meadow, so washingly. He went out into the shed and looked at the kayak he had bought his first wife years ago, before her rabbit hutch. He turned it over, then hauled it on to his bicycle. He could hear the children kicking their heels idly on the sides of their polished bunks.

Polly told him she was going down to the river next day to put in some May Day gratitude: we had been led out of the pagan world of revenge. 'Some day I mean to get down to the problem of evil and really tackle it. Get to grips with real evil, not just the failure of communities to support each other and forgive.'

'Could you leave me alone in my limbo? . . . Please?' he begged.

'Sure. Sure. But you know, limbo no longer exists. All that was put an end to with Christ's sacrifice on the Cross. Finito Limbo.'

But Conroy had wandered away and was plucking at his children's possessions and arranging them in rows and ranks, marshalling them like soldiers.

'But if you mean Purgatory, Joe, one doesn't stay in Purgatory for long . . . one moves on, and you will move on in this Purgatory of yours here below. One just moves on. I have it on the highest authority.' Polly saluted and moved on.

As Conroy stood there alone in the garden early on May Morning, the horror of the rape came to him again, and how he had connived. He quickly found himself back by the river in his mind, by its clear and pleasant waters washing his twins, separating them from self-infatuation.

The silence of the morning was a summoning one. It drove him on, with his kayak across his bike. The great trees along the river banks stood bolted upright into the alien pale sky, but the willows bending over the water were kinder and drew him towards their peace. He remembered wading as a child, trying to find secret fords to the other side, finding deep places under tree roots where no one had ever been.

The twins said the Ribena was bitter, but they drank it. Then he watched them, like two white handkerchiefs he had sent before him on a mission, two white flags, two white symbols of peace and truce being drawn down to where he could honestly follow. He had forgiven De Berry, he saw, and himself too. Such a harmony there was now he had made the breakthrough and got rid of vanity, cut it right off at its source and let the deep healing waters come instead. The sky was so white it seemed to pick up the peace of the meadowland he had reached. The place where there was no anger and no taint was blessing him. He had reached the place where the switch was neither up nor down, but neutral, so that flowers could rush over the meadows and run to him.

He had lit some candles and stuck them on the canoe, one at each end before he set his podlings off on their peace journey. Someone had said, down by the water, as the clock on Magdalen tower struck six, that someone had fallen in. Three people had.

Let's hope they could swim. But oh, it *was* cold. Then the sixth note had struck and the choir up at the top of the tower were floating down their hymn: '*Irato Deo Victima*'. The little cavalcade with Conroy bringing up its rear was identified by one of his pupils as Clare and Hari drove out with Polly and Grace towards Hedgencote.

'Many waters do not quench love.' The people of Judasland had placed their wreath on the waters in 1923 and waited for the rivers to leap up and gulp the flowers in. 'But many wreaths are not enough for our satisfaction,' Clare heard the cruel water reply, as black clouds banged across the sky on May Morning and the morris dancers tried to revive old and placatory dances.

X

No college flag flew at half-mast, but there was an unfamiliar sonority in the old stone cloisters and Tudor brick walls, and Long Quad echoed a silence that seemed to be warden of the newly dead. Even the maze that led into Judasland seemed to be a cerement, a white waxed cloth that surrounded the terrible events of May Morning: *Irato Deo Victima*.

The Fellows of Sanctus all seemed to feel an equal sense of their sinister silent exclusion from what had happened. They had all stood apart and watched Conroy construct the waxed sheath to enclose himself and his children in. Several Fellows didn't turn up at Common Room for days on end. One came again and again to Clare's office and whispered: 'It cannot ... He cannot ... He can't ...' But the fountain in Long Quad played on as though it were confirming a mystery more than a tragedy.

'If only we had known.' The Fellows seemed to contradict its lisping on by repeating, 'If only we had known.' They suggested that they had betrayed Conroy. They had killed the albatross, had been asked to watch one hour and had gone away to shave or ring a friend. But Clare sensed that what they were really feeling was not that they had let Conroy down, but that he had betrayed them monumentally by letting them think of him as the man in the pin-striped suit who went shopping in the Bullring, Birmingham and had once, long ago, composed a popular song. It was as though he had deceived them into believing his life had become littler than it was, so he had betrayed them on an unforgiveable scale by 'going away', and with his children, without even hinting, let alone sharing, one detail of his terrible odyssey, as though they were not worthy even of an expletive. No one can betray his fellow men and women more than by rejection on this scale. You don't count enough even for me to borrow your biro or your handkerchief. Conroy's silence dragged them on and into their own silences. It was they who were put beyond the pale now. His loneliness had been sealed, but theirs was sealed as finally in the silence of Long Quad where the fountain played on and on indifferently.

'We ought, sooner or later, to know what exactly happened up at the Herber,' Clare said. But the response made her guilty of putting the peripheral before the outrageous sacrifice. She felt so guilty that she did not notice that the college, and then the University, had closed ranks. It was the 'Pak doctor' who hadn't realised in his cultural ignorance that he was dealing with a major musical talent and had not sought the help he should have done. Clare defended Hari only weakly. She felt too guilty herself to do more than say from time to time, 'What did happen up at the Herber?' She sensed what her part in the affair had been when she came back from her visits there with his mail and tried to obliterate the grin on his damaged white face from her mind.

Polly Ives had stood there in the Conroys' house in Spide Street. 'But Polly,' Clare had tried to protest as Polly's eyes bulged with zeal. They had walked down to Balaclava Road together. The twins had been playing in the garden of the neighbour's house where they were staying. They had saucepans of water which they were tipping from one to the other when Polly had called in. 'All's well. Daddy's ready to have his children home.' An older child had twined his legs round the bannisters and nodded.

So Polly and Clare took the twins back to Spide Street. Conroy didn't seem to be in, and the twins had stood there thin and white. One had a brown mole by his white knee and this seemed to Clare to be his only bit of identification, so she had picked up a musical box from the floor and started to wind it. Out came: 'Now that the Daylight Fills the Sky', and the twins stared politely and nodded. Polly was embroidering bananas on their T-shirts and they stood there shaking their heads as they stared at the bright yellow bananas.

Clare asked them what they liked to eat and they said:

'Tomorrow. Twice ten thousand thousand.'

'Now that the Daylight Fills the Sky.'

They were such poor little specimens that Clare asked, desperately improvising, 'Do you love your teddy?'

'No.'

'Thunderblood,' said the other.

Then Conroy suddenly appeared like a white ship from a terrible land; a grinning peace smiled, desperately exalted, through his damaged face.

The musical box was now playing, 'There Stands a Little Mankin Beneath the Tree.' Polly was telling the twins a story about the bananas she had embroidered on their chests. Clare begged Polly to take the children back to the neighbour's, but then, as they twined their thin white legs with Polly's, she could see exalted Joe Conroy again, adjusting his bike at the front door, like a shining white sail blown there by a sudden and angry wind, from a terrible land of laughter.

Clare felt lightheaded again at the enormity of what had happened. She would dream that the college maze had been turned into swinging metal ladders and that her shoes had gone. Then she saw her feet had gone and then her legs. She would be woken up by the brightness in the May trees as though the two children were up there calling down to her, 'It's all right. It was only the candle-wax and sellotape.' Then she would dream that they had climbed the high wall surrounding High Lodge Hospital where her mother sat.

As she sat having her breakfast she could see the high top window in Spide Street where Conroy's face had so often floated at nights. Clare had again been cowardly. But what could she have done? What could any of them? She could have stopped Polly. She could have warned Hari. But these thoughts seemed merely janitorial ones, and she hadn't seen Hari since that evening after the picnic.

He had been hauled over the coals at the Conroy inquest. The Coroner had asked him to account for the prescription of a massive amount of a toxic drug to a patient known to be severely depressed and who had, once before, made threats on his children's lives. But Dr Sharma had maintained adamantly that the hospital had been at fault: 'I was given no information or guidance as to the circumstances of his discharge.'

The Herber Institute, still taking the view that the patient had walked out refusing further treatment, was exonerated from any responsibility. Conroy had left before any follow-up letter could be written. The matter therefore lay within Family Practice and none of the staff or the students working under Dr De Berry felt like contradicting the hospital's statements which were, in a sense, true.

The phone went and Clare hoped it might be Hari. But it was Nick De Berry.

'For Christ's sake, Clare, why didn't you tell me?'

'Tell you what? What did you need to know?'

'Look, can we meet sometime? Can I come round and see you?' Nick sounded anxious.

'What about?' Clare asked neutrally.

'Just the socialibilities. Just to say hullo. It's a long time since we met and I took you out for a . . . Did you know Joe Conroy well? You are having a pretty rough time, I imagine, and maybe you need a spin in this lovely May weather. Did he ever talk to you or confide in you? I know you can't discuss this kind of matter on the phone, so suppose I come over? I could come round at once, and afterwards I'd take you out to that place at . . .'

'After *what?*' Clare put down the phone before Nick could reply. She felt another chill round her as though Nick were preparing a dance for her to do. She thought of the circus ponies prancing round their ring in the little circus that came each year to Judasland, the ponies prancing up on to their back legs when the circus master cracked his whip. Then she could see Nick's grin shaped by his Irish beard.

So the Herber Institute managed to remain inconspicuous during and after the inquest. Questions about Hari's knowledge of English were raised, and his exact qualifications. One newspaper suggested he had none at all, and there had been a TV interview with a hospital Registrar about New Commonwealth doctors working in the UK, and an article in one of the quality Sundays discussed the influx of poorly skilled Third World immigrant doctors who needed, but were not given, adequate clinical supervision, and lacked rapport with the articulate, sophisticated and complex consciousness of the Western intellectual mind. They were obliged by their deficiencies to resort to the 'lucky-dip' method of medical treatment. The Herber Institute still kept a low profile, saying only that it had no statutory power over a patient in Conroy's informal category. No one at Sanctus felt like quarrelling with this. The Professor at the Herber often dined at their High Table, and was a personal friend of the Master's.

The rows and rows of neutral checkerboard streets in Judasland didn't seem to accommodate justice either. They were used to acquiescence in the ways of the Great and the Good, just as they had been a hundred years ago when only college servants lived there.

Grace Plasket told Clare roughly what she knew of Hari's mood. She thought Charles Mally had plans to terminate his contract. 'But you must both come out to Hedencote for a weekend again some time. You both need cheering up.'

Clare wrote to Hari commiserating and enclosing the college's formal invitation to Bishop's Benediction Night. She did it tentatively, feeling sure he wouldn't want to mix with perfidious Albion. But she wanted to give him the opportunity to come or to refuse. She was too numbed by the tragedy to give much thought to Nick De Berry. She was still trying to keep her thoughts off the white children flying round like soft paper in a wind. She went through Hari's book again, numbly; then wrote and told him she had finished re-reading his 'absorbing and fascinating book . . . And it is a *real* book, as I see it, in the sense that the reader wants to know what will happen next . . .' Then she stopped. The phrases sounded fulsome and patronising, as though she too secretly found Hari guilty.

She had had to defend him before the Fellows. She held them responsible, she said in a voice that wasn't familiar to them. 'Oxford's pursuit of excellence,' she heard her own voice quoting, 'automatically disqualifies it from respecting the outsider. And Conroy too. His crime was to have come from Birmingham and to have called New College "New" . . .'

The remark was in bad taste. There was no place here for small angers, and the reproach suggested that Conroy's troubles had been simply exogenous. Money-worries or a career at stake. But Smale and Pyecraft submitted to whatever Clare said. What was said in the college office during that terrible month of May seemed to belong to some other discourse than murder and suicide: betrayal.

But as the weeks went on, the quads unsealed themselves. The fountain in Long Quad became an irritant to those who lived near as it danced its independent jig over them again, and pattered its waters down lightly and indiscriminately. No one was prepared to point to the revival of *laissez-faire* ethics and the privacy of morality in connection with what had happened. Not many people, as far as Clare could see, wanted to talk about it at all. The fountain tinkled on *(In Usum Colleg. et Reipubl.)*, and the bells chiming over the city were picked up by the two rivers and reverberated as though all sorrows were equal, or as if the bells made them so.

There was a worse fate than being a neat and enforced college treasure. Clare would dream of 'Pa's Pop', and when she woke in the morning she saw Joe and his twins pedalling round to its music singing, 'We don't know where we're going till we're there.' Or she would see his two sons as the shining white scar tissue on his face. Or again they were singing: 'We don't know why we're happy but we are . . .' Or they were giving their father piano lessons on the towpath by the river, sitting in their coloured plastic thrones on the winged chariot at the back of his tandem. Conroy had been found at the bottom of the river tied to the bicycle after the massive overdoses. Another frisson would come over Clare. Children were like healing scar tissue over a wound. They were like white stepping stones over a river.

She didn't know how she had had the nerve to send off the college's formal invitation to Hari: 'The Master and Fellows of the College of the Holy Ghost request the pleasure . . . Decorations will be worn.' Decorations she could see all round her, white flowers in the trees, white children's clothes up there, white faces, wax legs and arms, votive limbs . . . She went to the surgery in Spide Street, but Charles Mally was on duty.

'Surely,' she said, again and again, as the Fellows drifted in to find out about Conroy's wife, 'someone must know why Joe discharged himself so suddenly. When I went up to see him, he seemed so much happier. He was writing again . . . A Requiem.'

But then she could see his twins again like white flowers high up in the great chestnut trees, and she still had no taste for angry investigation. It was silenced by all that green and white up there, that rowdy Punch-and-Judy show up in the trees that made her feel unreal. That *Grand Guignol* up there.

Conroy had no relatives who were likely to demand enquiries; no one even to find out what had happened to the Requiem he had started to write while he was up there at the Institute. But Clare was still too busy and too sad to think more about that. There was the Memorial Service to help organise. She had helped with so many christenings in the college chapel. The funerals were usually left to the Senior Fellows. What was left to her was the support of Mrs Conroy when she returned from Cambridge with her father.

Carey Conroy was too dazed to do anything but follow her father about. He had driven her back to Oxford and the two of them went over the house in Spide Street silently again and again as though they were inspecting it with a view to buying it, rather than trying to find out how to leave it. They would move from room to room in silence. Gradually little bits of the furniture began to disappear. Then one room would suddenly be emptied and Carey would just stand there taking in the empty room, as though she were waiting for something to happen. She would spend hours at the window of the narrow bathroom that had been carved out of the landing of the house. She would look out over the yard where her husband used to pace round and round trying to work the bad weather away, and where he had stood in the early hours of the morning when the voice of De Berry had stabbed him awake and his students' titters echoed as he reminded Conroy that he had solicited his rape. When Clare spoke to Carey, she just nodded as though Clare were counting out her correct change on to the wide impersonal counter that lay between them.

It seemed such a short time ago that Clare had seen Conroy and his sons at the little circus that had pitched for a few days on the recreation ground at the end of Parnassus Street. The twins had jerked their chins forward and laughed as the spotted horses went round and round the tiny ring, penned in by bits of soap-box and coloured dressing-gown cords. The ring-master would crack his whip and send the horses prancing round in one direction, and then crack his whip again and send them round in the other; or cry, 'Peanuts!' and set them up on to their back legs; or, 'Diamond!' and set them whinnying and leaping over small rods he had set on bricks, swinging them first into one position and then into the opposite while the audience tittered. Black flashes had been painted on the horses' grey coats and now they were beginning to wear off. A train would run past at the end of the Land beyond the gasworks and the horses would leap up again; or a child's sneeze would set them off, or a cough. Or a child, slipping off the wooden benches or bursting a crisp bag, would make the horses react. And then the circus ring grew bigger and had more and more animals in it. A boy would fire off a toy gun and they would all rear and whinny. Such was life.

Clare was wandering along the towpath when she met Hari.

'We all react too easily,' he agreed. 'It is much harder to respond genuinely. Or even, maybe, even to learn the distinction.' He told her he was looking for a job in London. She told him she hoped his book would be ready for the press before he went. He smiled and shook his head. He was impeccably dressed, but his smile was polite and detached as though she and everyone in Oxford were just clinical patients.

One of Clare's many painful tasks now was to find out discreetly what Carey Conroy's plans were, and exactly when she would vacate her college house, so that it could be got ready for the new French chef from Bourges-les-Trèves. M. Validot was Alec Smale's discovery. It was Alec who had seduced him from a small *routier* restaurant in the Haute Savoie with the promise of a house close to his work. Alec had promised to take Clare round the ancient college kitchens. M. Validot, it was hoped, would be inducted by Bishop's Benediction Night.

But Clare's new voice came again and she told him she was not in the mood to feel deeply interested in the new style of cuisine, or *Chèvre aux Poires* and *Champignons Bercis*. 'You could at least have made sure that a completely innocent newcomer and outsider wasn't made to get all the punishment.'

'You mean the little Pak chap? . . . Is he the chippy type?'

On top of this, Mr Bonnard rang again. 'Are you all right, Clare-pod? The press has been having a pretty nasty go at you Ivory Tower folks, and Academe. Shall we come up? Do you need our support? And what about this bean-feast you promised us . . . Bishop What's-Your-Line's Night? I suppose that has been cancelled? But if it hasn't, you know what a history-buff I am. We both want to come up and see how you are surviving this terrible ordeal. And we'd love to see some myth and magic and pageantry. And the glorious robes of yester-yore. It might do you good, pod, to have us with you. Us sane solid London people with our feet firmly planted on the ground . . .'

No one at Sanctus, naturally, wanted to talk about Benediction Night. At least, not until the funeral was over.

Throughout the month Clare felt light-headed. She was the one who was supposed to be supporting the Fellows. She was also left to deal with the police, the newspaper reporters and the enquiries from other colleges. The phone went endlessly, and her voice became a process: 'College secretary's office. I'm afraid I can't comment' became all one word. Hari Sharma never rang or came. She wrote to him and got no reply, but the Fellows still kept drifting in as though she could help them to understand; or as though she could shrive them; or as though she could assure them that it was disease they were talking about: not human relations, but pathology.

Behaviourist therapy at the Herber required that the patient should be discouraged from talking about his feelings, and when

Conroy had said, apropos his rape: 'I feel I must protect my children from myself,' the doctor had smiled and looked at his feet, and said 'Are you eating, Dr Conroy?' Then, 'Are you managing to get on with any work?' And now the same silence that the hospital had put round his horror had extended round the Fellows, Great Quad and Clare. No one put his head round her door any more and said, 'Clare, I really have got to dash. I'm not just making excuses for not coming in.' They needed her in a new way now, but she withdrew. She felt so lightheaded that they seemed like puppets hanging there in the room, their lips going up and down but nothing coming.

It had been suggested that Benediction Night should be cancelled out of respect for Carey Conroy and the dead. But the Benediction had taken place each year since 1473, and, it was pointed out in addition, Conroy's 'Guga Motet' was to be performed in the maze after the High Table dinner, so there was good reason to see this as the best tribute to their late colleague that the college could pay. None of his music had been publicly performed for years. But wasn't it the time to say 'Nevertheless'? The 'Guga Motet' was still being rehearsed in the maze, and if Conroy could never get back into the vein of his early healthy robustness and optimism, there was in this latest work a chance to encounter the troubled artist they had never bothered to get to know before. There was a chance to enter his larger world for the first time.

The Conroys' funeral had taken place at St James's Church in Judasland soon after the inquest. The Fellows had walked in procession following the coffins from Sanctus down the narrow streets of the Land, Parnassus Street, Inkerman Street, then left into Balaclava Road, their tread re-echoed by the narrow terraces, then suddenly muted as they passed the wider, larger semi-detached houses in the more prosperous streets, as though these inevitably echoed less of human tragedy.

The church bell tolled once, then once again. Then there was a long pause. Almost as an afterthought it tolled again. The old women of the Land remembered how they would be summoned from their scrubbing boards, from scrubbing down the clothes of the gentry, to hear their knell tolled on the great Creed Bell. The inhabitants of the Land proper got a smaller and harsher clapper-bell instead, one that sent the pigeons shooting from the church's campanile.

The Creed Bell now tolled again once, and then there was a

prolonged silence. The Tyler boys' father had been college cellarer, and Sacristan as well, so the Creed Bell had been tolled then for them as it was now tolling for the twins. It seemed to Clare that this was the age of child sacrifice. It was no longer an old man's or a soldier's death the bell would be charged with.

The great bell rang out once more. Then the cortège arrived and paused in the broad red-and-gold nave of the beloved church that had recorded so much of the life of the Land. Its great mosaic apse represented Him Who is the Light of the World, and the priest raised his hands as he led the procession up to the sanctuary gates. 'He who believeth on me shall not die but shall have life everlasting.' He led the way, initiating the faltering train. The three coffins followed him, and the mourners, led by Carey's father, crept behind, huddled, as he cried, *'Asperge me, Domine, Hyssopo.* Cleanse me. Forgive me.'

The phrases had a terrible finality. Conroy had been shriven. But the first hymn was William Cowper's, written from his madness with the gentleness of one who has injured rather than been stricken: 'Oh For A Closer Walk With God.' Its humility was an added pain. Conroy's monumental anger was ignored, and the Master in his address spoke little about Conroy's sickness. No one felt in a position to talk about the borderlines of responsibility except in a lecture hall, so he just recalled Joe's rugged individuality, his enthusiasm for East Germany; and his knowledge of trees. He repeated a few anecdotes to illustrate the dry humour of Conroy's college style when he was in health; how his many silences were succinct criticism of the place he had never really taken to his heart. He spoke briefly of Conroy's talent, and of Oxford sadly, as a place where the unschematised life was granted little respect. At Benediction Night, he reminded them, there would be a chance to hear Conroy's final work in its rightful context, and pay tribute to a troubled and stormy life. Finally he mentioned Conroy's genius for distinguishing between what mattered and what didn't, and how his final sickness had tragically worn this talent down. We were all at the mercy of life's quirky winds and its devastating storms. Conroy had never claimed to see life steadily.

> And To Conclude, I Know Myself a Man
> Which is a Proud and yet a Wretched Thing.

But no man or woman is innocent when a child dies.

Then they sang another hymn as the children's coffins were

wheeled away like two high chairs after a meal was over. But when Conroy's was moved, the hearse-wheels squeaked as though he too were being pushed away from life in a pushchair.

Clare felt herself choking, then unashamedly weeping. She felt someone touch her arm. Hari Sharma stood there. Outside in the street a few people openly gathered, and a few reporters. The sky was a glittering white like Portland marble, luminous and almost as though something good were being bestowed on the occasion.

Nellie Grainger came out of the church finally. This was the first time she'd come openly into the Land for years. Nothing would grow in her garden, it was said; not even wild berries. And no birds sang there. But now she publicly opened her front door for the first time since 1923, went in, then thought better of it, and, still in her slippery yellow dressing-gown and green pinafore dress, followed the mourners up towards Parnassus Street. The mourners began to quicken. One's existence is always reconfirmed, whether for good or not, by a funeral, and Nellie followed them. She had sat in the church as though she belonged there among the chief mourners.

But Hari had disappeared by the time the procession got back to Sanctus. Clare hoped he would come to the buffet, but he had shaken his head, so she stood alone sipping the wine that had been painstakingly chosen to give just enough warmth to the occasion to make it resonant. Things were done well at Sanctus as they had been done for centuries, and as none of Conroy's immediate family had come up to the college for refreshments, there was no one to inhibit the stories about Conroy's more lovable side that the Fellows were naturally elaborating in order to steer the real story to the place where it had to stop.

Clare could see Polly Ives standing there. Then she came over. She was pale and her face was swollen. She said she was going away to think things over for a few weeks. The Pastorate? She wasn't ready for that kind of work yet. 'I'm not a good thing.' She said goodbye remotely, and didn't even ask her friends for 'oodles and oodles of prayer'. She just strapped some bundles and a knapsack on her bike and wobbled away from the Land.

In the maze the green lobes of the trees hung bright and recording again. The spell was lifted. The green velvet tongue of grass and shrubs poured stealthily down through the Land again to the stone heart of the city.

Nellie Grainger had come to the reception, but she wasn't

wandering in the maze when Clare went back to Inkerman Street that night. Clare could hear two women calling across Balaclava Road to each other.

'She gorn up to the college too afterwards. You could smell it on her breath.'

'And not just her breath. I know someone who don't wash out her drawers every night! There she was, up there with the best of them. At the wine again.'

'In our days, you war in or you war out. If she thinks we've forgot . . .'

'She always war the type . . . used to go to the Masons Hall on a Saturday with a man. But she always come home alone. Or with the copper. Oh, she went into all the orchards and always come out with a crab-apple.'

'And they should really change the name of the place now, they should,' Mrs Gage was telling her friend. 'Judasland makes us all sound so dark and black. We want something brighter now, like Blossomville or Gardner's Corner. It's about time we changed our image . . .'

And so Nellie Grainger was rehabilitated and walked down the main streets of the Land holding her head up and forgetting about the maze for the first time for over forty years.

'It's always been the Land to me,' she told Clare, 'ever since the horses come down from the riding school and their hooves sparked on the cobbles and their eyes blazed forth. My father died when I was three months old, but *his* eyes still blaze forth at me too. "Nellie, I loves yer!" I've had six death warrants, but no husband. Not yet. But the man who come every morning to take his breakfast with me, his eyes said, "Nellie I loves yer!" even when he was up in the hospital with the S stuck at the end of his bed for "paralysed". His good eye was shut down tight and tied, but his other blazes forth, "Nellie . . ." Oh, how I loved those horses' eyes and them horses' hooves sparking on the cobbles in Parnassus Street. "Nellie! I loves yer."'

Clare felt better as she walked back to her lodgings, and less numb. But she wanted to get away from Oxford. She tried to creep into her lodgings without attracting attention, but Mrs Boden, who had taken to appearing like a bird on a perch behind the bannisters that led down to the kitchen called, 'Of course I'm the world's most discreet person, so you need have no hesitation in confiding in me. How has Dr Conroy's wife taken it? And who has taken the rap? And how is Sanctus behaving itself? I always said the Herber was the delinquents' college. Sanctus may have its absentees and mavericks,' Mrs Boden said with what seemed near delight, 'but the Herber has fielded the most actual sadists and psychopaths. The funeral must have been a terrible ordeal for you . . .'

Clare tried to spirit herself straight from the front door to the stairs. Mrs Boden went on, 'That rose next door is a disgraceful colour. By the way, a handsome oriental gentleman called. Looked rather a snob to me. You know how haughty they are. But perhaps it was just his pigmentation. He didn't say anything. Just said he'd ring. Left a note for you though, on the jumbly-jim . . .'

The note just told Clare how much Hari would like to come to Benediction Night. But please, no mention of his book. Sometime he would come round and collect it. He was very busy at the moment. Nothing more.

Clare still felt unreal. Carey Conroy had asked her to go to the Herber Institute some time and collect Conroy's things and see what could be salvaged of the Requiem he had started working on while he was there. But the thought of Conroy's grinning enthusiasm for the Institute chilled her – how he had jerked round the floor in his violent version of yoga, or sat at the dining-room table still grinning as he munched cornflakes, dressed in his hospital towelling dressing-gown, as though he would wear its regulation trousers and jacket too if that were required. Clare was filled with chill again. She could see Nick De Berry again, cracking his circus whip, and the children smiling down from the white trees. She felt almost nostalgic for her days as a college treasure.

She decided to phone Grace Plasket, who had been good to her since the tragedy. 'Can I come out to Hedgencote for the day, Grace? I need to get away from Sanctus. And from Inkerman Street.'

So Clare left her office; just told Alec Smale she would be away next day and held out her key for him to take. She took a bus out as far as Hedgencote Turn and walked down into the quietness of a lane that smelt sweet of wet morning hedges and quiet folded fields where elderly lambs bleated. It was a kind and pleasant walk and the trees seemed to have lost their menace. A river ran and then came back and ran again, criss-crossing the road. A few cars passed and then one stopped. Hari was opening its door to offer her a lift. Mrs Plasket had invited him out to Hedgencote too.

Grace was in the garden when they arrived. She made them

coffee and they drank it in the garden that looked up the steep side of a hill where crooked grey stone houses side-to-end straggled up to the church.

'How is the book going, Hari?' Grace asked. 'Your father was on the phone the other night, asking after you and after it.'

Hari stiffened and brushed the thought of his book aside. 'I shall be in bad trouble with my father over this affair,' he sighed. 'I think my culpability was in that I was too anxious to establish rapport with a man of artistic bent. It is true there was something I had not fathomed, but I had too little time and too little information to fathom it.'

Grace shook her head. 'It was just another of Oxford's cover-ups. Perfidious Albion. You should make a row about this.'

But Hari stiffened again, and silenced her suggestion of scape-goats. 'I had not digested the medical records thoroughly. It had to be.' But he looked very depressed again, and then detached.

'But your book?'

He shook his head and waved his hands. 'Let's face it. My book is of no significance or social value or medical worth. We must let it slide away as though we had cast it on the tides to work their wills.'

Grace sighed: 'Why don't you take Hari up to the church, Clare, and introduce him to our English religion of Ancestor Worship?'

So Clare and Hari walked through the village and up the hill to the church. The grass was long in the churchyard and chickens clucked and pecked between the graves. A bird flew low along the churchyard path ahead of them, following the path's course, then sprang up and away. The sun came out and threw black shadows from the tombs like helmets among the seedy grasses. The place was silent and empty. The church had decorated railings round it, ironwork swagger-and-fruit overblown with rust. More small speckled hens were pecking about. One followed them into the church.

There was utter silence inside. A bird shifted on the roof, then stopped. A tree shuffled for a moment outside, then stopped. A tap outside dripped twice into a plastic bucket and then was silent. The church smelt of newly-extinguished candles and the altar-cloth hung down roughly parallel to the altar but only roughly, like a carelessly spread bed-quilt caught and crumpled at one end by an indifferent nurse or attendant on the absent God. Damp surplices with chocolate and biro stains down them hung on pegs in rows and above them stood jamjars full of dead flowers.

Then Hari touched Clare's shoulder. In the Lady Chapel there was a glossy pink marble memorial to all those soldiers who had laid down their lives in two World Wars.

'*Dulce et Decorum Est*', the words had been chiselled out of the stone, '*Pro Patria Mori*'. Just beyond hung a row of rough grey worm-eaten crooked crosses with Flanders mud still caked on their spikes, a dark cruel grey on their crudely embossed sides, as though they had only just been torn from the wet mud of battle. Rusty nails were still roughly holding them together, but half hanging out, and the soldiers' names and numbers had been written in a clerical hand in marking-ink or punched out of metal ticker-tape, or discs like milk-bottle tops had been pinned on their stark cracked fronts.

Clare translated the Latin for Hari: 'It is sweet and fitting'. This row of soldiers' crosses were the only crosses in the church. The rest of it was given over to memorial plaques, urns and tablets to the great local landed families, their military relatives, stewards, retainers and victories, and faded regimental flags were draped round the nave walls and rafters and up the chancel, darkened by blood and time and battle and self-congratulation.

'Let's go,' said Clare, but they found themselves talking about the tragedy of Joe Conroy again as though outlawed gods had passed by with his little convoy too.

'I know so little about the lives of the academics,' she explained. 'I'm only a glorified typist, glorified because I'm called in to help with lonely undergraduates and visiting professors' wives and attend parties to make up quotas, and walk dogs and help out when a manuscript goes missing or a wasp flies up a trouser leg or a wife has to be rung, or a child fetched from ballet school . . .' But at the thought of children, the churchyard trees and their spring came at her again. So many white children up there.

'Let's go.' The convoy seemed to come again, but she felt better as Hari took her arm and they crossed a stile to the newer side of the churchyard. The turves covering recent graves were coming unstuck in the spring drought and peeling off. Round about stood ancestral yews with thick black globes, which great seas seemed to have moulded and darkened and set there, before the seas stalled and declined behind the flat dead fields where hot cows now stood and stared with the same dull glisten that the trees had. 'Let's go.' But once more, the convoy passed.

They walked down to the stream and watched some moorhens crossing from bank to bank. Bands of brightly dressed cyclists went past on bright bikes with bright smiles and big yellow badges, enrolled for some sponsored event that made Grace laugh as she peered out of the window of her cottage. 'It's a pilgrimage. They're going to St Remigius's to have their bikes blessed.' They waved at the pilgrim's leader who waved back, bearing a bundle on her handlebars of green foam-rubber crucifixes, swaying in the breeze.

Grace had cooked meat and made a salad and opened a bottle of wine. Clare and Hari both cheered up as they watched the smiling cyclists fluttering away down the hill. They ate and they drank, and Hari didn't mention Charles Mally or the practice in Spide Street, so Grace asked him what he did with his free time.

'Yesterday I went to the Sheldonian Theatre to hear Frederick Handel's *Esther.*'

'Oh, any good?'

Hari pulled a face as they sat there eating. 'I had to laugh. I was finding your musical tastes a little ridiculous. Here we all were, twentieth-century men sitting in solemn silent rows in a seven-teenth-century concert hall listening to elegant and cold eight-eenth-century music about the genocide of a race belonging several thousand years previously. Maybe a man of letters would better understand the cultural aspects of this. Maybe I am not serious enough. Maybe I was not meant to settle in Oxford, or in Europe even. Maybe I shall go to the States and take my chance.'

'We shall be sorry to see you go. You remind me so of my life in Bombay . . .'

Hari lowered his head. They drank more wine and laughed again and Hari cheered Clare up, saying that perhaps his book was not a write-off. He pushed his plate of half-eaten food away and thumped the table and said, 'My thesis is really an ethical one. I am throughout asking myself how far is one, in modern India, morally justified in using ancient magical spirit-beliefs as medical placebo techniques to drive away paranoid fears. We doctors are guilty of pretending to our patients that we believe they have been possessed. We deceive them into thinking we too believe the spirit doctors can effect a cure, which they often do. But is this any different from what you do here in the West? This deceit? Our spirits are like your Royal Family and your film stars. To ordinary people, these are common media to both our cultures. How far we are justified in pandering to simple needs to believe? It would be too cruel to tell common people their good spirits did not exist. It would have been too cruel to those soldiers in the church beside that pink marble memorial. Ancestor worship is also a form of placebo medicine. To sweeten old gods rather than to demystify ... This is the theory I am anxious to work out. But it is more philosophical than medical.'

Clare could see Mrs Plasket laughing, but by the time they had finished lunch and were sitting outside again under the gnarled old apple tree in the garden, Hari had agreed to come round to Clare's room next day and see how he could reconstruct his thesis with her help.

'Clare is not in a favourable mood at the moment,' he had told Grace. 'This is a bad environmental climate for a woman who is sensitive, too sensitive. But your distressing feelings will pass,' he assured Clare, and she saw him like a solid land or a new country on the horizon as he added: 'As for my own disgrace in this affair, I regard it as simply an aspect of post-colonial resentment.'

XI

Clare and Hari were both in the mood to sit down in the evenings at the table she had pulled away from the window because it looked down over the tall houses of Spide Street where Conroy used to peer down. She would spread Hari's book out and they would manoeuvre its material round like a kaleidoscope till the same pieces fell into a different shape, with a different emphasis.

Clare was also making its index. Drawing up lists and categories, she found, was a way of imposing the order that they both wanted at that moment, and it amused her to think of them both drawing up such exalted lists of all the things there were in the world, such indiscriminate celebrations: abstract, anchovy, aspirin, authority . . . beef, Bemax, blind dates, boils, and Brahma. The haphazard headings of life. Their promise of random bounty.

And Hari who had, Clare felt sure, been made the scapegoat for British defects, seemed to be cheered up by this act of ordering and making sense of the world in a totally unideological sense, putting everything there was into ranks and files and marching them this way then that. Then they would sit there drinking the good tea his mother had sent him and making up their own 'Tables of Contents' . . . absolute . . . affluence . . . ankles . . . ants . . .

'Clare,' Hari would continue, 'caution . . . clarity . . . cream . . .'

'Cowardice . . .' she would add, 'craven . . . creeping . . . crimplene-controlled credentials . . .'

'Oh?' he would raise his right eyebrow non-commitally, look a bit puzzled, then smile ruefully as they went on feeding words into a box-file. The work was good for them, imposing this arbitrary order not just on the book. And the events of the last few weeks had reminded Clare how much she was alive. She had noticed other people too, walking from Conroy's funeral with the decisiveness of the dazed undazed.

Sometimes she and Hari would go for a walk for a break, or stroll down to his flat in Parnassus Street, where he would show her photographs of his home and family. They would look out of the window where a stream ran away into a river that fed the Thames that flowed down to London before it left for the sea.

And it was here that Clare began to feel detachment from what had happened and began to step out of the Land in the way she had once stepped outside Sanctus. When it was warm they sat on the roof, or in a still bare, blank garden with cement benches and one geometric tree that Hari's block of modern flats turned its back on. They could see the old houses of Candid Street with faded signs still over them: BOWERS CASH DRAPERS AND CLOTHIER; or TRY OUR TEAS THEY ARE THE BEST. 'I am afraid not,' Hari read sternly.

A small printer's shop was working behind them and the clanking of its press re-echoed through the front-rooms of the small two-up two-down houses as though they were all involved in a monumental effort. Then the press stopped banging and loud TV voices came from the shop next door. It had once been a Co-Op, they saw. Then Clare remembered a corner shop starting up there, then a boutique, then the workshop of a *luthier*. Now it was a Chinese take-away, but the memorial plaque for the Co-Op shop assistants who had died in 'The Great War' was still stuck on the side of the shop, stained by graffiti and take-away but still legible: EACH FOR ALL.

The streets were silent again. Clare could see men cycling past looking like Nick De Berry, but she and Hari were succeeding in placing a grid over the tragedy and found it was safe to walk on. They walked on it and were slowly graduating from the horror of the murdered children, they thought.

'Let us take another drive out into the country when this rather geographic chapter is completed,' Hari suggested. It seemed a good idea, another picnic, to get the reminder of May Morning and its terrible judgements and monuments out of their minds.

Sometimes when Clare got in at night, Hari was already there and Professor Boden would call out as she inserted the key in the front door. 'Your medical-wallah has gone up . . .'

And Mrs Boden would peer up from the basement and call through the bannister, 'Is he by any chance connected with one of the colleges not a teapot's tip away from here? They are getting round to having Commonwealth Scholarships from the hot places now as well.'

Then her husband would interrupt with a shout, 'For God's sake woman, don't let my toast burn. And I want three slices and they must be soft in the middle . . .'

Clare would go up and see Hari sitting there fingering his text.

'I was too concerned, as regards the Conroy tragedy, with improving my own rapport with the English and my own standing in the University. Charles Mally has hinted several times now that he wants a woman partner.' He smiled and dismissed the subject. 'It was the immutability of fate, and in any case I was not made to work among the ingrowing toenails and dandruff and the frozen shoulders of the NHS. There is no place here for preoccupations with the great sicknesses of the spirit. I am applying for a job in London. But', he raised his thick eyebrow sadly, 'whether I shall get the required references after this tragic affair . . . A doctor is always bound to take risks when he prescribes, and I was given no hint from the Herber Institute, not an inkling . . .'

'Hari, we know, and we are backing you.'

Hari pulled a face. 'I am backing the Queen, and Clare is backing Hari.'

'Sorry,' Clare reddened, 'True. It doesn't make sense.'

He took a deep breath and smiled and unwrapped a parcel he had brought and slowly produced two shiny black fishes like bright silk evening handbags with elegant gold studs along their spines.

'Maybe', he said, firmly pressing his lips together, 'your landlady would let us use her stove. I have been so tired lately, and have longed for my revered old professor to advise me, and for my mother to cook me good Indian food.'

They stared out into the back garden. The maze seemed to have sent its green right out over the Land again this evening. One of the Bodens' grandchildren was watching a great beige boneless rabbit pouring itself out of a home-made cage to sample the Bodens' flowers. The smell of orange-blossom came, and the contented sound of cricket bats. The green expanded into a bowl round them.

Hari looked down and sighed, 'A patient called me out this afternoon because his ceiling has moisture on it. It may have made his TV set damp and he wants me to advise him how to claim another, or how to get a mortgage. Or some sleepers. I was not quite sure which one it was he wanted. What did you think of my restructuring of Chapter Three? The Politics of Psychosis?'

'I gave your book pride of place yesterday when I got in,' Clare heard her clipped little Oxford vowels and phrases come tapping out of her machine, followed by scones, neat summer salads and sachets of herbs marked 'Fun with Flavours'. Then the staircase spirit left her again and she teased him. Surely he needed her as much as she needed him?

'Hari's higher haspirations hindered and hurt by hernias and haemorrhoids.'

'Ah yes,' he nodded, and she went on thinking about his index, then constructing some higher index of life in general with its random and outrageous entries: Purse, people, pluperfect, poison, prison, pity, pox, perhaps, prelude, passion, potatoes, putrefaction. So much or so little, according to how you chose to see it. Hari was fidgeting again with the two shiny fishes and Clare's thoughts wandered on from fish, feathers, fear and futures to Drawberry Road where her parents were sitting at their little round table, really too small for three people, and her father was pressing apricot stones to the side of his plate and Clare was easing them on to the regimental badges decorating hers as he beamed and said, 'Some young folks take the easy way out, Clare. Or make the easy link-up with the folks from overseas. But Mardi and I are both grateful you don't go for run-of-the-mill ways of doing life. Have you ever thought of acting with the National Theatre, eh pod? You're a good-looker, you know.'

Or it was winter and instead of summer salad and stewed fruit, there were tangerines to be battled with: rich fruitcake, then nuts and tangerines, and as her father peeled and pursued his Christmas fare he was still saying, 'Mardi and I are such a couple of grateful old bods having you here to share our lives when you might have been off with the other summer fledglings. You name it. Life, Clare-pod . . .'

Then Clare would watch the little bit of pith that he had inadvertently carried up to his eye. He would wink, lunge at it and bring it down, transferring it first from his thumb to his index finger and then wiping it back to his lip and his eye again as he winked. Mardi poured out small portions of very sweet sherry into their small cut-glass egg cups and they all cried, 'Cheers. Here's to us.' The little thread of pith would go up and down as though it were the crane that was constructing their life of little things together. Finally the thread of pith had settled on Clare's shoe, she saw.

Then, that summer, the Bonnards had gone on holiday without Clare and she had met Ambrose and gone to Slack Street. It seemed so minor now, this fear of hers that things were falling apart. But the police had come and wanted Ambrose, and she had come home and taken to standing by the window on the watch in case he should come and Miss Pugh get the door first. And Miss Pugh stood on watch too, always hoovering beside the phone and round the front door, polishing at the blue glass door till her duster left bits of fluff caught on its leaded panes.

'*Duw*! He's been standing out there since I came back from Bethesda and the Recitative League. They should send him home. Barry Sands to goodness. *Diawl*!' she read a picture postcard. 'There's no telling with my niece. Once she gets to Barry. However, this won't buy the baby a new bonnet, so I'll leave the hoover out on the stairs for you good-girl. And I'll put the Tidy Tilly out too. In case. *Duw*! when is it, Clare-bach, that your parents come back from their annual?'

Then a card flopped on to the doormat. Mardi had written: 'I hope you're having lots of fun and lots of friends in, just as we did at your age.' Clare's father had added as a postscript: '*Bellissima signorina, make hay while the sun shines.*'

Then Clare had felt sure she saw him, lolling on the pavement outside, rotating on one heel and reading a magazine, his eyelids big and heavy and a look of anger and impatience on his face. He seemed so much more black now that she had seen him with the Toshidis, and Clare could hear Miss Pugh at the front door, then feet coming up the stairs, followed by Miss Pugh banging her feather duster along the bannisters. A door opened. She pictured herself and Ambrose in hot summer parks, coffee bars, by the Serpentine, swinging to Beatles music, sharing food beside the river, or arm-in-arm in a tube train standing up lazily when it stopped. It hardly mattered whether it were Balham or Knightsbridge. The whole of London was equally theirs.

But instead, at Slack Street, the hot retex smell had come up from the dry-cleaners below, and Mr Hood lay in his coffin; the police were looking for Ambrose and control had gone and things were falling apart. She felt almost reassured as she thought of the pith going up and down against her father's face and the stones being expelled genteelly from the stewed plums, and laid in careful rows.

'I left the stage, I left London,' – they both stood looking out at the green of the maze that the evening was still slowly spreading round the Land – 'because things seemed to be falling apart.'

'You mean the immigrants?' Hari asked neutrally.

'Oh no. Just the growth of chaos, bad transport . . . lack of work. I knew I'd always just play bit-parts. The English rose.'

'Uhu. Maybe the last paragraph should end as a question rather than as a statement.' He leafed through his manuscript.

'Maybe.'

'In the meantime,' Hari gathered up the two black glossy fishes, 'we should ask your landlady if we might use her stove.'

Clare led him gingerly downstairs. 'Mrs Boden,' she called in her best crimplene voice, 'may I introduce a friend of mine?'

They shook hands politely. Mrs Boden's big eyes were like an owl's as Hari asked for the use of the kitchen. Clare was alarmed as she frowned, expecting her to say, 'How abnormal!' as she gazed at the two shiny black fish, or to screw her face up and cry, 'I just can't stand coarse fish. It's pathological how you two adult people can stand there and tell me . . .'

But she just gazed at them and said, 'Robin fish . . .'

'It is not Robin fish, Madam,' Hari corrected her in his gentlest voice, as though he were dealing with a very dangerous patient, 'we call it loshi.'

'Excuse me!' Mrs Boden exploded, 'but my husband and I lived in Kuala Lumpur for three years and that fish was named after an anthropologist friend of ours, Dr James Robin.'

'That may be so, but we are arguing with different economic concepts here, using perhaps different cultural and social tools. If we might be allowed to use your grill and a few of your cooking utensils . . .'

Mrs Boden ushered them silently down to her kitchen, but it wasn't all that clean. There were bits of muesli in yoghourt tubs, and bits of yoghourt in coffee cups. A bar of dirty soap with grey cracks was melting into a salad-bowl, and a grey film of sticky liquid like rice-water held all these things to the stove.

'I think,' said Hari, still the therapist, 'that perhaps it would be best to cook our fish in the open air. Over twigs.' So they got some tinfoil and matches and took their supper down to the maze.

Clare gathered sticks and they lit a fire and Hari unwrapped the two decorative black handbags and cleaned them and gazed at them. One of the fish had an eye missing.

'It looks rather doleful,' he observed, 'as though someone had robbed it of its birthright. What is it trying to tell us poor humans who have never experienced the ocean deeps? The little you once saw', he reproached it, 'you shall now see no more.' He gouged out its second eye.

'That sounds rather Shakespearean,' Clare said as he gutted the second fish.

'It has evidently and enviably never suffered from divine discontent.' He plunged his knife into its gall bladder. 'Revenge is always a strong motive.'

'I suppose you believe in reincarnation?' Clare asked as they ate.

'I am a scientist but the belief is deep in us, it is true.'

'What would be the reincarnation for a college treasure?' Clare went on. 'Would she go up in her next life for serving men so well, or down for an unlived life?'

'We don't have that concept for women.' Hari ate. 'Are you not satisfied with your status at the University? My sister would regard such a position as entirely within her social status as an educated woman. But perhaps your colleges are not so venerable as they used to be. I happened to visit Cambridge last week. A colleague had invited me.' He sighed. 'I haven't fathomed the British yet. I travelled to Cambridge to seek out this spirit of Ancestor Worship. But alas, I found that I had to take shelter in Woolworth's where many score of schoolchildren were making sketch maps of the supermarket and weight-watchers were demonstrating so that a lorry was obliged to swerve and knocked a religious enthusiast off her bicycle. There were few vantage points to view this once famous city. And in our restaurant some dust or other matter caught fire. In a chandelier. Cardboard or paper. Or just dust. But the management came out to support us and each of us shared their war experiences until the management came back to tell us "All Clear". It was just dust in the candelabra and no doctor or ambulance was needed. Everyone seemed so sad to have missed a great experience. The great works of English literature do not prepare us for this aspect of your life.' Hari smiled ruefully and Clare felt he was suggesting that she too was hungry like this.

'I don't blame you for feeling like that,' she repeated again and again, with banality.

But Hari wasn't prepared to be the object of her compassion, though he seemed to want to help heal her wound. He changed the subject and told her about some form of suttee still being practised in his grandparents' day, in India.

'Maybe it's because nothing has happened to us for a thousand years. No great tragedies or surrenders or rethinking,' Clare said, thinking aloud. 'How funny. Nothing has ever happened here. Only private griefs, and they aren't attached to anything public, so they can't be shared and never have a permanent meaning.'

'Even at the great gates of your castles, cathedrals and libraries it seems you first require a notice of instruction to reach the toilets,' Hari yawned.

'You haven't had at all a good introduction to Britain,' Clare sighed.

'My father's was a good one,' Hari smiled. 'He made many friends.'

'You do really feel very bitter about what has happened?' Hari shrugged. 'And I don't blame you,' she added.

'Maybe I could exonerate myself. I could wear a T-shirt saying I AM BACKING THE QUEEN – and all the British with bad backs and damp ceilings.'

'You are very hard. But I don't blame you.'

Hari held his hand out towards her, then put it round her waist. She eased herself uneasily away and laughed as nervously as she had at Slack Street.

'Oh Hari, I'm not sure we're along those lines yet.' And she could hear her college-voice carrying on: 'I hardly think that would fill the bill.' It was such a poor little world she was still inventing for herself. Such a cosy tea-room built over other peoples' crises. Their conversation ground to a halt and they wrapped up the remains of the fish.

The trees hung over them in the maze. The wind touched them gently and then more sternly. There still seemed to be someone living up there, and white faces peered down out of the pink-and-white chestnuts, moist lips glistened and soft mouths pouted. The children were still up there. The May Morning wreath had been gulped down by the waters, and then the children had risen and were hanging up there with the birds. Clare needed Hari.

'My mother died of an infection,' she was telling him. 'You're lucky still to have yours.'

'Yes, but I am unfortunately still in over-reaction to her authority. Aware that she is too strong a figure . . .'

Some children had climbed the bough of a tree and dropped over into the Sanctus maze and were creeping through the bushes to where a stream ran through to the Cherwell. They reminded Clare of the children at High Lodge Hospital, who weren't allowed on to the wards but who gathered out here to see their parents. She thought again of the children who used to climb the hospital's high wall and stir in the bushes and trespass closer to where the patients sat, hiding behind the loaded trees, or peering from behind the hot-houses where the bloated Paeonia Rubra and scaly Humber climbed up the iron window-crank and clouded the glass with their breathlessness, and mocked the patients with their glossy wholeness.

The faded green sunhouse where Clare's mother sat had a gear at its side to make it revolve, and there were two little rooms at its back where cricket bats and croquet mallets were stored; there were three pink gilt boudoir chairs with red roses on their upholstered seats and moulded gilt foliage and smiling cherubs on their backs and sides, as though the patients were to be received at Court. Suddenly the sunhouse would revolve and a door open and Mrs Pax, Mrs Bonnard's companion with the thick white hair, serene blue eyes and porcelain complexion, would sit smiling there. The intruding children would whisper that she was a murderer – not just a murderer but a poisoner too. They would look at the secret herb beds round her and the purple lobes of the Crown Imperial and call her the Imperial Poisoner. Clare held back, the dutiful daughter, as they peered through the sweaty blooms and advanced on Mrs Pax, trying to read her poisoner's thoughts.

'My parents', Clare's mother would begin, struggling to deliver each syllable, 'sent-me-to-a-very-expensive-boarding-school . . .' But the children were creeping closer to her guardian, Mrs Pax, as though they were all taking part in a game of 'Grandmother's Footsteps' when the nurses' backs were turned. It was the Poisoner's serene normality that compelled the children. They wanted to get a little nearer to the place where she conceded, yes, she was going to 'swing'. Clare could see a sudden rush over the lawns of ox-eye daisies, then the children would be standing there. They had played truant from school to the grounds of the forbidden hospital, turning somersaults, playing football, or just waiting there with wide eyes till Mrs Pax should say the word that would lead them to where she would soon be.

But instead she would just lay down her sewing and smile at

them, spreading a great Union Jack over the summer-house floor in front of her and promising it to the one who could answer the riddle of how to make a Venetian blind. The trespassing children could have made themselves drunk on the obsessive neat deft stitches of her tapestry-work, and the smooth hands stitching to make the pink flesh of a soldier, or the white face of the King Trooping the Colour, so dark the adult mystery they probed: 'Is it nice at Chalstone, Miss?' They'd invented the place where she was to swing.

Mrs Pax would nod serenely. 'Passable, but I shall miss my kitty. One, two months old.'

'What's his name?' the children would tease, then turn their attention to Clare's mother. 'Are you a poisoner too?' they seemed to ask, but Clare could only remember her mother demanding: 'What are you doing in my house?'

'In those days there were no antibiotics,' Clare told Hari, as they sat in the twilight over the remains of their picnic supper. But Mrs Pax was still stitching at the tapestry pageant spread out on her knee. If the children could get really near her they might hear her 'real' Poisoner thoughts. But Mrs Pax just sat there serenely like a Florentine painting and called for more matching wool to finish the horses' fetlocks, or the Imperial Guard, complaining that the wool had to be an exact match 'so that my horses can ride proud'. Mrs Bonnard still sat there with the strange smile on her face, leaning over sideways till the nurse came and propped her upright again, and the trespassing children leaned over at Mrs Pax and asked her to sing, 'Oh I Think when I Hear that Sweet Story of Old'.

They would widen their eyes and pretend to swoon in ecstasy when she sang. 'Do you really love that sweet story, Mrs Pax? And what a funny name you've got, Mrs Pax.'

'It means peace,' the Poisoner smiled back at them serenely and matched her tapestry wools again and went on inserting the thousands of even, meticulous stitches that seemed to go so oddly with murder.

'So you see,' Clare ended. The trees' boastful excesses reminded her of the carefulness of her own life. But the reminder of High Lodge Hospital was worse, and the vast celebration there seemed to be of human weakness and infirmity, and of Conroy's children.

It was getting dark in the maze now and Clare didn't want Hari to leave her alone with so many probing children. The trees were full of voices now:

> Go, said the bird, for the leaves were full of children,
> Hidden excitedly, containing laughter.

'Let's go,' said Clare. The children unnerved her. She touched Hari's arm, took his elbow. The voices of the children still sounded so laughing, as they improvised and feigned innocence of Conroy.

At half past ten it was still warm. They stood under the now silent velvet trees, and Hari touched Clare's hand again.

'Would you like to drive into the country with me tomorrow? Charles Mally is on call and I am free. Maybe you could show me some beauty spot, and then perhaps we could take a meal in a restaurant.'

'An Indian one?'

'Oh dear me no. Indian restaurants in this country are provided only by a low-caste people who have been expelled from their native communities for having tried to poison their clients. Or maybe you would like to come up to London next weekend with me and meet my sister? She is studying at the Imperial College.'

Clare opened her mouth but the squeamish little Drawberry Road voice in her said, 'I'm afraid I'm booked next weekend.' She saw herself taking Alec Smale's dog for ever on a walk, then peering over a dead squirrel on the tow-path. 'Something must have attacked it,' as though that were always to remain her response to the burgeoning trees.

Hari nodded, then stood there enquiringly as Clare read the notice Mrs Boden had printed in big telegram capitals beside the telephone table: 'MR BONNARD SEEKS TO GET INVITE TO VISIT LOVELY DAUGHTER IN GROVES OF ACADEME, she had printed out maliciously.

Hari stood there puzzled, just giving his small lip movements. His eyebrows shifted a bit.

'My father always has had a rather quaint way of expressing himself,' Clare dismissed the note. 'My parents would like to come up too for Benediction Night.'

Hari's face lit up. 'It is always a great pleasure when one's parents are genuinely willing to entertain one's projects and share one's experiences.'

'Of course,' Clare hesitated then explained, 'only the Fellows and their distinguished guests go to the dinner proper at High

Table in the college hall. We college 'associates' are invited to drinks afterwards in the maze. And to the concert. They are going to perform Joe Conroy's last work. A motet, I think.'

Hari nodded. 'I have a feeling that I may find this modern music more suiting to my spirit than the Handel one. I would like to pay my last respects also. And it will be . . . one will wear evening dress?'

Clare nodded miserably. Mrs Boden had pinned up another malicious telegraphic notice by the telephone: YOUR PARENTS RANG AGAIN TO SAY THEY HAVE PLANS TO MAKE OXFORD THEIR HOME-BASE FOR A FEW WEEKS ARRIVING ON JULY THE FIRST.

After Hari had gone, she thought of him and cried; thought of the weekend in London and cried; cried also because there was still this reed in her throat: this valve through which someone else would suddenly talk.

Clare heard a noise from her room as she climbed back up the stairs. Perhaps Polly Ives had come back. Perhaps Alec Smale had brought his dog round again. But a large pigeon stood at the open window. Clare threw a book at it, but it neatly side-stepped as it told her it had come in from Slack Street. It ducked as she threw her shoe at it. She couldn't bear to touch anything that had touched the bird, so she chased it barefoot round the small room. It made little complaining noises as she drove it out of her larder or from under her bed. It had an ugly rash on its claws and her moisture-cream dripped off its beak. She remembered how Yani had sprayed stray pigeons with aerosols and jabbed scissors at their eyes: 'In Bomba we no longer have these poor-country problems.' But now the bird just strutted proudly back at Clare and stood there taking stock, opening its legs obscenely, parting its feathers, putting one scabby foot on hers as she sat at her biscuit-supper. It watched her digestive processes and burped when she did; yawned when she yawned, murmuring: 'The more we are together . . .'

Hari had gone but the bird stood there. 'Change your mind?' It seemed to cock its head on one side and grin at her. 'Didn't fancy him, after all?' It stood with its phosphorescent claws shifting. 'Here's to us.' It was lifting up its dirty wings as though it were trying to open a big dilapidated umbrella in an over-crowded bus. The bird posed its foot on Clare's again and she saw now it came unmistakably from Drawberry Road, and not from Slack Street. Perhaps it was this pigeon who had sent all those Valentine cards, and all those bouquets to the stage-doors in the days when Clare had been an actress.

Clare called after Hari but he had gone. She stood weakly in front of her father's messages by the telephone. He and the bird seemed to be marking time patiently. Clare called again after Hari, but all she could hear was the sound of his car turning the bend. Then it was gone, and she heard the final stroke of the church clock's chime.

XII

'What part of London do you come from?' Professor Boden asked Mr and Mrs Bonnard as they sat side by side on his broken settee and sipped his wife's strong tea. 'West Hampstead? Ah yes. Kilburn where the Irish boys used to hang out. And now the Bushmen . . . What made you want to come and work in Oxford then, Clare?'

The sound of violent clapping came from the basement. 'That's only my wife,' the Professor went on. 'She's trying to get rid of her double chins. Trying to slap them down. Swat them off. So what made you want to work in Oxford, Clare? One of my pupils comes from a weird place called Seaham Colliery, and another wears earrings. God knows why they always have to choose Oxford. And who's the exotic Mahatma in silk ties who keeps coming to the house, Clare?' The Professor planted his legs wide apart and shaped his lips into rubbery rings so that they looked like bits of sports apparatus. 'And what exactly is he a doctor of? Non-violence? Ancestor worship? Or proving that the British Raj was really responsible for the holocaust all along? Ah well, we must keep abreast.'

The Professor wandered away, then came back suddenly. The sound of slapping accelerated in the basement. 'We have to move with the times.' The swatting stopped. Mrs Boden was calling up angrily: 'Look at that!'

It had been raining and suddenly a rainbow hung over Inkerman Street. Mrs Boden was quarrelling with it vociferously. Clare wasn't sure whether she was ticking it off for having such a simple unimaginative colour scheme, or simply because the rainbow had anchored itself into the back of a lorry loaded with rusty clamps. The driver in its cab looked surprised as she ticked him off for his charge, then he went on eating a hot dog calmly, with a slightly injured air.

Now they could hear Mrs Boden psycho-analysing a blank-looking man who had come to the door to try and persuade her to subscribe to a Life Boat Fund. He too seemed as dazed as the lorry driver in the cab at her taste for strong meanings, and the Jungian significance of the Polperro Life Boat Bazaar. The Professor arrested her analysis with a complaint. There wasn't enough cake for the five of them so the guests would have to have toast. He fumbled about for some bread and found there wasn't any, then he reappeared wearing a bee-keeper's outfit and dabbing at some rubbish that had been stacked in a corner, poking it with a tennis racket and calling out to his wife, 'What are we eating for supper tonight, Mrs B? So that I know what to get up out of the cellar.'

'Not for us,' said Mr Bonnard, cheerfully deprecating.

'Sorry?' the Professor asked, puzzled at the area suggested by his guest's remark. 'Sorry?'

'Don't get out the good wines for us, Professor. No potable potions up from the cellars for us plain, day-by-day folks. We don't aspire to those levels.'

The Professor, who had never even hinted that his 'levels' extended to non-university people, just looked puzzled and asked, 'What? Wha? Wha?' and dabbed his tennis racket in the pile of rubble again and poked at a piece of an old invalid carriage. 'It'll have to be the '54 then.'

'Just something everyday for us everyday people,' Mr Bonnard reassured his host genially. 'Because this evening we want to look up an old friend of Clare's, and perhaps invite him out to a drink on the town. Nick De Berry is the man for us. Dr Nicholas De Berry of present fame, I believe. At St Martyrs' College.'

Clare had been longing to see Hari again ever since she had refused his small invitation at the end of May to spend more time with him. Ever since then she had dreaded this visit of her parents as though the great pigeon who had planted one foot of its on one foot of hers were still there.

Mardi was explaining to the Bodens that Clare and Nick De Berry were old friends: 'They had deep things to think about together. But now Nick's gone to higher ones: Aesculapian adventures. Higher healing. Trick-cycling, so we are hearing on the grapevine.'

'Didn't Nick used to come round here, Clare?' the Professor asked. 'Give him a ring. Ask him to drop in for drinks this evening. You know his number? He's the Medic at St Martyrs' and Junior Proctor as well. Go round and see him. Bring him back with a pupil or two. One of his pupils is a De Beer, and another's Dick Graçart's son. Related to the Le Michaels as well. Just back from Princeton with masses of girls. They have lovely girls there. Princeton does.'

'Talking of girls,' Mr Bonnard went on. 'Nick gave Clare-girl here a good education in music. The things they used to get up to four-handed on the jolly old joanna.' But this aspect of Nick's togetherness didn't interest Professor Boden, and he just munched the pieces of sponge cake his wife had set out for the Bonnards while his wife gulped quantities of tea very noisily out of a huge breakfast cup.

He stared at her. 'It's a pity I don't really like you.' Her throat went on working up and down as though it were a predator in action. 'You women do have to take such noisy action. A life of actionation. My nurse used to have to tell me again and again to bite my food.'

'One bite for nanny,' Clare could hear her voice come out as though for once she hadn't fallen into the spirit of the staircase. 'One bite for the soldier at the Front, and one for – '

But the Professor perhaps hadn't heard her small clear voice because he just grinned and went on, 'Came the day when I could scrub my ankles and discover that the black marks on them weren't there by nature's unalterable decree. No, they were just household bootblack. The kind the maids use. Not a permanent fixture on my small boy's small body.'

'So one bite for the small boy's small . . .'

But Mardi interrupted Clare: 'Small boys love dirty knees.' Then Mrs Boden started clapping at the remnant of her chins again.

'Never had a cold either,' the Professor recovered himself and went on. 'As soon as I start to sneeze she puts a dob of Vaseline at the back of my throat so that as I lie there in my truckle bed at nights . . .' The Professor went on talking and eating the amount of cake that would have been his due if the Bonnards had not come, and his wife went on working on her chins. Her husband had got on to the subject of who was to be next Dean of St Martyrs', and filled them in on the rest of university and college politics, the crisis in the English Faculty, the second language ruling, college excats, gate rules and music hours. The De Beer youth, he told them proudly, was a damn nuisance in all of these tiresome businesses.

Clare was afraid Mardi was going to press the subject of students, and raise the Conroy tragedy. But she just said, 'So now we know,' and they rose to go. 'It's so exciting for us ordinary mortals to get these glimpses into the lives of the illustrious.'

'I wouldn't go so far as to say that,' the Professor grinned modestly. 'The tomes and the hundred-or-so modest articles I've pushed around tend to get dust on them, and, as I say to my colleagues in LA and Cornell . . .'

'Do they still all come from the Public Schools?' Mardi interrupted this curriculum vitae.

The Professor frowned and turned to his wife: 'I've had this pain in the lower calf of my right leg now since yesterday.' Mrs Boden peered at his left leg and he shouted at her impatiently: 'No, my *right* leg. Right calf, woman. As-I-have-just-told-you. I've always had a tendency to weakness just there ever since I was in Pop at Eton.'

'Ah Eton!' exclaimed Mr Bonnard. 'What is your view of the future of the Public Schools?'

'My right calf,' the Professor was hissing at his wife.

'*Caesar et sum jam forte*,' Dad grinned, 'Caesar ate some jam . . . but my dog-Latin days are a thing of the past. So they still come on coming from the great Public Schools?'

But the Professor was looking steadfastly at the calf of his leg: 'That's the spot!'

'Daddy, shall we go out now?' Clare suggested, unfreezing a little.

'A leg stretch? Right. Show us the way, daughter of ours whom now, perforce, we are obliged to share with the high-ups. Are you game for Nick De Berry's?' he beamed at her. 'Lead us on to St Martyrs'! Lead on MacDuff and cursed be him who first cries "Hold Enough".'

'Onwards,' Mardi supported him. 'Now to storm the citadel of St Martyrs'. Ambassadors three from Curley Hill, we.'

'Daddy, Nick may be very busy.' Clare was horrified at the prospect. 'He may be teaching,' she protested.

'No, no,' the Professor urged them on. 'Bring him back with his dancing girls and we'll open up all that '55. Bring us back the latest news from the home of hired assassins and find out about that lodge porter they got rid of last week for indecency, and that new chef that gave them British plonk in their . . .'

'Daddy,' Clare begged, 'Nick's a very busy person. He may be writing a lecture or . . .'

'Clare pod,' her father reproached her solemnly, 'Nick De Berry's family was so good to us after your mother died, that time when *we* were very much alone . . .'

'Yes, but I feel I've paid for that. I mean, Nick's life's not like that. He's not alone, and he and I haven't got all that much in common.'

'We were newcomers at Curley Hill after your mother died,' Mr Bonnard repeated ceremoniously. Her father's stubbornness made her conjure up Nick De Berry as she stood before him naked in her bedsitter and he called angrily: 'For Christ's sake, secretary, get some clothes on before you sound off about Joe Conroy and Dr Sharma's bread and butter.'

'Lead on, MacDuff,' her father went on relentlessly as they left Inkerman Street. They could hear the sound of Mrs Boden slapping at her double chin again and her husband crying, 'Sic Transit Gloria Mundi. My trousers are growing too tight. We shall both have to diet.'

They got to St Martyrs' and as her father yarned with the college porter about Curley Hill days, Clare was praying that Nick would be out. The porter rang through and said there was no reply from his rooms and Clare was just leading the Bonnards away with a sigh of relief when her father, prowling round the College, met a Fellow in a gown who asked, 'Can I help you? Are you looking for anyone?'

The Bonnards had hit on the most alcoholic and most expansive Fellow of St Martyrs' who was eager to tell them its history. 'The history of graft.' Then he gave them a run-down on the Fellows' lives in graft. Mr Bonnard told him about Nick at Curley Hill and the Fellow told him that he would probably be out of luck where Nick was concerned. He was their latest and brightest star in the human genetics scene, had just won a Research Fellowship for the college by his work on certain types of mental illness.

Clare trailed along behind them, longing for Hari to be there with his hold on certainties and his indifference to what was making her feet feel like lead now. The don was leading them across a quad and down a narrow tunnel and in at a small wooden door where he called up to the top of a narrow flight of stairs: 'Nick! Nick! Have you got any of that Bourbon left? I've just been telling these friends of yours about your latest victories in the heredity sandpit.'

Nick was in fact giving a tutorial. A girl feeding a baby was sitting beside a folded pushchair. She had put a packet of nappies on the floor and Nick was kicking them round the room gently as he tried to unravel an argument. 'Ha!' he called as the don poured the drinks. Then he let Mr Bonnard get on to his Curley Hill days.

'Of course!' De Berry smiled and nodded smoothly. 'And Clare and I are old friends. But I'd no idea you would still remember me. It is good of you to call.'

'I was telling them, Nick, about your breakthrough in – is it? – Huntington's Chorea.' The don lowered himself into an easy chair and fingered a slender cigar, trying to make the group more sociable and to jell there for an hour or so. 'It is Huntington's, isn't it?'

Mardi fidgeted. Dad cleared his throat. Nick pulled at a pile of offprints and offered them, but Mr Bonnard interrupted uneasily, 'We're not applying for places in your college.' He grinned and lit his pipe, making the room smell of bonfires heaped with old rags so that the baby started to cry. 'We're just rather humdrum ordinary folks who like to see how things tick. Up top. Do you remember how you and Clare used to play duets together? "High on the Giddy Bending Mast"?'

Clare sweated and fidgeted. The pupil on the settee put her baby to her breast and said, 'I'll come back later, shall I, Nick? And Toby and I will see you tomorrow at the Dicks?'

'Dad,' Clare pleaded. 'Nick is giving a tutorial.'

'It's quite all right,' Nick replied, with clear and deadly politeness. 'But I mustn't keep you.'

Clare was trying to help his pupil get her pram unfolded but she could hear the conversation by the door. The don had poured himself another Bourbon and lit a cigar: 'Nick, it *is* Huntington's disease and not Parkinson's? Your breakthrough?'

Mardi stirred. 'We didn't want you to feel we'd neglected to do the courtesies,' Mr Bonnard interrupted, 'been in Oxford, you know, without sparing a moment in our point of time for the timeless places and for a short trip down memory lane. The Curley Hill mob . . .'

167

'As you say, Curley Hill,' Nick conceded, 'it was at Curley Hill . . .'

'We have good reasons to be very grateful to the De Berry family then. At Curley Hill,' Dad said munificently.

'Well, that is reciprocated as far as I'm concerned. It was when my parents first got to know you . . . and your wife . . .'

'Of course, I'm Clare's stepmother,' Mardi said hastily. 'Clare calls me "Mardi" by the way. I've never thought I could be any kind of substitute for a real mother. So "Mardi" does for me . . .'

But Nick was in full flood. 'I'm sure it would be hard to be a substitute for her. And I have good reason to be humble too. And grateful. It was after Mr Bonnard's tragedy that I first started getting interested in medicine, determined to get to grips with hereditary diseases. It was because of Mrs Bonnard that I first decided on my career. As I was explaining to my pupil.'

Clare was still at the door, her attention fixed by the recalcitrant pushchair and the conversation at the other end of the room.

'Just recently a lot of new ground has been broken apropos Huntington's Chorea, and there's sure to be a genetic break-through fairly soon. Yes. It was at Curley Hill I first decided,' Nick went on as though he was still giving a tutorial. 'Yes, in the next few years . . . a lot of light thrown on it by what Rabin and Kartwee are doing in the States. It's only a matter of time before *in vitro* engineering will take care of the inheritance factor for a start . . . And of course, *in vitro* means . . . genetic . . .'

Clare had always been told that her mother had had a breakdown 'because of the war'. 'She has just let herself go,' Clare and her sister would lament as they lay on the piles of mattresses touching the hotel ceilings where they were now living while their father made his hotel inventories. The inventories were for the duration and they had thought of their mother's illness in the same way and that she had died, as her father had told her, of a hospital virus or infection.

A bell chimed and then a deeper one. Mardi was looking at Clare and trying to stop Nick from continuing his guided tour of mental illnesses with a hereditary basis. Then another bell chimed and he looked at his watch as it dawned on him that Clare was not Mardi's daughter but the first sick Mrs Bonnard's. He had never had a clear idea of Clare's claims on him, and now he was slightly tight and confused.

'We must make a date. I mustn't keep you now,' Nick murmured.

Clare's father got out his diary as Nick widened his eyes in a way that was all too familiar. Mr Bonnard hadn't grasped that in Oxford that remark, 'We must meet sometime' was merely performative. But Nick sorted this one out. 'We must get in touch when Clare and I are less under the thumb of squalid suffering students.' Then he widened his eyes at Clare and repeated the concession: 'Give me a ring some time and we'll have another outing. That's a deal.'

The rest of the day was a nightmare. The Bonnards went to Evensong at the cathedral and sang Ascensiontide hymns to Christmas tunes, then they went into a pub and sat in chilly silence among groups of students laughing across to each other.

'No. They were only mental pictures of her periods.'

'Inducing superstition in the great apes.'

'And mine's garrulous as well.'

'He managed to unload the lot. Let's go.'

Then the Bonnards crept back to Inkerman Street, hearing Mrs Boden searching for galoshes in the garden and trying to squeeze the beige rabbit back into its cage, then squeeze out her cat's piles and then squeeze into her galoshes crying, 'I simply hate galoshes that are too loose round the final toes. They and tepid food . . .'

'Clare-bird.' Mr Bonnard listened from the open window upstairs with a grim face. 'You're leading a rum life here up among the gods, but aren't some of you heading for catastrophe? Eh? or a real headlong crash? Your stepmother and I have been thinking. Now that I've retired, the bonds that hold us to London are sadly being fast worn down by our new Commonwealth friends. We've got nothing against them, your stepmother and I. We've got to know plenty of them and we've had some good times together. Mardi actually asked Mrs Nandy how to make a vindaloo! Really hot! We've got good friends in Drawbery Road too, but the time has come when we want to spread our wings where the winds aren't so strong. And garlicky. We've been putting our thinking caps on and going through our pennies and our pounds with a pretty shrewd young accountant – coloured, yes – and we've come to conclusions.

'Is this for keeps, Clare? The Prof's house? Don't you think you want to spread your wings further? It's grand having pals like Nick De Berry around, but how do you get on with the Prof?'

Her father dropped his voice. He had been into the huge bathroom strung with semi-rude notices about washing greasy pots in the hand basin and leaving tealeaves in the bath. He had noticed another notice, this time in the Professor's hand. It was pinned to an enormous set of bathroom scales like rusty gallows and announced: 'Will all students weigh themselves weekly and record their weights in the appended book'. A large arrow 'Book' directed the student to the food-stained book which contained nothing but abusive words written there by the students, plus a few messages from girl-friends who didn't trust Mrs Boden's message-board downstairs, and her huge brown challenging eyes. Mr Bonnard didn't like the look of the book and scales any more than the students. 'Exciting as these digs are, are they for keeps?'

He and Mardi had been at the estate agents. 'We've come to the conclusion that we'd be able to afford a modest house here in some goodly suburb of this great city of dreams where we could join the United Nations and the wine-making ditto (if there is one among the dreaming spires. Or is it now the screaming tyres?) . . .' And so Clare's father proposed that they should pitch their tent here; should come and make a home for their daughter too, somewhere where there was a decent patch of grass 'to turn by our own private family alchemy into a garden where daughters can flourish and invite their friends . . .'

They looked round Clare's bed-sitter with the pans behind the thin cotton curtains and the little gas ring with spaghetti hoops stuck to it, and the screen behind which she hung her clothes. They looked at her bedside biscuit-tin and the Majolica vase where she hid the cotton night-gloves she wore to keep her hands smooth.

'It's very nice,' Mardi had said. 'Top notch. First rate for a high-flyer.'

'But is the Prof straight with you, Clare? There's a lot of funky business about these days.' Clare was still frozen as she walked them back to Grasslands Hotel where they were staying. If only she had responded to Hari, instead of blindly reacting.

The Bonnards had a chilly little meal at their private hotel in North Oxford. There was tepid brown soup out of dazzling white bowls that were too hot to hold and shifted about on the place mats, then tiny pies like little sewing-bags that squirted a thin brown fluid over the highly-polished table and the hunting-scene place-mats. They drank water powered with fluoride and chlorine from the Thames Valley plant and told her they were going to spend several days house-hunting.

'Nothing pricey . . . nothing fancy . . . just a bit of flair . . .'

'And style.'

'To give us all a second wind . . .'

Clare was so numb that she couldn't eat. She panicked again as Mardi went on separating bits of pale green cabbage and then putting them together again as though she did not like what she found inside: 'A bed-sitter is fine *pro tem* but it's no substitute for a strong home-base to be moored to when you've had a fairly competitive day in a fairly pushy kind of society. Fawning and feuding as well as dreaming. We don't want our daughter not to get a fair deal . . .' Clare could see from the way her parents spoke that they were preparing her for Huntington's Chorea; had been, perhaps, all Clare's adult life. She watched the family meal from a distance greater than at Drawberry Road; watched the knives and mouths go in and out; up and down.

The damp little brown cushions on their plate turned out to contain threads of chicken. Clare also found a piece of sliced date beside hers and three red currants. Her parents were staring at a big leaf of red cabbage with a blob of cottage cheese lodged at its curly edge. Then after a 'mango mousse' that was a piece of pale yellow blancmange perched on a piece of water biscuit, they sat in big chunky tweed armchairs by a dead grate and drank weak instant coffee. The room smelt of damp people and damp dogs.

Mardi went through the estate agents' particulars. Clare murmured weakly, 'But my flatlet is really very convenient. It's so near Sanctus. And Judasland has a very active community feeling . . .' But they were telling her of future dependence. They had come with a mission, and now it had become a crusade.

They met again next day at Grasslands for salad with shreds of cheese and cress hanging out, and drank little sweet drinks out of glasses shaped like penguins. 'Here's to us,' Mr Bonnard held up his little sweet liqueur and Clare wondered if he would begin to sing when he got lit up, 'How Sweet Is My Store', and when he got to the last line, 'Nor Envies The Monarch His Throne', Mardi would shoot out more estate agents' particulars.

'The house we've got our eye on is in a really flourishing community. Of course, Judasland must be steeped in history and simply fascinating, but is it "you" for keeps? I mean, there's such a lot of student drift these days. The world where anything goes. But we've seen our dream house out at St Andrew's Mead. The houses out there aren't all rooming houses and impersonal set-ups which are not such fun – ' oh how they were preparing her last rites ' – as, as, as you enter the maturer middle years, rejoicingly albeit but remembering that riches have to be *taken* then, as well as *given* . . .' Her mother entering her mature and middle years at High Lodge Hospital.

Clare felt weak and cold. Her parents seemed to be talking to someone else as they sat by the blank fire-grate. But all the same, they were taking her back to 1940 on the Isle of Wight, preparing her for her throne beside Mrs Pax. The shop her father had kept then had been a seaside shop where rubber rings and water toys and pink rock and pink sand shoes hung outside round its door, and darkened an inside smelling of sweets and rubber and suntan lotion. They had to close the shop during the Battle of Britain. But they would have done this, in any case, because Clare's mother had taken to raiding the till and giving away the sweets and sea shoes, as she wobbled round falling over the camera equipment and opening the films.

France fell in May 1940 and they prepared for invasion. The Island was closed to tourists, and the Army arrived. The Battle of Britain had started. Mr Bonnard's shop was closed for the duration, but he got a job as a caretaker in a huge empty hotel on the Downs looking over the sea, and his children spent their time counting cutlery and china, folding linen and blankets and piling up layers of mattresses on beds, then lying on the tops of these mountains while their father padded about down below checking pillows and chamber pots.

It was here that, resting their feet on the ceiling, Clare and her sister, Hazel, discussed why they thought their mother had 'let herself go'. She would totter round the hotel with a rubber swimming-tyre round her neck and then get lost in the huge rambling building. They might find her in the cellars, or trying to climb over the chimneys, smiling when the fire-brigade brought her down and looking at her daughters as if to say, 'Ought I to know you?'

As the girls lay on the mattresses with their feet pressed on the ceiling they would try to remember their mother as she had been as a young woman, dark-skinned in summer, wearing a gold tussore frock, long ear-rings and beads round her dark carved neck. And she was smiling as she played for them to dance to, chased them naked round the garden with a hoseful of water, helped them clean out the thick green pond, took them on the common to eat bread with rhubarb or stewed apples on it, let them make a camp there and sleep all night, gave them apples for finding the first foxglove in flower, or ran out of money, but never out of love or good humour.

'She looks like something gaping on a fishmonger's slab, now,' Hazel had said to Clare as she recalled this other self at the beginning of her mother's illness, when their mother had cut the warty buttons off the back of a skate she had bought and stuffed them into her mouth, and munched and guffawed: 'The Vicar took me to Southsea for a dirty week-end.'

She told the doctor, 'I'm feeling a bit mischievous.' Clare and Hazel would grow angry, but their mother would sit there eating as innocently as a thirteen-year-old maid being accused by the mistress of the house of seducing the youngest son. It was only later in the strange white sunshine of the early autumn that they saw the size of their loss and the size of their guilt. Clare couldn't help thinking the real woman would come back. She dreamed she was walking past the railway-station and her mother called out: 'Cooee Clare! It was only the hot-water-bottle that burst.' Or she would be leaning out of a sea-breaker saying: 'Wasn't it silly of them to send me the wrong time-table like that?'

And so, half-consciously trying to prevent more of her family from doing this Dr Jekyll and Mr Hyde, Clare would tether them with her well controlled self. The empty hotel denied them grief. The rows and rows of empty rooms suggested that there had never been anyone in them. There was no proof of Mrs Bonnard's existence here. The girls would see their father disappearing down the long corridors as though he too had gone after his wife 'for the duration'; 'the duration' being a normal season like the winter, or a routine day of the week and both would come back like Wednesday after Tuesday.

A German ship, black and smoking, had been driven up on to the rocks under the Downs, and people fed off its silence. No one had seen it rammed by the rocky cliff. No one knew how or why, one morning, it had suddenly appeared. Some people said it had been full of troops the Germans disembarked at night. Some said it was carrying poison gas. Others said that Hitler's right-hand man had come to negotiate a peace. Mr Bonnard simply said:

'Never be blabbers, girls. I don't want my two girls to become the babbling type.'

Clare had lain on top of the pile of mattresses for hours on end watching the dead black ship the seas had tipped on its side. Then, mysteriously, the ship had gone, but she could still smell the less mysterious smell of her mother's fishy hands as she ate the black warty buttons she'd cut off the skin of the skate when they had turned on her: 'You've just let yourself go, Mummy. We hate this war just as much as you do.'

And now that Clare and Hazel had at last seen the finality of this change, the strange silence between them grew stronger and stronger, as though the body of their real mother had been stretched taut over the white sky like a tent pinned out there which they sat inside, far from the dirty salacious woman. Once in an upstairs cupboard, as they were clearing out their flat above the hotel, Clare had found a pair of her mother's white slippers, pearly white dancing-slippers with delicate criss-cross filigree straps. And now this pearly white was above and accusing them for their compassionlessness.

The schools had closed after the Fall of France and most of the children had gone away. Clare and her father had been in the large garden when the first dog-fight started. It had been very hot and the sky a brilliant blue. You could see every detail of the silver sword-fights going on up above. There would be the gentle tapping of their guns like a finger's on wood, no more. Then the sudden animal munch of the ground guns. Then shrapnel fell and hissed and singed the lawns. Clare found herself taking shelter in the toolshed, trapped there and unable to get back to the hotel so near. Her father had crawled in as well. She had beckoned him and as he made his way to the toolshed through the screen of noise and aircrafts' careers, it was as though she had always viewed her father's life from the other side of a busy road. But he was so near now she could hear his pumping heart, and pity came.

By this time Mrs Bonnard had been admitted to High Lodge, up on the top of the Downs about an hour's walk away. Hazel and Clare dreaded their weekly visits. Sometimes they would climb into the hospital gardens over its high wall and approach the summerhouse where their mother sat beside that other patient, Mrs Pax.

The stately Madonna of the Lilies, with blue eyes and a pile of white hair drawn into a full opulent bun on the nape of her neck, would simply smile serenely when the children, who had climbed the wall and raced up behind her, started playing 'Grandmother's Footsteps' with her again, whispering that she was the murderer and the Imperial Poisoner and that she was going to swing when the Germans got here. The Queen, as they called Mrs Pax, was so much more interesting to talk to than their own mother. The girls would try to make her talk about her tapestry-work and the royal horses, Trooping the Colour and the Battle of Waterloo, all depicted in bright wools on her murderer's lap. Her bracelets would click together as they asked her again and again whether it was nice at Chalstone, widening their eyes in communication with each other, or persuading her to sit in the swing that stood near their summerhouse, swinging her higher and higher till her hair came undone, the Poisoner's hair flying loose round her laughing face before she was hanged.

Was evil really like this? Clare would ask herself as they continued to taunt: 'Do you go to Holy Communion on Sundays?' The summerhouse would revolve: did they give twenty-four-hours-a-day sunshine to Chalstone women who were going to swing? Clare could hear the children asking. *The leaves were full of children.* Behind Mrs Bonnard and Mrs Pax she could see the trees the trespassers climbed, the high full trees they sat in staring down, and the conservatory where the nurses on duty would go for a cup of tea. Clare could still see the chipped china cups they used, and the tin teapot and the cheap tin clock that gave out a shrill alarm when it was time for them to take off their caps and snap them shut and pack their india-cloth bags and go to their bicycles. Then the pattering feet came on, and the shouting child-voices. The Pluck and Phlux, the Coryliss and the Distended Rhee were banging on the sweaty glass of the conservatory and taunting Clare herself now she knew the truth: 'Will *you* like it up at Chalstone, Clare? Will you come with us?' Then it was Conroy's children again, who seemed to be shouting at her now, up in the trees and shouting down: 'Will *you* like going up to Chalstone, Clare? Like us?' But Clare could only hear Mrs Pax's serene voice replying: 'Oh yes. Provided I get my wools to match the white of my proud horses' fetlocks.' She was holding out her tapestry. 'But I shall miss the jolly trees here.'

'Why, Miss? Please? Why the jolly trees?' they teased the Poisoner.

'Because trees cast such a blind eye on our faults.'

'What *are* your faults, Miss? Please,' they went on asking the Imperial Poisoner, wide-eyed at having pinned her here at last.

'Perhaps that I spend too much time among my favourite pussy cats and horses when I should be improving my mind . . .'

The tin teapot in the glass house clattered among the sweaty shouting blooms. The sound of water came, dripping into a tank, and the patients shelling peas into a pillowcase. It was Clare herself, not her mother and the Imperial Poisoner, who was being mocked now by the ogling flowers and gloating trees as she grumbled mildly that the directions in the cookery book weren't quite correct, and that Hari didn't need her, didn't think of himself as a victim and so didn't need her. The children were still peering from the trees though, with pink wet mouths. They were growing clamorous, then rowdy, as they listened to the steady breathing of the woman who was about to hang at Chalstone and who sighed because she missed her matching wools; who sighed again: 'We are not always as careful as we should be about broken fingernails;' and who sighed finally: 'I'm afraid, Hari, I shall be busy all weekend catching up with my mail and my friends and getting through my domestic chores. They simply eat into one's time.'

XIII

'Mardi,' Clare shouted, standing by the big double bed that smelt of Morgan's Pomade, 'Mardi, you and Dad are interfering with my landscapes and horizons.' She went on like a precocious child, 'You are interfering with my higher inscapes and my outscapes.'

They were in the bedroom of Grasslands Private Hotel, or they were back at Drawberry Road, and Clare could still feel the warmth of her father's hands against her, and the warm fug of the flowers near them in the hospital hot-house. Or the warmth of her father's thighs in the hotel's toolshed where they had taken shelter when a dog-fight started in 1940. She could still hear his heart beating and see his wet eyes, and his clumsy lonely body separated from her, and so totally unable to talk about his sick wife that she had put a hand on his tweed shoulder and kissed the back of his neck and he had drawn her on top of him as they huddled from the shrapnel in the small shed in the hotel grounds and silver planes slid here and there, somersaulted while the woodpecker tap-tapping of machine-guns came from up there, then the great gun started up from the Downs below.

Her father had asked softly: 'Is everything going well, Clare? You know I mean, inside?'

'Well, Mrs Anders seems quite happy about coming twice a week, so we're managing. Is it the cooking and the shopping . . . You mean?'

'No, Clare-pod. I didn't mean inside the house. I was thinking of – ' her father slid his hands from her shoulder which he had clasped as a plane wound down. He had patted her armpits and slid his palms through them. 'I was thinking of my own true daughter's inner well-being. One day she'll be grown up and want to marry and we'll both want to know that everything's shipshape inside – England too hath need of thee, daughter-o'-mine. After this terrible war, it'll need people like you. Do you ever go down to Dr Maynings and get yourself – ' he asked shyly, ' – get yourself physically – and all the other things a budding young woman should do? Just to make sure things are running along like clockwork in the inner home as well as in the one you and Hazel look after so jolly well for oldies?'

Clare had got up as he put his hand out towards her again, and ran through the dog-fight down the road. He came after her a little way, sadly in his baggy old tweed jacket. Then he stopped and went back to the hotel and she pretended she had set out shopping when the dog-fight started and went into a neighbour and said, 'Could I shelter here till this lot's over?'

Soon after this Clare got herself a job as a properties mistress in a small repertory company, taking the place of a woman who had been called up. She got jobs occasionally too, in pantomimes, standing shoulder-to-shoulder or with linked arms in the chorus, kicking up her legs and crying: 'All Together Feeling Fit and Fine'. Her father would come to every production he could manage, while Hazel went to Australia and stayed there. Then, when Clare was on tour with ENSA, her father took to going to tea-dances and met Mardi at the Metropole.

Now, as Clare stood by their double bed, she could almost hear her father rustling the garbage bin in the evening, wandering around the flat in Drawberry Road while Mardi was knitting or reading, then picking up bits of paper, fumbling like a giant moth and humming to himself: '*All Together Feeling Fit and Fine.* Clare, what about an Away Day?' and they would take the train to Slipsham-on-Sea. Or fly kites, father and daughter, on Parliament Hill, or tinker with the two-stroke engine on the model boat Mr Bonnard was making to race on Kenwood Ponds, or go to tea-dances: 'Quite right. Follow your stars, Clare, take stock.' Sometimes a little tomato soup had leaked down his lip to his chin. 'If you've got a healthy body and a sound mind and a cultivated personality, you need a decent bit of time to find out what use the boffins have for you. But, more to the point later on, what use *you* have for *them*.'

But now, although Mr Bonnard was in the arm-chair asleep, he had won. Clare could see the back of his neck as she stood at the top of the flight of stairs and Miss Pugh banged about them with her broom. Clare could see his mouth open slightly as he let out a slight gasp. She saw herself pop a kumquat in. Or something brighter and rounder and rosier, and harder. But instead both Bonnard seniors were standing there as captors in the hotel lounge, going through estate agents' particulars. A small map was helping them to find the way to their dream house, and telling them which bus they needed to get there where an invalid could be installed.

'We're looking for a community where there's a keen sense of mutual interest, give and take,' Mardi was still saying, and Clare could see the rows of semis with their bright gardens round them like felt padding, dyed such a bright green, green swaddling or bandage, and neighbours who would pull their weight with installed sick daughters. 'St Paul's Crescent, we feel, is a real live community with a proper appeal to all age groups . . .' Clare felt she ought already to be feeling physically ill and ready for St Paul's Crescent. But instead she just felt dazed, as though she were in an express train and the towns and the landscape were flashing loudly past her and quite out of her reach, already installed on her throne of sickness.

'Dad, I must make it quite clear,' she was saying again, 'that my life has its own inscapes and outscapes and inturns and outlooks . . . I have my own commitments and dimensions.'

But her assault was only against the wind because Mardi just smiled and said, 'Judasland could be a fascinating place, but is it for keeps, Clare? After all, it has become rather steeped in tragedy for sensitive people like you. Clare!' Mardi suddenly barked. 'Wake up, Clare! This is the bus stop and this is the bus to take us out to St Paul's. We've got big plots to hatch out at Fands Park Gardens or Myerly Drive. Wake up Clare! . . . Does this bus go to Dapplewell Road? Good. Thank you. On we hop,' she commanded.

Rain faltered and fell. The river was a brown crescent leading to more grey rainfields and more grey houses caught in the bright green. The faces of the people in the bus queue seemed stunned too, and amazed that the Bonnards should keep up energetic rapport with such a world. The bus doors sprang open and Clare's parents bundled in. 'Wake up, Clare,' Mardi called again, marking perhaps a new stage of Clare's illness where she should exert a bit of edge. But Clare was so cold and stunned that she was still standing there when the bus-driver closed the doors, and she only gave a faint smile as she saw her parents through dirty bus windows shooting off into the world of red brick and bright green bandages

and arcades of shops, announcing 'Cara's Cards . . . Pru's Fruits
. . Spin-a-coin-Launderette . . . Pat's Snacks . . . and Spicelands
Mini Mart . . .'

Clare didn't know how long she had been standing there at the
bus stop when she saw a car drive up and heard Hari call: 'Are you
alright, Clare?' The rain had stopped and the sun was making the
pavement smell warm. He opened the door of his car and said,
'Where shall we go? Where would you like to go? I have been away
in London for the last few days. I have had several interviews in
London and the provinces. How is our book?'

Clare was supposed to be dining at Grasslands tonight. Mardi
had announced triumphantly that dinner was to be *Beef Entente
Cordiale*. But the thought made her ask Hari to drive her right out
of the city that was now starting to steam in the tepid sun. They
drove out towards Hedgencote and by the time they reached the
forest of Cotnose, near where they had their picnic on May Day,
the sun was coming kindly through the green leaves and Hari was
taking her away from the future that her parents had always been
plotting for her.

They got out of the car and Clare could hear the wind in the
black dense trees of Cotnose. Then the forest was towering over
them in black sea-breakers. They hadn't gone on inside it on that
white and sacrificial May Day. They had approached it from a
different direction and today they hardly recognised it as the same.

Hari was examining the little wrought-iron stile in the wall's
side. There were two decorated steps up, two neat iron cobbler's
lasts for ladies' slippers. Hari helped Clare up, and there were two
boot soles like it leading down the other side.

'The lady of the house must have thought well of herself,' Hari
remarked. They were in a clearing. Old beehives were scattered
over the rough grass. The hives were old cones made of plaited
rushes and battered by the winds and birds' maraudings. And they
reminded Clare again of the battered old summerhouse at High
Lodge. It seemed to be revolving so that Mrs Pax could step out
suddenly on to its stage and ask: 'Huntington's Chorea, is it
hereditary?'

'Oh yes, onset at age about forty . . . By the age of forty-three
the very distressing process . . .' The hospital hot-house was full of
damp sweaty tumescent blooms, all taunting again; Wart Burum
and Spotted Race waiting for secret carnival sacrifice, as the May
Morning hymn came from somewhere in there:

'But of course,' Hari's voice went on reassuringly, 'the offspring do not necessarily get the disease and in any case, science is advancing at such a pace that great progress may be made very soon in genetic engineering.'

After Mrs Bonnard's death, Clare had dreamed that Mrs Pax was sitting at the piano, playing an Andante of such sweetness that Clare had woken still hearing its first hesitant statement, then its sudden resolution. It was so full of assurance that she had had to break it to herself again that her mother had just died among the full trees bursting with birds whose songs were gloat and boast; had died among the ferny Mock Caestris and hairy Pluck. All of them inside the conservatory were nodding at humans, then waiting till they had gone to start the real May celebrations that were to take Clare out to Chalstone. She panicked again.

Hari had gone ahead, and the sight of his back as he thrashed away at stinging nettles comforted her for a moment. But then the flowers came back, Volux and Pluck, quilted Angist, Aquilla Nauta, spongey plush Clox, glistening Nongest and swaying Solomon's Seal, all chanting noisily with huge upturned sweaty faces. It was nature's Public Holiday. The clamant flowers blocked the gravel paths. Their May Mornings had nothing to do with humans so they gave them 'rough music'. The onset of the disease came at about the age of forty. The flowers were choking her, aloof and intact as they confirmed human misfortune.

Clare tried to catch Hari up, but he had gone too far ahead. Mightn't Nick De Berry have got it wrong about her mother? But the flowers only seemed larger and more gloating. May was so unmasked, she said, as she caught Hari up and clasped his arm.

'It is *all* hereditary. Life is hereditary.' And in the days and weeks that followed this trip of Clare's with Hari to Cotnose, she had to remind herself again and again that the flowers, the trees and the children in them were taunting her primarily for having life too firmly under control, for never playing. If she didn't keep reminding herself, she might freeze into the posture of Mrs Pax by the little sun house, forever snipping and lamenting her wools that didn't match.

Clare was sitting beside Hari, his arm round her and against the high grey wall of the forest again, but the children taunted on:

'Will you go to Chalstone unaided? Or with Mardi carrying your floral sponge-bag and pink nightie?' Hari was clapping his hands at some mosquitos. Then he was looking at his watch: 'Shall we go further into the forest or shall we go back to my flat where I, maybe, shall try to make a very mild curry?' He kissed her gently as though he knew she agreed now.

They drove back to Oxford. Hari's sister had given him spices from home, and tea. He was going to cook and had wanted for a long time to cook for Clare, he said, in Parnassus Street. She didn't know from the muddle in his flat whether he were packing to go, or unpacking after a long weekend. However, his book and its index were still on his table: 'dog-bite . . . dolls . . . Dutch courage . . . duration . . . death . . .' Clare was grateful again for this grid of the neutral, the arbitrary and the random to tread on to stop herself falling through into panic and thoughts of High Lodge Hospital. And the moon stood also large and neutral, a white globe resting on a bed of white cloud. And Hari stood there like a route that lay across a foreign land, and invited her to walk steadily.

They said goodnight under the moon's neutral bulb and agreed to go out to Hedgencote again. Grace Plasket wanted them to see an old house that was up for sale there. It was the old doctor's practice. But it would have to wait till after Bishop's Benediction Night.

'Black tie?' Hari was querying his invitation card again.

'That means evening dress.' He frowned, then they both laughed as they looked up at the cold and indifferent moon on its white tablecloth. It was as though it had made a joke up there and they both wanted to laugh.

Clare's parents had rung again, but she tore up the message that Mrs Boden had left out for her. Tomorrow Hari and she were going up to London for the day. He was going to hire his evening dress and she was going to buy herself a dress. Then they were going to have lunch together and walk in Regent's Park. Clare wondered whether Mrs Pax and her tapestry would refrain from coming with them. The moon hung so beautifully blankly up there as they said goodnight.

XIV

Preparations were well under way for Bishop's Benediction. College servants in starched white jackets were already moving smoothly about on wheels. Then they melted into the kitchens, cloisters and Hall. From the buttery came the happy voice of Nellie Grainger: 'How those eyes blazed forth! Nellie, I loves yer.' And from the flower beds under the Master's Lodgings came the voice of Mrs Plasket, telling someone up above exactly why she had decided to discontinue the education of Dr Charles Mally of Judasland.

'I could have taken him back to Peshawar. I had already improved the health of Akim's wives no end. I was already teaching them French and German and how not to be subservient to our common lover. But Charles Mally has grown old before his time, and knows nothing about obstetrics in the East.'

M. Validot from Bourges-les-Trèves had already been installed in the college kitchens and Grace had already seen him in the covered market ordering three hundred tins of Double-Serve Double-Quick Consommé and five hundred Petts Pies with white liquid seeping out. 'They remind me a bit of Charles Mally,' she was calling sadly upwards.

In the maze the band and chorus were having their last rehearsal for tonight. Conroy's 'Guga Motet' was extremely demanding in its tessitura, and the tenor had to keep leaping a sharpened eleventh while the conductor was trying to get the right degree of rapport between the singers, and the right amount of bleep from the piccolo. Then the distinguished guests started arriving and the college was full of swift dark shapes and starched shirts.

Ever since the college had allowed its Fellows to marry in the 1880s, their wives had been permitted to sit up in the gallery at the end of the Hall and watch their husbands entertain their guests on Benediction Nights. The women's seats were in the rickety but richly carved gallery, built – along with a large part of the college – from the proceeds of the Dissolution of Sanctus's own monastic foundation in the early part of the sixteenth century.

The gallery was the glory of the great dark tudor Hall with its smells of four hundred years of beef, and its faded murals and rich panelling. The carvings along the gallery's face were a famous example of anti-clerical art: a donkey was shying at the Consecration of the Host, and a vast nun was comparing her great bare thigh with the thigh of a large pig waiting for the knife. A few boys were playing truant from the High Altar and an aged priest was using his Missal as a fly-swat.

At the end of the gallery was an early attempt at psychometrics: the heart of St Rendocrinius had been neatly divided into equal segments of a circle, each one representing some aspect of the saint's character: '*Journey to the heathen Teutoni . . . Bee Keeping . . . Thirty days of fast . . . Geometry . . . Calming of storms . . . Huge fish caught with a jewell in its mouth . . . Curing of an Ague . . . Three eggs a year . . . Chastity . . . Bubonic plague . . .*' His soul hung there in his heart and in the great halo round his head, and no one was sure whether the saint had cured the Bubonic Plague or succumbed to it.

At any rate its representation of character had been preserved from the wrath of the Reformation and the Civil War, and Clare, who had been needed in the gallery to replace a wife who had pleaded a headache and withdrawn from the occasion, found herself placed next to St Rendocrinius's dissected heart. Its analytic segments reminded her a bit of Hari. She found herself trying to divide his soul into similar segments: '*Ideas and theories, European and Oriental . . . Love of Fresh Tea from Bombay . . . Tenderness . . . Tennis, inability to play . . . Sternness . . . Lack of resistance to colds . . . Reservations about the British . . . Reservations about tea bags . . . Kindness . . . Many paper handkerchiefs in use . . . Fortitude . . .*

Would she ever know more about Hari than this? Down one side of the college Hall, its celebrated sons were represented in oil paintings. The other wall of the Hall was blank and for a moment Clare thought it might have been left like that to record all the stoical people of Judasland who, over the centuries, had been invisibly good or courageous. Perhaps Hari belonged on that wall, but if she were beginning to love him it was for the order he imposed on her frightened mind. It was Hari who was teaching her to convert reaction into response and she was happy as she pictured him standing out there in the maze with her after the dinner was over, listening to the music and watching the fireworks go up. Hari had fabric and texture, she thought, as she heard the Fellows talking to their guests below in the Hall.

'Esther plays divinely,' one of them was saying above the clatter of plates, 'but the thing I really love about her is her way with the cats, and the garden and the kids . . .'

Clare looked out of the high hall window and down at the rows of streets, the red and blue checkerboards of Judasland, and the tall houses of Spide Street tiered behind. The great bell of Christ Church sounded. The wind blew outside. The trees in the maze seemed to stretch as far as Cotnose now. Clare had been there several times with Hari. She sat there in the gallery, in her new dress, longing to see him out there among the trees and bushes perhaps feeling fairly at home.

The wives all sat there in their coloured dresses like butterflies pinned in a glass case on the wall. Then, in a hush, a little hatch door opened in the side of the hall below and the Fellows, led by the Master, entered almost on all fours, heads emerging first from the hole that led from the Delta Room where they had just finished their drinks. Then they mounted the flight of stairs that led up to High Table. There was a popping sound as the Latonège 1953 was uncorked, and voices began to rise.

'God is already dead, Charles, so which side *are* you on? . . . Too many *incredibilia* for my taste . . . and the Papacy was so afraid of incest . . . Preferred the German kind to the French, poor Pio Nono . . . No, Milton is far too nouny for Bill . . . Of course the Coroner was correct . . . inexperienced barefoot Commonwealth doctors . . .'

Clare pictured Hari getting into his borrowed evening dress and puzzling over 'Decorations will be worn'. She could see the Master below, his mouth sagging slightly at one side and wine dribbling a little as he leaned over his guest who was repeating loudly, '. . . relative to bonnets, I should say pigtails are messy breeders . . . and more prone too to anaclytic depression.'

'We should have frozen their investments,' Clare could hear Professor Boden, who was Dr Pyecraft's guest. 'Our militia should have acted first. And then asked the questions. No one has ever been Socialist enough for me.' The Professor sighed in protest and cracked a quail's leg indignantly in half. It leaped off the plate and splashed rich sauce on to his glasses and he laid them angrily down beside the quail's broken spine, the coralled professor repeating an epitaph: 'I repeat, nothing is left-wing enough for me.'

Then Dr Pyecraft's wife, who was sitting next to Clare, was telling her what she did about children's schooling when she was abroad. But when she got on to her au pair girls and the time off they were demanding now, Clare no longer had any instinct to reply, 'Too true . . . too sickening . . .' She no longer hankered for the staircase spirit either. Things were not so frail as that now. Words were serious.

The Master was banging his hammer on the High Table; the scouts stood back and a hush fell. The Junior Fellow, dressed in black with an object like a dead bird on his head, walked with deadpan selfconsciousness up the Hall, followed by the Manciple muttering a Latin prayer that Clare had coached him in.

A Swedish woman on her other side whispered too loudly, 'We too have that ceremony in a small part of North East Sweden. When the pupil fails his exams, he can go three times to the Chief Professor and call up to his office window, at the same time throwing up a piece of – what shall I call it? A small piece of lard as proof of his motivation. And then if the pupil can show . . .'

But the Swede was gently shushed into silence and the ceremony went on. The prayer for the soul of murdered Richard II was mumbled. The Amens were repeated three times. A long list of conditions connected with the foundation of the college were read. The drinking water and beer were tested by t! e Manciple, and finally the Master read out a piece about the relationship between Plato and Socrates that had caused a constitutional rift in the college during its Platonic period in the sixteenth century. The Fellows now all agreed to the relationship. 'Stet, Stet.' Out in the maze Clare could see Hari in the crowd talking politely to Mrs Boden, and jingling the money in his pocket.

The waiters were moving silently around with trays of glasses, and dishes of ice-cream, and strawberries. The party was in full swing.

'. . . complained about what poor sportsmen the mad were . . . And the meat-loss is at sixty per cent . . .'

'Still use the medial "f", but there's a glorious little sun room . . .'

Clare stood awkwardly beside Hari trying to find someone to

introduce. Hari saw Mrs Plasket. She hadn't been invited but she was still there stooping over a flower bed with a trug and calling to a waiter, 'Sure, but their self-immolation fears are worse than their fears of fouling . . . whereas if you move further East the picture is reversed.'

Hari stood in his borrowed evening dress. It made him look slightly ill. They all stared as a bad-tempered black procession trailed past. The Mayor and the Ward Councillors of Judasland followed the Senior Proctor, then came the Vicar of St James's and his choir of boys in scarlet cassocks and dazzling white surplices, who were to sing in the 'Guga Motet'. As Clare was still looking for someone to introduce Hari to, she heard the voice of Dr Courtland from Judasland: 'No, the Coroner didn't give it to him too hard. There'll have to be an enquiry into the lucky-dip method though, that these second-language doctors use.'

Clare could see Nick De Berry but couldn't hear his reply. She drew Hari away. 'Let's go into the maze. I think the music is going to start . . . I'm sorry my parents couldn't stay. They had to get back. They decided after all that their roots were in London. But they hope to meet you soon.' What did it matter if her father told Hari about the West African sidesman in their parish church, or Mardi told him what fun curry-making was and how she had made one out of some scraps of sardine and an old butt of cheese? What did it matter, her embarrassment, if they leaned over Hari and told him that Indians had a lot to contribute to our rather stodgy way of life, and that there was a lot to be said for the idea of reincarnation? 'We all feel we've been here before – even in pedestrian Drawberry Road. You Indians are here to make us more sensitive . . . It's good to meet you captains of this lofty ship as it tosses on the high seas of the future.' Hari would only have been amused.

'Are you keeping a friendly eye on our big girl?' they had asked Dr Pyecraft when they met him on their visit to the college before they abruptly left Oxford.

'Clare is the one who keeps the eye on all of us.'

'That's as we suspected really, all along.'

But the Bonnards had quietly packed and left Grasslands Hotel as though Clare had caught them red-handed.

'How are you enjoying your work in Judasland?' Dr Pyecraft was asking Hari. 'It's a good healthy practice, I gather?'

Hari shrugged. 'A gentleman patient consulted me yesterday about the state of his cracked ceilings. And a woman patient consulted me about the design and the cut of her trousers. Were they suitable for Rome? she asked.' Clare could hear Mrs Plaskett telling Nellie about a lover in Kuwait.

'Ah well,' said Dr Pyecraft, 'my pupils consult me about their mother's lovers. Do you know Oxford well? Have you been here long?'

'How vain is man! So vain, Again I say, Again this strain,' the choir started up. Then Alec Smale laughed and turned to Clare: 'Hi Clare. How's the Albert Hall? Have you been dancing the Farandole there recently? Clare dances every summer at the National Woman's Guild of Farandole dancers.' Then he saw she was with Hari and stopped. 'Clare, I've upset you.' Alec flung his arms round her as she moved away. She turned and saw Nick De Berry again standing there facing her.

'Oh Nick,' she started and smiled too big a smile. Then: 'You know Hari.'

'Of course.' They shook hands again and Nick gave his dark broad grin and Clare was surprised at how warmly he asked after the book.

She had gone back to the Herber to try and retrieve Conroy's last manuscript. She had knocked at the door of the ward office. The staff sat there inside drinking tea and doing crossword puzzles. They shrugged when she asked them about the manuscript. 'Try the Occupational Therapy department,' they called out. 'And if you want your clothes back, lovely, you'll have to earn them,' they added to a patient standing in the door.

In fact the bundle of manuscript papers had been tidied into the Occupational Therapy cupboard, but a bit seemed to have been used on a huge communal mural that was being pinned on the ward wall: 'I'm Janet from another planet' someone had written over Conroy's *Requiescat*. The hospital collage had been entitled 'Laughter', and Clare could see decorative flights of his demi-semi quavers like flights of stairs leading to the birds that crowned the mural. Then she found other bits of the manuscript stuck between sheets of sticky paper or interleaved with painstaking copies of 'Amazing Grace' and scraps of tortured poetry hidden behind games boards and Scrabble sets and papier maché paper-clip holders. Then she found another note of Conroy's that she took away with her. 'Memo: invite Nick De B to Benediction Night? Perhaps dedicate the lot to him???? . . .'

Now as Nick De Berry stood there talking warmly to Hari she

hoped the Requiem might have value. The unfinished manuscript might not be performed for a long time or perhaps never be 'cashed'. It seemed as much a matter of touch-and-go as her own life, also waiting for a verdict over the next ten years. Perhaps in five years' time both would be forgotten or performed. She herself could do nothing in either case. So she had filed the manuscript carefully away and taken a day off work to go to London with Hari.

He had always wanted to go round Fortnum and Mason's so they decided to have a cup of tea there, and then wandered round trying to see if there was anything they could afford for their supper. Clare wanted to go to the lavatory, but the Ladies was out of order and she was directed round to the staff lavatories by the store's entry. She passed two baths where assistants were washing and calling to each other, then she went into a cubicle.

'Is that you, Sharon?' the girl in the next cubicle tapped on the wall and called out to Clare, but before Clare had time to say 'Oh no,' the girl had gone on, 'I've got a nice surprise for you. Coming over! Catch!' An enormous bloody parcel of what felt like meat flew over the partition that divided the cubicles, hit Clare, and splashed the front of her white crimplene dress with the blood of two game birds that she couldn't identify. The college-treasure dress, decorated with trumpets and drums, was ruined.

Hari stared at her when she got out with her parcel. 'It may have solved the problem of your future career,' he observed, nodded, then stared again at the stain. 'But in the interim . . .'

'It must have been meant as a baptism.'

He laughed. They both did, as though this were the first time she had been blooded.

'And also solved the problem of what to have for supper,' she held up the blood-soaked package. 'But what are they?' She unpeeled the paper and Hari peered.

'Pheasant. Or grouse. Or partridge. But whatever they are, they only throw minimal light on the British character.'

'Just shop-lifting, I think. International, global shop-lifting.'

'But shop-lifting even in undeveloped countries hardly involves such terrible stains.' Hari stared at Clare's dress. 'Also, there may be little point in our exploration of outer space when certain features of our life down here below demand explicit explanation. Let us first buy you some new clothes.'

They strolled up Bond Street staring in the shop windows, then they came to Oxford Street and bought Clare a T-shirt and some jeans.

'And I must find Moss Bros to hire a dress suit for Bishop's Benediction Night. And also some decorations. Which order of merit am I most suited to, would you say? I never had any taste for the soldier's life. Nor for the taxidermist's or stamp-collector's.'

'Perhaps, when your books are written . . .'

So he came to Benediction Night without decorations, and voices were coming again from the maze: 'Oh no! Dan was the author of Time and Sue Lee its editor . . .'

But the Handel was under way and the oratorio came leaping out:

A Public Monument Ordained
Of Victories as Yet Ungained.

But there was a sudden sharp wind as the conductor raised her baton for the opening bars of Conroy's 'Guga Motet'. The electric wiring had blown down and the chances of singing such an intricate work without lights were slight. Even with full lighting it was a very complex score to decipher. But everyone knew 'Pa's Pop' by heart, and the conductor and choir broke into its *In Templo* as the wind attacked them; and so the 'Guga Motet' was never sung.

In fact, it wasn't about a rubber-band factory near Dresden, nor about a whole-foods co-operative in Fulham. It was about some animals, and the terrible mistake they made when they found the Babe of Bethlehem – a man among them. It was a strange song cycle, about life between the acts; human life as 'not normal'. The animals had come to the manger of the Christ-child, and had gone away disappointed. A misunderstanding. They hadn't come to greet a man so obsessed with suffering. They had come to wish him long life and prosperity.

Hari gazed at the demure English women with smooth clear complexions that made them look much younger than they were. Who were the people who wrote things on walls, and dropped bottles full of petrol in at Asians' letterboxes, then came to him to have the burns treated? Was the British race becoming feeble-minded? Or were there two races?

Someone was striking a rod on a bench. Someone was doffing another great hat like an exotic bird that the wind and rain tore at as everyone hurried back to the college Hall to shelter. Then Clare could hear Grace Plasket's plangent voice as she crept behind them in her jeans and muttoncloth shirt, drawing her long fine greying hair from her large sad eyes in the half-light, murmuring as she gazed round at the distinguished guests:

> Being Certain that They and I
> But Lived Where Motley is Worn

Then she was silent. The guests had all moved back to the hall but the lights in the college couldn't be made to work either, so thick gold Paschal candles from the chapel were lit and they all silently agreed to abandon the 'Guga Motet'. But because everyone knew 'Pa's Pop' they all started singing Conroy's *In Templo* again, standing by the long benches that ran the length of the Hall:

> With hands I take those Hands that make . . .

They had all picked it up in their youth or in their children's childhoods, and the performance was a rough but cheerful one. When they came to Conroy's last movement, 'Give Us a Peace in That Dark . . .' they all, in a sudden and spontaneous respect for Joe, fell silent and let the choir go on alone till it came to the final narrative: 'Nevertheless'. The 'Folk Mass' ended on such a hopeful note – 'But if . . . And yet . . .' – that it suddenly didn't matter that Conroy had later taken back his treasure; had changed his mind. Who was he to know what his music had once done, and what it hinted? Who was he in his cracked spectacles splashed with paint to validate his work? Or not? Is the artist really in charge of what he has said? Perhaps he is better off with an interpreter. Perhaps he is better off without a portfolio. Perhaps better off stumbling blindfold among the furniture in cracked glasses, the innocent victim of life's indifference. Conroy's 'Nevertheless' had come and gone for the last time. It was as though in the distance a door opened. It didn't matter now that Conroy had backtracked. Clare and Hari, in his audience, were invited not to lose sight of hope and happiness. So the last 'Nevertheless' seemed to end by saying: 'Where you look for him, he's gone. The message can do without its messenger now.'

Then Handel's Fireworks Music started up and the party voices faded away and a set-piece of fireworks went up into the sky. They all laughed as it became clear that it was the medieval 'Ship of Fools' that sailed away up there. The Handel still went on, loud and repetitive as though it were celebrating a military occasion; as though the death of an artist or children had to be bruited noisily abroad as well as silently lamented. Tears could be purified of guilt and the waters made clear again, the wells cleaned and the springs reconsecrated. Judasland seemed to have echoed the evening's noise and now echoed its silence. As Clare drove away to Hedgencote with Hari, she thought she might be beginning to learn the difference between forgetful happiness and the mindful kind. She leaned over and kissed him and he smiled:

'I have a feeling that affairs will become much happier for both of us now.'

XV

Mrs Plasket had shown Clare and Hari the Hedgencote pub where the row about the double yellow parking-lines had broken out. She had shown them the old hat-factory the calves had leaped into on their way to the slaughter-house on market-day in 1903. She had shown them the barber's shop where Prince Charles had been shaved clean after the Battle of Worcester in 1629 and the spot quite near it where the vicar's wife had been caught lifting snowdrops from the churchyard.

Then a lady in a hat like a saddle-bag had stopped them and asked them to take sides in the war between the two rival Hedgencote drying-up cloths, one depicting a stone tump that had been the site of a Danish defeat in 701, and the other celebrating Hedgencote's 'Sleepy-Badger Tea Rooms (1669)'. And they were also asked to be enthusiastic about the Spearhead Art Gallery, where pen-and-ink sketches of eminent Parish Councillors were displayed beside the watercolours of Hedgencote at different seasons of the year: Hedgencote on Boxing Day, 1960, and Hedgencote on Good Friday, 1963.

'The mind boggles at the possibilities,' Hari observed as Grace Plasket read out a notice outside the Parish Hall: Miss Dimmick would gladly show groups of 'Coters' round her old cottage where it was reputed that Prince Charles had drunk mead before going to the barber for his clean shave. The barber's however had a notice out about Durex Delphin and picture-framing.

'Appassionata fabulosa vivace,' Grace murmured, 'a visit to Miss Lampedusa's stream-lined cottage! I can just see the hot-water bottles ranked round to keep the place warm . . .' But Clare and Hari arm-in-arm had wandered into the old dead ancestors' church, where women in print overalls were dusting and arranging flowers and calling over to each other in their flat Oxfordshire monotones.

'Our ballcock's got stuck again, so we has no water . . . No, as I said, it don't do to get took to the hospital. But my sister in London, she says it's worse there. You see, she got took to the Nuns'! If you please! And they do keep praying for you, if you get took in there.'

'Yes, if you war on your last legs,' another woman in a feather hat with a feather duster called indignantly as she reached up over the regimental flags, 'they'd still keep on with all this prayer.' She stopped dusting to adjust the flowers on the High Altar. 'And sprinkle you with Holy Water if you give them half a chance. And even if you war took real bad. They say', her indignation rose, 'they're selling old New Nock House to another doctor. A coloured gentleman from Oxford, they do say.'

'That's news to me,' Hari widened his eyes at Clare.

'Yes, a coloured gentleman . . . Got into trouble with the colleges.'

'But what's a coloured gentleman doing here? What would he be wanting here? After all, it's just sheep and fields and grass around here. But still, they're all doctors these days, aren't they? Even in the schools and the supermarkets, they've all got to be doctors these days.'

'Yes, and what do you think? An artist lady's moved in to Baychess. Did you ever? An artist lady! Now what did she do to get like that, I asks you?'

The church volunteers knocked the flowers' heads up into place and went on: 'And they say she's a sculptress. A stone carver. Makes angels for the graves. Now, I ask you, how did she get like that?'

'It's all these newcomers.'

Hari and Clare pulled faces at each other and went on through the churchyard and up Church Hill where two old men on zimmers were leaning across the parked cars. The birthright inhabitants of Hedgencote frowned and shook their heads. 'Jest set there, they be, like lemons, these city folk, in them skemmy old barns. Bass says . . .'

'And them old barns of a house been set there since the War! and before I war too!'

'And they do be so old and so clammy that I takes our Rose's hot-water bottle when I goes to work for Lord Banks.'

'Yes, and they say Lord Banks sleeps in the toolshed now the bats have got into his bedrooms and his sitting-rooms. Them bats is conserved, so they say. So he can't call the infestation!'

Then the women church cleaners joined them.

'And they do say the new doctor's wife is coloured too.'

'But it's nothing but fields all round here,' someone objected again. 'Mrs Hacker went to Italy on a tour, but she said there war no toilets there.'

'Nor war there in Spain when our Jean got the sack and went. She lost her teeth but they gave her a really lovely cheese cake. Not too cheesy. And not too foreign. Just right, so she thought she'd try Yugoslavia next time, unless it's the same about the toilets.'

'The cheesiest cheese-cake I ever had . . .'

'. . . and them bats is a protected species. Rose has to have them even in her front room.'

'Well you would do, wouldn't you, if they war protected. They should've pulled down all them skemmy old barns of a house years ago, when our Bass first went into service . . .'

'That's right, when they had the old trees down, and the dirty old Jubilee Drinking Fountain and the slaughter-house and the old Butter Cross. In them days there warn't no moither about a few bats and old barns . . . and the old ice-house up Grimmers. Blam the lot.'

Everything was suddenly precious to Clare. She clung to these human voices as though they guaranteed her survival. They moved on. Hari still seemed uncharmed by Hedgencote, its leaden-voiced people, and its anticipations of a new doctor. Grace wanted to show them New Nock House though, and they left Church Hill and went up Praise Hill to where the Lamb Hotel stood, and beside it, the old doctor's house, at the crest of the hill.

It looked as though people had, through the ages, first tried to align it with the seventeenth century, and then with the eighteenth and then with the nineteenth. They had failed each time and it grinned its defiance through its worn brick and mortar, and allowed nothing to digest it.

'New Nock's as old as "Edjcot",' two more indignant women said as they pushed their bikes up the hill. 'All this old stuff gets on my nerves. They should've got rid of it in the War when they did the others. In London. My niece out at Sandlands says why should she go out cleaning when they's nothing really nice in them gentry houses. They say Lady Banks dabs out her smalls up the towers of the colleges, Mondays, and she don't have any nice things. Maybe the new doctor? . . .'

'But they say he's coloured, Maud.'

Hari hardened his face and looked stern. 'One of my patients has announced that her navel has disappeared,' he said. He went on ahead and was reading the menu pinned up outside the Lamb Hotel. There was a notice board outside it announcing the meetings of the Hedgencote Harriers, the Hedgencote Pathfinders and the Hedgencote-Slipfield Heritage Foundation.

'The mind boggles again,' Hari announced as they caught up with him; then he went on reading out to Grace Plasket: 'In a recent raffle, E. Pulls has won a Bulgarian Dancers' Trophy and Mrs Brief came second with Fruit Fancies and Yesteryear. And there is soon to be a talk on Chaucer and the Isle of Wight, and another on Flowers in the Age of Nell Gwyn. And look!' he added, peering back at Grace Plasket, who was trying to attract the attention of some ex-lover who was making his way towards the Lamb, 'Mrs Grace Plasket is to read a paper on "Books I Have Not Loved", and another on "Places I Have Not Loved".'

'And another,' Clare added, 'on "Men I Have Not Loved Either".'

'I have loved them all too much,' Grace protested sadly. 'It was *they* who have always betrayed me. Men alas, only need mothering.' She looked at Hari and then at Clare. 'What do you think of New Nock House? Do you see a great future at Hedgencote, Hari?'

'That is, as yet, a problematical question.'

They all three went into the Lamb and watched a woman who was trying to wash out the pub curtains as they still hung at the windows, holding a plastic basin underneath their ends and letting them swish in and out, up and down in the soapy water as they ordered their lunch.

'So what about Oxford?' Grace leaned over to Hari as he gazed sadly into the weak beer-liquid in his glass and the curtains swished methodically in the basin of water behind them.

'Oxford is certainly very full of celebrated people,' he conceded. 'In the Cornmarket yesterday I recognized two distinguished MPs who advocate the sterilisation of backward women and camps for immigrants who have no skilled labour to offer on the market.'

'I wonder how they would have acted if Hitler had invaded,' Clare murmured as she seemed to have murmured such a short time earlier, and yet a time before she had ever met Hari or thought of a real context for such a question.

Grace Plasket kicked idly at a table leg. 'Oh, the academic world would have worked out some *modus vivendi* with the Nazis. So sacred is scholarship that they would have traded scholastic freedom for the agreement to remain studiously at work on the price of eggs in the manorial economy of 1267 in return for not noticing when the trains ran through to Otmoor full and came back through Judasland empty. No one would notice when the doors creaked open at night, except perhaps Nellie Grainger who thought her father or her lover might be standing there calling, "Nellie I loves yer . . ." '

But Hari still looked judicial and simply said, 'Your judgement is too harsh.'

'That seems rather over-generous,' Grace scowled.

They ate their ham rolls and drank their weak beer and weak tepid coffee and wandered out again past the washed curtains, now dabbed out and dripping noisily on to the lino on the bar's floor. Then they walked down Praise Hill again, towards the old Grammar School and the narrower streets of grey stone terraces that ran down to the hump-backed bridge that led over the railway to the river beyond. They walked on and on past the graveyard to the allotments where the town's birthright inhabitants still lived and worked and dug their belly gardens.

As though Grace had touched a small bell, the hard monotone of authentic Oxfordshire again came banging out at them from a farm-labourer's wife as she dug for potatoes: 'Yes, at Grimmers it war, warn't it, Fred? We had to put all the Foot-and-Mouth animals down the lime pits. Even the farm tiddies. Even the dairy herd they only had for the girls. All of them down the pit. You ask Mrs Tell if it warn't the Grimmers Field.'

An elderly woman in a long brown cardigan dragged down by heavy pockets pulled at the cardigan and then at her pulled-down hair and nodded and agreed. 'I been set here over seventy years, and as for those poppies there,' she stared over to where a rash of bright poppies had rushed up to the edge of the allotments, 'I been set here since 1907 and I've never seen such a sight of poppies there in that old field of Grimmers where they put them in the lime. After the Foot-and-Mouth.'

They all gazed at the brimming field of scarlet poppies. 'Don't ever let them stop,' Clare thought.

Beyond, a lane led up to some falling-down cottages with young trees growing through their roofs and corrugated-iron holding the water out. A thin child with a stye on her eye watched them balefully from a pile of newspapers stacked on a broken windowsill.

'Hullo,' called Grace, just missing a teapot full of tealeaves that was emptied out of the window and splashed her smart pink shoes. A woman's voice shouted at the child, 'Give over now, or I'll learn you.' The child cried suddenly.

Mrs Plasket sighed and wiped her wet pink shoes. 'I suppose women's violence is always against pink cotton slippers,' she said bitterly.

'Yes,' Hari agreed, 'a woman's anger is much more stupid than a man's. A woman will go to the forest and carry home a gaping head dripping with blood and cry triumphantly: "Husband, look at the tiger I have just slain in the forest!" But alas, her poor husband is obliged to point out that it is really her own firstborn son she has just slain and is proudly lugging along behind her, his pink tongue being trailed by a jackal.'

'Have you never killed the thing you loved, Hari?' Grace asked angrily. 'Anil told me he had killed you, in thought at any rate, dozens of times. Not by tearing your head off but by never delivering you from your torpor. Oh you youngster Indians are so languid, and – ' she wiped, then rubbed at her pink slippers, then wandered away, 'I suppose even Anil never really understood a woman's needs,' she sighed as she stood there. Hari turned to Clare: 'Grace too does not appreciate the difference between reaction and response.'

He didn't mean to take Clare into the forest of Cotnose so soon again. But it was their only way of getting away from Grace. She followed them a little way and then she stopped, calling wanly, 'Perhaps the University would have pointed out that the Court of Richard III or Henry VIII was as vicious and violent as the Nazis, and just settled for living in violent times. Or perhaps, one by one, we would all have been picked off and disappeared . . .'

Grace stooped over a ditch where she had seen something move, then the last of her they saw was her big straw hat waving behind her idly as she poked at a hedge. A car drove up just then and she called to someone inside it, then got in and disappeared.

Clare and Hari walked on and climbed the little cast-iron pedals that mounted the great wall of the forest. But they were at a different place this time. Clare inserted her feet into two different 'shoes', then Hari was leading her down the corresponding shoelets on the other side. It was an arboretum they were in this time, not a forest. There were huge Chinese and Greek trees, Australian gum-trees and smoke thorns, Canadian maples and a huge catalpa shedding white cotton petals beside a cobbled courtyard where water dripped into old lead tanks from wooden leats.

They sat down on a bench. In front of them was a grim Victorian conservatory with glass façades decorated with black ironwork lace. Inside, the same great rowdy blooms Clare thought she had escaped from were peering out, jeering. The great rabble seemed to have gathered here again, as Clare told Hari she thought perhaps her mother had died of Huntington's Chorea. He plucked up one nostril and his thick right eyebrow.

'And maybe you want a confession from me, too? My mother has written proposing that my uncle seeks out a bride for me.'

'Maybe you should tell him you don't want a bride yet.'

The conservatory echoed the long silence. 'True. My career here has not yet been destroyed,' Hari said at last. 'In India we also have these lies and dishonesties and cover-ups of the establishment. The colour of your skin and your community also determines who gets off the hook and who takes the rap. And we also have communalism which is as ugly there as it is here, in your colleges. Communism to me is a less ugly idea.'

No, Hari was not interested in scapegoats or victims. Clare had been afraid but now she felt suddenly that nothing had been taken away from her as she sat again beside Hari leaning against the grey wall that encircled the forest. They could see a wind picking itself up from the ground and gathering strength as it blew over the rough poppies, spreading through the daisies and then the poppies again like children racing over towards them, and then stopping: 'Mrs Pax! Are you sorry you couldn't stay?'

But Clare had to exercise a new limb. The more you delayed using it, the harder it was for the graft to take. The limb became an artificial one if you let the children ask: 'Is it nice at Chalstone?' Who were 'they' after all, who were coming to take her away there?

Beyond the arboretum they could see corn that ran full of little nemesias in the barley, and more poppies defying agriculture's rules that the area was designated for oats. Then they were back at the great lead tanks with their wooden leats where water dripped away steadily on three distinct notes. But the flowers had stopped gloating and the trees were dull. Clare reminded herself again that nothing had been taken away from her.

'This is a gloomy place,' Hari was saying. 'Shall we take a more cheerful path back to the sun? It is getting late. Perhaps we ought to be getting back?' He looked at his watch.

'Let's go and look at New Nock House again first,' Clare suggested. So they climbed the wall of Cotnose and walked away from it down the track that led to the road, passed the river and railway and the graveyard and the allotments, and were just standing there looking up at Praise Hill where New Nock and the Lamb stood when they heard a jolly voice call out towards a very old man sitting on an upholstered chair by his garden gate.

'Hello, Mr Dark. How are you, Mr Albert Dark?' A well-dressed woman in a big straw hat was leaning over his garden gate and calling in with enormous enthusiasm, 'All well, Mr Dark?'

Mr Dark stared and scratched his head and frowned and looked worried as Hedgencote's local historian repeated, 'How's the world been treating you today, Mr Dark? Some time I should like to come round with my notebook and make a stab at getting down to the everyday life-history of our town. Your goodly experiences of days gone by.' She got out her notebook briskly and poised her biro.

'Eh?'

'Do you find that in spite of the passing of the good old days . . .'

'Eh? If it's that blammy pension-book of mine you be after, I reckon it's gone and got legs again. Or if it's the meals-on-wheels plate, well it's boy moy gasunder.'

'Good days, were they then, Mr Dark?' the local historian poised her pen again. 'Or were they bad days? Answer me for posterity. I suppose you can remember the terrible Foot-and-Mouth plague and Grimmer's Field. And Hungerberry Copse when hunger really bit . . .'

'Warn't Hungerberry then. War the Sibden.'

'Ah. The Sibden. A much more authentic name. Can you tell us more about the Sibden?'

'No, because I war out in service all my life. Oxford I war. In Judasland. Only comes back here when I war seventy and too bad in the joints for the professor I works for. "You're no more good to us here, Albert," his wife tells me, "What with what we pay in food and stamps for you. You aren't worth your keep any more." '

Mr Dark repeated this and roared with laughter. 'And some of them says we won't have nuclear weapons,' he roared even louder. 'But Oi bin set here or there all right. Nearly ninety years.'

'You have indeed, Mr Albert Dark. And a very rich inheritance you bear with you. I suppose your grandfather must have remembered the old Hedgencote yoke-plough and pick-hoe and set-horses?'

'Oh no. He war in the cellars of the colleges too, till the damp down there got into his bones. Then he went in for the gas. Down by the station'

Then Mr Dark shuffled away laughing. 'They's been on about the Sibden,' he called in to his wife, who was concentrating on the blue sky on the TV set, inside. 'They's always bin on about something daft. What do they be thinking on? I can't never have heard them right. Two funerals last week and old Toby gone this. So what do they want, eh? They got the telly too, aint they? So what they want now?'

'Nock House would probably be too damp,' Hari said judiciously, 'and in any case I am probably leaving Oxford. I am hoping for a job in London.'

As they walked away, they could hear the old woman with the pulled-down cardigan and pulled-down hair calling across her garden again about the poppies that had come back.

'And I been set here since 1902 and I never seen poppies come there in Grimmers Field before. Them should by rights be oats in Grimmers.'

Hari and Clare walked on. 'Let's have one more look at Nock House.' It still stood there in the twilight as if to say, 'Hate me if you want.' Clare wanted to laugh again at the faint grimacing smile on its crooked old face.

'It needs feeding. Loving.'

'Subsidence, perhaps?' Hari pursed his lips.

'Maybe it just needs to be lived in, to make it stand upright again. Like Lazarus being raised from the dead.'

'Maybe.' He kissed her.

They went round the back, to the black pump and the privy discreetly surrounded by roses, and the waterbut and the larder with the broad shallow stone sink and the marble slab smelling of rancid butter. There were a few wizened apple trees in its garden, an old broken seat, and a huge and vulgar clematis lolling like painted Easter egg against a wall. They stared at the old house. 'It needs loving,' Clare repeated.

It was as though some mocking adult had dumped a hat on its head, far too close to its large and stupid eyes. They stared up at the crooked parapet of stone that girdled its steeply-pitched roof. New Nock house stood there askew on the top of Praise Hill, perched there making a permanence out of its celebration of the temporary.

'It makes me feel so sorry for it.' Hari still made no comment.

They found a door at the side was open and went in and stood in the empty rooms; went upstairs and looked down at the Lamb on one side and the railway station up beyond the allotments and the churchyard. The station was shaped like a medieval castle and they could see a train run into its battlements, then run out again. A dog ran into a garden, then ran out again as the train bounded away and the dog went on barking after it. Then they climbed up spiral staircases in wooden cupboards to some hot dry attics. They sat on window seats looking out over the valley that had never heard of Oxford. There was an old abandoned rag doll on the other window seat with a faded blue-eyed smile. Sawdust and straw were bleeding out of her neck, but she was smiling prettily, not knowing that her head sagged not in becoming modesty but because rats had gnawed at her neck. No. She smiled, it was her touch of distinction that made her lean and list.

'I can see why you hate Oxford,' Clare said. 'Are you really going back to London, Hari?

Hari merely shrugged and said, 'This was once a grand house indeed, but now it bears only pathos. Maybe I shall return to London. My brother has a flat there. In Bernard Street. Charles Mally and I have parted with no bad will.'

They wandered downstairs again and out into the garden. Flowers stood all round them but they were no longer insolent or jeering. They walked down to the bottom where rubble bled out of the old drystone wall. Clare looked tenderly back at the old and abused house. Hari just repeated, 'Subsidence and damp.'

'But what will they do in Hedgencote without a doctor?'

'The NHS will arrange that. Shall we enquire at the Lamb Inn as to whether they can provide a cup of tea for us? We could talk more easily than we can at Grace's.'

While Hari was staring at the menu at the Lamb's front door Clare was laughing at the two polished brass doorbells beside it.

One was marked 'Day' and the other 'Night'. Both signs had been painstakingly painted in bold black print that was now faded, and beside them in a cursive hand the signwriter had added: 'Press Once', then an arrow with a flourish for a tail, 'Bells'.

Clare pointed at the candytuft that was growing in the flowerbed underneath: 'Candytuft,' she counted off, 'bell, flower, leaf'. Then she saw a dog gnawing at a bone and then at a stone and added: 'Dog, stone, bone. What a lot of hope there still is in the world. Dog, flower, house, and a man militant,' she pointed at Hari and laughed, 'man keeper of all these things ranked in order round him and naming them: air, sky, finger, and man standing like a guardian beside them.' Their guardian had no intention of becoming anyone's victim. Hari was presiding somewhat severely. 'And what a stern father you will make. What a Man of Decorum.'

'Yes, I am somewhat over-authoritarian by nature. Over-reaction.'

'And so optimistic about the Indian rope trick you preside over. Dog, stone, candytuft and man all in rows, all in dutiful ranks waiting to climb the Indian rope. Rose,' Clare laughed. 'Dog, man, woman.' She imitated Hari's severe expression. 'Man, upright . . . two legged . . . man in thought. Such optimism . . . about its importance.'

But Hari just lifted his eyebrow and frowned for a moment. 'I think this hotel may furnish us with some tea.'

'We've just lost our little kitten,' three little girls in matching dresses announced proudly, bouncing up to them from behind a wall as they came out of the Lamb. 'We've just lost him.'

'Then he is probably over there,' Hari pointed at some wild black shrubs that had run over the edge of the garden at New Nock House. 'I have just seen a pair of fiery eyes staring out from among those bushes.'

'Oh no,' the little girls exclaimed in shocked unison. 'No, you see he's been *killed*,' they repeated proudly. 'He's *dead*.'

'That I cannot help you with, then. Categorically not. I am a doctor and consequently merely concerned with the living.'

'Are you our new doctor then?'

Hari took Clare's arm, and it was then that she agreed to leave Oxford and go back to London with him. It was his stern optimism about the Indian rope trick – 'bell, flower, men and women' – that she had grown to love.

And yet even as he stood there judiciously in his stoic absurdity, the daisies and the poppies were rushing cheerfully up at them as though they wanted to be embraced. The Queen Anne's lace where wheat had been sown; and the scarlet pimpernel threading its way in and out of the beady barley; and the red poppies pouring through grids made to hold them back. . . . There was something so unexpected and gratuitous about this new version of Jack Frost. Such an abundance of life in spite of the farmer's cold will. So Clare blessed the riot and disorder, and decided to ask her father about her mother's disease. In a sense, she told herself, we all live with the same amount of chance. And without it life would be merely cyclical. Because it wasn't cyclical, she'd have to tell Hari in full.

He stood there staring at some very small white flowers. 'Those little flowers make a very modest statement about life.' He examined their tiny cup-like petals with blue stigmata inside and rows of dots all round.

But Clare didn't have to worry any more about the very modest statements she made about life. She needn't worry any more that her life belonged among student files and picture postcards of New York, and the day Alec Smale's dog ran away, because Mrs Pax still sat there working at her tapestry of Trooping the Colour beside the noisy greenhouse flowers, and would sit there forever to remind Clare that each day might be her last day of wholeness, and to treasure it.

And Clare needn't be worried either about spending the rest of her life in bedsitters, at church teas, or sipping small and careful sips of very good sherry at six in the evenings on well groomed college lawns and fitting the right replies on to the Fellows' small remarks about the weather and the gardens and speeds on the motorway and who would be next Principal of St Martyrs'. She needn't be afraid of a life of small hopes and marginal satisfactions, because Hari had finally rejected Hedgencote and they would move to London, to the Borough of Tower Hamlets where Asians were attacked in the night streets, firebombs were dropped through their letterboxes, and the police curled their lips with insouciance when appeals for help came: 'Yeah. I got my problems too. Got any enemies? Let's see that passport first though.'

For Clare and Hari would both inevitably be drawn into race relations campaigns. They would both suffer humiliation and disillusionment and learn to tear each other apart instead of the enemy, and hate each other after each encounter with the police and the National Front. And after each defeat they would learn to bicker about agendas and points of order, and rage over the powerlessness of MPs and the indifference of the Great and the Good. And all the time Clare would be discovering that Hari was indeed an autocrat, not a libertarian, and they would rend each other further when there should have been healing. The future was not going to be blinkered for either of them. Clare could see Hari disappearing in despair, alone and with his book abandoned for the more serious concerns he had been thrown against.

But now he just put his arm round Clare's waist, as though it would always be like this, and led her along.

'I am afraid I am getting too far from my roots,' he sighed. 'The longer I stay the more of a stranger I shall become on my mother's farm and within our community. I am becoming increasingly cut off from my nieces and nephews and our whole family network and culture. Do you feel like a holiday in India?'

Clare smiled and nodded and they wandered on. The flood of white daisies and the riot of red poppies went rushing along beside them as though the children playing by the river had forgiven an adult crime, or just forgotten it, and had come rushing over to them instead, saying they wanted to show them the shallow part of the river where you can wade across and the field of red poppies beyond. Clare found herself thinking again, 'Let it come. Let it all come. Don't let the flood of poppies ever stop.'

As they lay side by side that night on Hari's settee she could still picture the children waving to them and lowering themselves from the willow tree beside the water and calling, 'Pretend you haven't seen us here.'

It seemed impossible not to respect this play of theirs. Hari and Clare had had so little of that, rather than whispering to herself in a new access of horror: 'But suppose you are like your mother this time next year!' she said instead: 'Don't let the rush of the unexpected poppies ever stop.'

'Nose . . . cheek . . . tooth.' Clare had daubed Hari's face with face cream as they went to bed that night. 'Floor . . . ceiling . . . man . . . purpose . . . power . . . prunes . . . how funny life sounds when you put it like this.'

They both laughed at the arbitrary headings that people had to live under. But both of them knew of something fluid and evolving behind the haphazard and static lists of life. They both knew the distinction between forgetful, knee-jerk happiness and the unblink-ered remembering kind.

They could hear Mrs Boden on her bicycle below in the street loudly denouncing a bird she had heard this morning for singing so loudly and rhythmically. Then other voices called down the street: 'Too big for the Rotunda or the CIA . . . No, I haven't met him as often as I have met Mandela. Nelson is a strange man . . . we can trace our family back to 1607 . . . Cloning genes since he met her . . . laying out the duvets ever since . . . We'll take both cars . . . But first I want to work on my mind . . . And his eyes blazed forth at me – Nellie, I loves yer!'

Then Oxford began to melt away like a snowman when the sun starts to shine leaving only the two stones that were his eyes, still staring proudly though the snowman was gone.